LIA
AND
BECKETT'S
Abracadabra

LIA
AND
BECKETT'S
Abracadabra

AMY
NOELLE
PARKS

AMULET BOOKS · NEW YORK

Cataloging-in-Publication Data has been applied for and may be obtained from the Library of Congress.

ISBN 978-1-4197-5344-2

Text copyright © 2022 Amy Noelle Parks
Title page illustration © 2022 Andi Poretti
Book design by Deena Fleming

Printed and bound in U.S.A.
10 9 8 7 6 5 4 3 2 1

Amulet Books are available at special discounts when purchased in quantity for premiums and promotions as well as fundraising or educational use. Special editions can also be created to specification. For details, contact specialsales@abramsbooks.com or the address below.

Amulet Books® is a registered trademark of Harry N. Abrams, Inc.

ABRAMS The Art of Books
195 Broadway, New York, NY 10007
abramsbooks.com

This one's for my girls almighty, Chloe and Sophie

IN OUR MAILBOX, I FIND A POSTCARD FROM MY MISSING GRANDMOTHER AND A SONNET FROM MY BOYFRIEND. ONLY ONE IS ADDRESSED TO ME.

I'm standing on the doorstep reading the poem when Camden's car fishtails into our driveway. He pops out, leaving the car running, which is not like him. This boy says "eco-conscious" more often than I reapply lip gloss.

"Tell me you didn't open that," he says, rushing toward me.

I hold up my hand like a crossing guard, because I don't want him any closer. "I did. And we're done here. Unless you want to hand-deliver it to your muse?"

Camden winces and brings his fist to his mouth. He's so cute, and a little twist of pain flashes in my stomach. We haven't been together long enough for it to be my heart, but I thought we were headed in that direction.

A couple months ago, I helped Camden bring up his chemistry grade with Grandma's haunted house trick. You turn all the things you need to memorize into vivid images that you picture in a Gothic-style mansion. Using this system, Grandma can memorize a deck of cards in less than an hour. It took me a week.

The haunted house thing worked for Camden, and when he aced his test, he took me out to celebrate. Since then, we've spent most weekends together, and I've lost a bobby pin or two—although nothing of importance—in the back seat of his car.

"It was just a daydream. I never intended anyone to see it." He comes up the steps to stand in front of me. "You know what you're like. Can you blame me for one little fantasy about someone more serious?"

Yes. I can. This whole situation is ridiculous, but my throat tightens the way it does when I cry. I'd sort of thought that Camden, with his eco causes and scruffy shoes and homework dates, took me more seriously than his predecessors. If he didn't, what was the point of all that boredom?

I hit back because I don't want to give him the satisfaction of my tears. "Maybe don't call me silly when you're the one rhyming 'elocution' with 'pollution.'" This was not the most disturbing part of the poem, but it's all I'm willing to say out loud. "Years of therapy will not undo this."

Camden puts a hand out, but I yank my arm away.

"I wrote one for you too. That's what I meant to put in the mailbox." He holds out a folded square of paper. "Do you want it?"

OK. I'm a little tempted. I haven't had so many poems written for me that I can afford to reject them out of hand, but there's not a lot of dignity to salvage here, so I'm going to take what I can get.

"It's over, Camden," I say before turning to go inside.

He grabs for the door. "Lia! You can't take that in there."

"Oh yes, I can." I push the door shut, but he shoves it open and follows me in.

"Be reasonable," he says, and I shoot him an outraged look.

Mom comes out of her office. "Hey, Lia. Camden. How's it going?"

Camden looks at his shoes. "Hi, Mrs. Sawyer." His face is bright red. As it should be.

"Camden and I broke up. He is no longer welcome here."

Mom's eyes widen. "What happened?"

"Do you want to tell her, or should I?"

"You wouldn't."

"You want to bet? Two days ago, you told me you couldn't stop thinking about me. You said every single day you'd give me a new reason to stay together. Good plan. Terrible execution."

"Volume, Lia," Mom says, and I glare at her. I swear I was eight years old before I realized my given name wasn't Volume Lia.

The piano goes silent. I'm so used to hearing Emma play, I didn't realize she was home until the music stopped.

"What's going on?" she says, coming out of the living room.

"My boyfriend wrote a romantic poem about Mom."

"Lia!" Camden shouts.

"I want to see!" Emma says at the same time.

"About me?"

To her credit, Mom is horrified. She and I don't have the smoothest relationship, but she's never been one of these mothers who dresses like a teenager and flirts with our boyfriends. She's a lawyer who consults for environmental organizations and mostly works from home. Today, she's wearing leggings and an oversize T-shirt that says STOP THE FRACKING MADNESS.

Her hair, which falls straight to her shoulders, is the same indeterminate shade of beige that grows out of my head, although every eight weeks I return mine to the golden color I was born with. (I don't think of this as dyeing my hair. I am a heritage blonde.)

From what I gathered in his poem, Camden's fascination stems less from her appearance (a small consolation on the weirdness front) than from her intellect (ouch).

I hold out the poem to Mom. "Would you like it?" Camden makes a grab for it, but I vanish it into my sleeve.

Mom shakes her head rapidly back and forth and steps back into her office, shutting the French doors. The lock clicks and the blinds close. A better person might feel sorry for Camden, but I can't quite manage it.

"You're really not giving it back?"

"No. Consider it insurance. Come up with some flattering reason we broke up, stay away, and no one will ever see it."

"Except me, obviously," Emma says.

"Well, yes, except Emma."

"Lia," Camden says.

"You're lucky this is as bad as it gets."

The frustration on his face slowly morphs into embarrassment. "I *am* sorry."

I nod and he leaves.

"Wow," Emma says. "You were super tough."

That's when I cry.

Emma pulls me upstairs to my room and lies down next to me until I stop. It doesn't take all that long. I was maybe more interested in the idea of Camden than the reality of him. And maybe not even the idea of Camden, but the idea of me as a girl who could attract a boy like him. Because I thought Camden was not the sort of guy to fall for someone silly.

Upside . . . I guess I was right about that.

Emma kisses my forehead and wipes away the last of my tears. She is two years older and perfect. And not knowing-her-makes-you-feel-inadequate perfect, but truly perfect. This year was hard without her.

She chose Oberlin for college so she could get a music degree while double-majoring in something meaningful (environmental studies) because my parents insisted. Grandma thought she should ignore them and go to Juilliard, but rebellion is not Em's way.

Thinking about Grandma makes me remember the postcard. "Can I show you something?"

"Please. I'm dying to read it."

"That's not what I meant, but here." I fish the poem out of my sleeve and hand it to her.

"That sleight was nice, by the way. I didn't catch it."

Emma's sweet, but truth is, it was clumsy. Grandma would have called me out if she'd seen it—even mid-breakup. I've gotten sloppy over these last two months. Camden wasn't all that interested in my magic.

"This is awful," Emma says, looking up from the poem. "And not just because it's about Mom."

"I know. He has no imagination." Which, believe me, I am plenty grateful for right now.

"But you stayed with him almost two months. That's like a personal best. Looking at this, I can't understand why."

"I figured dull wasn't so bad after Liey McLiarface. Plus," I say with a pointed look, "Mom liked him."

Emma laughs. "Well, if you didn't want to show me the poem, then what?"

I hold up the postcard for her, letting her see the picture of the donkey before flipping it over. The message, written in the purple ink Grandma always uses, says It started with this.

Emma takes it out of my hands and studies both sides. "When did it come?"

"Today."

"The postmark's from two days ago."

"I know. What do you think it means?"

Emma shrugs. A few weeks ago, our grandmother took an Alaskan cruise and disappeared. The cruise line insists an accident was impossible but can't explain what happened. Everyone believes this is some stunt of hers. It wouldn't be out of character: Two years ago she vanished, and the memory is still fresh. She resurfaced after three weeks with a face-lift and pink hair.

Most of the time I'm sure the same thing is happening again, but sometimes, late at night, I'm afraid I'm the only one who loves her enough to worry. Mom and Emma see Grandma Matilda as a cautionary tale, but for me, she's more #goals.

Emma began piano at age five and has always divided her time equally between practicing and schoolwork. Mom, for all her environmental activism, spends most days alone, working through scientific reports and government regulations. Dad is an actuary.

This is the royal flush of boring jobs. Actuaries make insane amounts of money calculating risks for investment firms and insurance companies because so few people have the stamina for the mind-numbing, soul-sucking nature of the work. (In fairness, Dad would probably explain his job differently.)

The only thing Mom and Dad really understand about me is my aptitude for math. Their love language is enrolling me in gifted programs, and they're sending me off to another one as soon as Emma leaves.

But I'm not looking forward to it. It's not so much the work—that part's OK—it's the "fun." Video game tournaments, binge-watching sci-fi, and trivia nights aren't enough for me, and math camps never have night classes in tightrope walking.

Unlike everyone else in the family, Grandma Matilda—who left home at eighteen to become a magician's assistant—gets me.

Got me?

No. She's got to be OK.

I examine the back of the postcard again, searching for a secret message, but nothing leaps out.

The doorbell rings, and Emma, expecting it to be Camden, takes my hand. Mom calls, "Girls, can you come down?"

Puzzled, we look at each other and head downstairs.

Mom hugs me. "Are you OK?"

I nod.

"You know I never did anything to encourage him?"

"I do," I assure her.

"OK. There are letters for you both. You have to sign."

Emma and I exchange another confused look.

"They're from Grandma," Mom says, and I grin as relief sweeps over me. Mom shakes her head. "Fasten your seat belts."

I rush toward the open door, and Emma follows. The man waiting there holds out a white-and-green envelope to each of us. I sign the little card, give it back to him, and look down at the letter. This must be the explanation I've been waiting for, but something about how official it is makes me nervous.

"Ready?" Emma says.

I turn to Mom. "You didn't get one?"

She shakes her head. "You know Grandma."

I do.

The letter is written in Grandma's purple handwriting.

Darling Lia,

I have a little proposition for you: Spend the summer doing magic in Mirror Lake.

The Society celebrates its hundredth anniversary in August, and, truthfully, it could use a little attention. Which is where you and the other young people come in. I've set up a competition that should generate some outside interest. I promise to make it worth your time.

All my love,
Grandma Matilda

PS You were born to do this.
PPS Don't forget what I told you about Blackwell boys.

This must be good news. Emma and I exchange letters. Only the first postscript is different. Hers says *I'll understand if piano is more important, but look out for Lia if you can.*

Humph. I don't need a babysitter.

Mom, who's been reading over my shoulder, says, "You're not doing this."

She's speaking to me, but Emma answers, "No. This tour's too important. And if I back out now, I may never get another chance." She looks at me. "But it's only two weeks. I could meet you after."

I squeeze her hand, because I may not need her, but I want her all the same.

"Lia. No," Mom says. "You start Solstice next week. That could make a huge difference in the kinds of colleges you get accepted to, which will affect your whole life. Not to mention it's a chance to make a commitment to something worthwhile. Something you have a real gift for."

"Maybe I have a gift for this too?" I say, ignoring the "worthwhile" part. I reach into my back pocket and pull out an ace, showing the card to Mom and Emma before twirling my arm through the air like a flamenco dancer as I change it into a queen. Completely loyal, Em claps. I curtsy because I deserve it this time.

But Mom is unimpressed. "That's not a gift that gets you anywhere. This fall you choose a college and maybe a major. It's time to get serious about something that matters."

Mom has a gift for wounding me, but I am used to being not-Emma. The truth is, I'm not the kind of person who gets serious about anything . . . or anyone. Camden and I only broke up thirty minutes ago, and I am well on my way to being over him. I have zero desire to stay here this summer and see if we can get back together.

"Grandma needs me," I say. I'm sure of this, at least. That's why she sent *me* the postcard, even if we both got letters.

Although what she wants me to do about the donkey is a little unclear.

"Grandma's not even there," Mom says. When Grandma vanished, Aunt Julie moved into her house, and Mom knows she would have called right away if Grandma showed up.

"Please," I say. I know I spend too much time on trivial things. Like riffle passes and trends in nail polish and the seventy-fifth digit of pi. And I know Mom wishes that instead I would devote myself to solving climate change or creating High Art or generating Important Knowledge. And maybe I will. Eventually. But I'm only seventeen. Is wanting to spend one summer on magic really so bad?

"Lia, you are not pulling out of one of the most prestigious math programs in the country for some ludicrous contest organized by your whack job grandmother. Dead or alive."

"Mom!" I say, genuinely shocked. This is her mother, after all.

"Well, I'm sorry. But no."

"You're letting Emma go on that tour. That's not work. And it's not academic." Emma gives me an injured look. It's not nice to bring her into this.

"She's learning to be a pianist, not a sideshow freak."

This hurts more than I want to let on. "Why are you so against this?"

"I'd like you to do something with your life that isn't completely ridiculous."

"What if it's only a little bit ridiculous?" I say, trying to make her smile.

We all look toward the garage when we hear the door opening. Mom sighs. "Let's see what your dad has to say."

When he comes in from the side hall, he says, "What's up, ladies?"

"Camden wrote a sonnet about Mom, so Lia broke up with him," Emma says.

"And Grandma Matilda sent us a certified invitation to come to Mirror Lake and do magic," I add. "So she's alive. But up to something."

"And now Lia wants to run away to join the circus," Mom finishes.

"So, same old, same old," he says and kisses my forehead.

Two

DAD TELLS US TO GET IN THE CAR BECAUSE WE'RE GOING OUT FOR PIZZA. IT'S FUNNY—HE SPENDS ALL DAY WORKING WITH NUMBERS, BUT HE'S MUCH BETTER THAN MOM AT READING THE EMOTIONAL TEMPERATURE OF THE HOUSE AND NUDGING IT IN THE DIRECTION HE WANTS IT TO GO.

Once we've ordered and salads are in front of us and they have wine, he says, "Now, what's this about Matilda?"

I pull my letter out of my back pocket and hand it to him. After he reads it, he looks at Mom. "Twenty-five years, and I still cannot believe you're related to this woman."

"And yet . . ." Mom says, and gestures to me.

"Is it so bad that I'm like Grandma? Seems like she did all right."

"Lia. She was a magician's assistant and had three husbands and still disappears on the regular. I'm not sure 'all right' is the phrase I'd use."

The waitress clears the salads. When she's gone, Dad says, "You really want to spend the summer on magic, not math?"

I smile, because he says this like he can't quite believe anyone would willingly make this choice.

"I do." I look at Emma for help, but she lifts her shoulders. She'll support me because this is what I want, but she doesn't get it. "I do math all year long, but I only get to do magic in Mirror Lake. Plus, magic is the only thing I've ever done that makes people gasp."

This is not entirely true, but I'm assuming my parents don't want to hear about the first time I took my shirt off in front of Camden.

"It's fun and you're good at it. I get it," Mom says. "But is magic really something worthy of devoting your life to?"

"I don't know. That's kind of a big question for the summer after junior year."

She shakes her head. "It's not too early to think about your future. You've been given a lot of advantages. You need to do something that's going to leave the world better than you found it." She smiles at Emma. "Or more beautiful. And I'm sorry . . . but I just don't think Mirror Lake magic is going to do that."

I change tactics. "I'm worried about Grandma."

Mom rolls her eyes. "She's fine. This is one more attention grab."

"Maybe. But what if it's not? She's not going to be around forever."

Mom presses her lips together. I'm fighting dirty, but desperate times.

The pizzas show up, and we stay quiet until we're alone again.

Then Dad says, "I don't think we can force Lia to go to math camp. And we certainly can't make her stay."

"True," I say, and Mom narrows her eyes.

He looks back at me. "At some point, you'll need to pay us back for the camp deposit."

I can't help grinning. "Of course. Absolutely. I can get a job in Mirror Lake if I have to."

"OK." He looks at Mom. "It's probably not the worst thing if Lia spends the summer with your sister."

"I'll agree *if* you also do that online SAT class."

Mom has been pushing me to do this ever since I got my disappointing (to her) verbal score this spring, but the idea of doing a whole class in test prep on top of school was too horrible to contemplate.

One of the problems with having a lawyer for a parent is they try to negotiate everything, but I grew up playing this game.

"Not the live instruction one," I say. She's been pushing me toward a version that's practically school. You have to go to class at certain times, plus do all the homework, but there's another one that's mostly videos on demand and practice tests, and that might be bearable.

"OK, but I want you to do the math prep too."

I open my mouth to argue.

"Anything not perfect can be improved," she says. "You have a shot at scores that could get you in anywhere."

"If I do this, I get to go. The whole summer?"

"Yeah. If you get those scores up, it won't be a total waste of time."

"Also, if I find Grandma," I say.

"Sure. That too."

Two days and sixty-seven meaningful maternal sighs later, Emma and I are finally in the car. Mirror Lake is a couple of hours northwest of Milwaukee but seems much farther. The closer you get, the more the hills and dips in the road feel like a roller coaster, especially since the thick evergreen forests that spring up once you're away from the city make it seem like you're winding your way through Space Mountain.

Just before the town, the road drops steadily down toward the lake. Even in the summer, a faint layer of fog clings to the ground until noon, and because there's only one major road, cars enter the downtown bumper to bumper.

"How can there be a traffic jam?" Emma says, leaning her head on the window. "Only eight thousand people live here."

"It's almost twice that in the summer."

At some point in the distant past, Mirror Lake pulled itself out of an economic depression by becoming a magic-based tourist trap under the leadership of Thurston Carter, one of the most famous (and wealthy) magicians in the world. It's an odd place, full of palmists, magic shops, fortune-tellers, and sellers of herbal teas and essential oils.

People slow their cars to gawk at a man sticking flaming torches into his mouth to advertise a barbecue restaurant. Across the street, a mime juggles bowling pins, while in the gazebo by the lake, women gather in a circle to hold crystals above their heads.

A few blocks down the busiest side street, I can just barely see the little theater where Grandma's former partner, Henry Blackwell, performs magic shows Saturday nights. His grandson does some kind of mind reader bit there Fridays, and novices try out their acts Sunday afternoons. I'd like to do that someday, but I'm not ready.

Emma scowls out her window at the mime. He bows to her, twirling an imaginary top hat. "I hate this place," she says.

"I know." But I'm smiling so hard my cheeks hurt. Emma and I spend every July here with Grandma. It's my favorite month of the year, but Emma—not so much. When we were kids, she loved it as much as I do, but the last few years, she's been atypically crabby about our visits.

Grandma lives in one of the big houses along the lake. I honestly don't know if all the money came from my grandfather—husband #2, who owned a construction company before he died—or if she made her own fortune as a performer. She and Henry (husband #1) were pretty big for a while with television specials and Vegas acts, but she was the assistant, and Henry lives in a more modest neighborhood behind the downtown. Grandma had one more husband after my grandfather, but to hear her tell it, he didn't have any money at all.

When we get to the house, Em and I go in the back without knocking. I'm a little worried about how it will feel to come in without Grandma, but Aunt Julie flies down the back steps, making so much noise it's impossible to feel sad.

She wraps us in her arms and pulls us upstairs to the kitchen, pouring iced coffee and putting chocolate chip cookies in front of us. Aunt Julie is a taller, more vibrant version of Mom—both in the way she dresses and the way she moves through the world. She works in reality TV and lives wherever the next show is.

"Are you staying the whole summer?" Emma asks. "Even if Grandma comes back?"

"Until September either way. We're shooting in Chicago next season, but I don't need to be there full-time yet. Mirror Lake's close enough that I can pop down for the prep work." For the last few years, Aunt Julie's been working on *Schooled,* which isn't the biggest reality show going but has a pretty good cult following.

"What's the next season about?"

"Clowns, if you can believe it." The premise of *Schooled* is that it follows a group of novices entering some kind of training program. So far, they've done hairstylists, pastry chefs, and pilots, but I like where they're going with clowns. "Are you ready for the big event?" Aunt Julie asks me.

I shrug. "Who knows?"

"Do you know who else got letters?" Emma asks.

"Just you two, Theo, and the Blackwells."

"Really?" I say. Theo is the grandson of Grandma's old manager, Peter Yoon. We're in and out of his house every summer, and Theo's a friend, so I'm not surprised Grandma included him, but Henry Blackwell's grandsons? That doesn't make sense. She threatened to disown me if I ever so much as spoke to them, and Henry's just as eager as she is to keep us apart.

"But she hates the Blackwells," Emma says.

"It's complicated," Aunt Julie responds, looking out the window. "When you perform together for that long, you're connected in a way the rest of us can't imagine. She can't let that go, but she resents him too. Because he was the reason she stopped."

"What did he do?" Emma asks.

"Made her sign an NDA and a noncompete as part of the divorce."

"What does that mean?" I ask.

"The nondisclosure agreement meant she couldn't reveal how any of their tricks were done, and the noncompete said she couldn't work with any magician other than Henry."

"She couldn't do magic at all she after she left him?" I ask.

"Not for money, or she'd lose the house. They bought it when they were married."

"That's horrible," Emma says. She's thinking about how it would feel to give up piano.

"Well, along with the house, she got a fair bit of money. He complained often enough that she bankrupted him. And she was mostly ready to leave magic to have kids. At least that's what she always told us."

Still, it doesn't seem right she had to make that choice while Henry got to do both. "Why did they stop performing together?"

"I think their personal life made it too hard, but I don't really know. She doesn't talk about it. Growing up, my dad had a fit whenever she mentioned Henry."

I can imagine. I've seen old photos of both Henry and my grandfather. Henry was gorgeous. Grandpa not so much.

"Why on earth would she invite the Blackwells into this event of hers?" Emma asks.

"Maybe they're not as bad as Henry," I suggest.

Emma and Aunt Julie exchange a long look. Then Emma says, "They're pretty bad."

"Yes, they are," Aunt Julie agrees. "But you don't do a magic event in Mirror Lake without inviting the Blackwells."

Emma stands. "I'm going to head back."

"Already?" I say. "We just got here." I know Mirror Lake isn't Emma's favorite place, but I thought she'd want to spend some time with me before she left for Europe.

"I have packing to do."

I walk Emma to the car, hoping that once we're alone she'll tell me what's really going on. When she opens her door, I say, "Spill. What happened with you and a Blackwell boy?"

"What do you mean?" she asks, and drops her eyes to the ground.

"Come on." I am not having it. I saw the look she gave Aunt Julie.

She shrugs. "It was a long time ago. I don't want to talk about it." This is strange. Emma tells me everything. "Just be careful around them. They're like doughnuts—super tempting but really bad for you."

She gets in the car and drives away, leaving me to wonder when she found time to secretly date a Blackwell.

✦

I head down to the beach and settle into one of Mirror Lake's trademark purple Adirondack chairs, closing my eyes and tilting my face toward the sun. I don't know how many hours I've spent in this spot. Enough that—much more than Whitefish Bay—this place feels like home.

Although today, the familiarity is bittersweet. It's not just that I miss Grandma—I do—it's that I feel both uncertain and betrayed. Because she didn't trust me enough to tell me what's going on. I'd never say this out loud, but I always thought I was her favorite. She has to know, whatever screwball plan she has in mind, I'll have her back. But what if she planned to return by the time I got here . . . only something happened? Magic is full of escapes and disappearances gone wrong.

For the first time since Aunt Julie called to say Grandma was missing, I let myself cry about it. At home, I couldn't, because Mom and Emma weren't worried, and my sadness would have been one more example of my drama queen tendencies.

After a while, I wipe my eyes on my sleeves.

"You OK?" a voice next to me says, and the most beautiful boy ever lowers himself into the chair alongside mine. I could fall right into those brown eyes, and his dark hair is just long enough to be mussed by the wind. Or my hands.

"I'm fine. Thanks," I say, giving my eyes another pass with my cuff to make sure I don't look like a raccoon.

"Boyfriend trouble?" he asks.

I take a moment to appreciate this move. He's made it easy to wave him off if I want to.

But I don't.

I shake my head, feeling suddenly grateful to Camden and his ludicrous sonnet. "I was missing my grandma. No one else in my family gets it."

He nods. "I hate it when people say, 'They had a good life.'"

"I know." I don't want to get into the whole complicated story, so I don't bother to correct him. Besides, I had to deal with plenty of insensitive comments when my other grandma died two years ago. "People who say 'They're in a better place' should lose their speaking privileges for a year."

"My grandfather in India died in January. Even though we only saw him every other year, I miss knowing he was there. It's terrible when your family gets smaller."

"It is." I feel cold all over at the thought that Grandma Matilda could be gone for real.

Down by the shore, a toddler sprints into the water, and his mother follows, yanking him out. He arches his back and screams, while his older sister takes advantage of her mother's distraction to plunge in herself. When her mother pulls her out, she joins her brother on the ground, screeching. The sound could legit be used as torture.

After watching for a while, the boy says, "You know what I can't believe? That people walk around their whole lives seeing how kids act, and then at some point they think, *Yeah, let's make some more of those.*"

"I know, right? If parenting was actually fun, I don't think nature would need to incentivize it so heavily."

He looks at me blankly for a moment, but when he figures it out, he laughs, which is a sight to see. While I'm watching him, I notice the book on the arm of his chair. David Foster Wallace's history of infinity.

I need to find out this boy's name so I can decide if I should keep my own or take his when we marry.

Gesturing at the book, I say, "What do you think?"

"I like it, but I don't think you'd be interested." He moves it to the other side of the chair. He's been taken in by my pink sweatshirt and painted toenails. I'm used to this, but that doesn't mean I enjoy it.

I tell him, "My favorite part is when he tells you to 'deal' after he gives that detailed explanation of Zeno's paradox."

He blinks.

"But it's a little old. I think I agree with the physicists who are saying that infinity is mathematically useful but not empirically real."

That gets the biggest smile yet. "Oh. You are fun."

"Yes, I am," I say, delighted. Sometimes boys are not pleased to learn I know as much math as they do, but this one is not irritated or skeptical. He's intrigued. And so am I.

"Hey! Beckett!" a blond white boy about our age calls from the top of the hill, giving me a name. And a nice one.

"My cousin," Beckett says, giving the boy a just-a-minute wave. "I need to go."

I can't help looking at him curiously. Beckett and the boy on the hill do not look like cousins.

"On my dad's side. My mom grew up in Mumbai. My dad grew up here."

Beckett is a Mirror Lake legacy and a math genius and a dreamboat. I am all the swoons.

"What?" he says in response to my smile.

"Nothing," I say, all innocence. He looks like he knows better, so I change the subject. "How'd they meet?"

Beckett tilts his head. "Who?" My smile returns. I am not the only one distracted here.

"Your parents."

"Right." He shakes his head a little. "My dad's a CPA, and my mom's a programmer. He spent six weeks doing some training at her branch in India. One day he got my mom to walk him around her floor for a ridiculous amount of time so she could help him look for a meeting that didn't exist. Then he offered to take her out to dinner as a thank-you."

"Smooth."

"Hey, for a CPA that was A-game material. My mom would want me to tell you that she knew what he was up to immediately." He clearly loves his parents. I like it.

"I'm growing old here!" the boy on the hill shouts.

Can he not see that his cousin and I are having a moment?

Beckett stands. "Same time, same place tomorrow?"

I nod.

"Oh, and one more thing?"

"Lia."

"Nice. But actually, I wanted to follow up on the question I asked earlier."

Now I tilt my head.

"When you said no to boyfriend trouble, was that no boyfriend or no trouble?"

"No to both right now," I say, looking into his gorgeous eyes. "But I'm not opposed to either."

Three

MY PARENTS' PRIMARY CONSIDERATIONS IN BUYING GROCERIES ARE ETHICS (MOM) AND PRACTICALITY (DAD). BREAKFAST OPTIONS AT HOME CAN BE BRUTAL. COFFEE IS BANNED FOR BOTH ENVIRONMENTAL AND FAIR-TRADE REASONS, AND MORE THAN ONCE I'VE BEEN OFFERED A BOWL OF SOAKED PEANUTS—WHICH TASTE EXACTLY LIKE THEY SOUND—AS MY MORNING MEAL. ("BUT LIA, THEY'RE SO EASY TO CHEW!")

So I'm a little overwhelmed this morning by the joyful possibilities of Aunt Julie's kitchen. I can't focus because I keep bouncing back and forth between the shelf of primary-colored cereals in the pantry and the collection of artificially flavored creamers in the fridge.

"Is mixing salted caramel with cinnamon a mistake?" I ask Aunt Julie, who's sitting at the little table drinking her own whipped cream–covered coffee.

"Yes," she says. "Although the vanilla and caramel are good."

I prepare my coffee, following her advice. The sugar component of my morning meal taken care of, I search the refrigerator and find a bag of little oranges and a cardboard container of eggs marked "hard-boiled" and pushed toward the back. I pull both out and put them in front of Aunt Julie.

She picks up an orange, looks at it skeptically, and returns it to the bag. Instead, she peels an egg but stops halfway through, sets it down on the table, and says, "This is why I mostly prefer prepackaged food."

When I look at her curiously, she pushes the egg toward me. In faint, gray letters, right on the egg white, it says "clowns."

"Huh," I say, and finish peeling the egg. There's no other message. I attack the rest. When I finish, I have four eggs, each with one word: "clowns," "two," "there," and "were."

I rearrange them to get: *Two clowns there were.*

"You think Yoda's sending us a message?" Aunt Julie asks.

I try again, producing *There were two clowns.* "Is this for your work?" I ask, thinking about clown college. *Schooled* does all kinds of crazy stunts to keep things interesting.

She shakes her head. "My mother."

"How long have these been here?" I ask, mentally adding grocery shopping into my plans for the day.

"Since I came? I'm not really an egg person. She must have left them for you."

I get out my phone to take a picture.

I have no idea what Grandma is up to.

✦

As I sit in the sun on the little balcony off the room Emma and I share when we're here, I study the picture I took of the eggs and Grandma's postcard. I retrieve the illustrated history of magic from our bookshelf and flip through the pages but find no mention of clowns. Or donkeys.

Aunt Julie sticks her head in my door. "Walk or drive?"

"Can we drive?" I say. "I'm going to wear heels."

I've put on my navy dress with little white polka dots and pulled up my hair. This is as close as I get to battle armor. All Aunt Julie knows is that Peter Yoon, as Grandma's manager, has a letter to read to all the people she invited into this contest.

We're going to the Society of American Conjurers, the second-oldest magic association in the country. It was big when Thurston Carter—who made his name by disappearing the Brooklyn Bridge—was in his prime, but it's a little down at the heels now.

"Ready?" Aunt Julie says.

"You don't have to come," I tell her. "I can drive myself."

"It's OK. I want to check in with Peter. Maybe he's heard something." The little bit of hesitation in her voice makes me squeeze her hand, and she pulls me into a hug. It's nice not to be the only one worried.

The purple-painted mansion that houses the Society is up on a bluff, so I'm feeling pretty grumpy about my shoe choice by the time we get to the porch.

She presses the doorbell, and a gong sounds somewhere inside. A few minutes later, Peter answers. "Members or guests?" he says with a smile.

Aunt Julie says, "Peter, you've known me since the day I was born."

"And yet, despite my frequent invitations, you've never gone through adjudication."

To be admitted to the Society, you have to be recommended by two current members and successfully perform a ten-minute show in front of the membership. Right now, there are 137 members. Fifteen are women. And that includes my missing grandmother.

Aunt Julie sighs. "You know why we're here."

"Do you know what she's up to?"

"I only know what you do," Aunt Julie says. "Less, probably. Can we come in?"

He steps aside. "Hello, Lia."

"Hi, Mr. Yoon."

"What happened to 'Uncle Peter'?"

Since we were little, Emma and I have always used "Uncle" as a courtesy title, but everything feels more formal here at the Society.

Nothing's changed since the first time I visited. The windows are stained glass portraits of magicians—Houdini thrashing about in chains, Herrmann shooting cards out of his hand, Abbott with his floating orb. The only light in the foyer comes from wall sconces and lamps.

Peter tells me I can join Theo upstairs in the library. As I walk slowly up the staircase, I study the photographs on the wall, which go back in time as I climb. I spot four pictures of Grandma and Henry performing and, nearly at the top, their wedding photo, which was taken here. Unlike her performance updos,

Grandma's wedding hair cascades down her back, and her high-necked, sleeveless dress clings to her body. She's looking up at Henry like he is the sun at the center of her solar system, and if I had to name the emotion on his face, I'd say awe. It's heartbreaking, knowing how they feel about each other now.

Just as I'm about to keep walking, I notice the date in the corner of the photo: July 10, 1971. But that can't be right. Grandma always says she got onstage for the first time at eighteen, the summer after she graduated from high school, and she told me she married Henry just six weeks after they started working together. She always said they got married quick to save money on hotel rooms when they traveled for shows, but now that I've seen this picture, I no longer believe her.

If this date is right, the math on her stories doesn't work. She was born in 1951, which means she was twenty in her wedding photo, not eighteen. It's not like her to get a detail wrong. So if she got onstage right after high school, where was she performing—and with who?

I sigh. More questions to ask if she ever decides to come back.

When I come into the library, Peter's grandson Theo puts his sketch pad aside and stands. He seems like he's grown into himself some over the past year. Still bookish, but now with geeky-love-interest-in-a-K-drama vibes.

He pushes his glasses up. "Hey, Lia. Emma said to say hi."

"You talked to Emma?" We always hang out with Theo when we're in Mirror Lake, but I never think about him when I'm away. It's news to me that Emma does.

"We talk all the time. We both ended up at tiny liberal arts colleges in the middle of nowhere and had to pool survival strategies. We swore if we both still hated it after a year we'd transfer to Madison together."

"You don't like Grinnell?"

"I love it. Now. But the first six months I kept having nightmares about cornfields."

"Poor baby," I say, walking over to the shelves.

This library is members only, so I've never seen it before. One quick glance tells me there are dozens of books I've wanted to read but could never find out in the world. Magicians are careful about their secrets. I take a book on mirrored illusions to the couch.

Theo sits beside me. "Do you know what's coming?"

"No. You?" Since his grandfather is in charge, I'd hoped Theo might have some inside information.

But he shakes his head. "When's the last time you talked to your grandma?"

"Almost two months." Last time I called was before everything started with Camden. Putting him at the center of my life made perfect sense while I was doing it, but now that he's gone, I kind of can't believe the way I sidelined my friends and family. Especially since I don't even miss him.

Theo takes my hand. "I'm sure she's OK."

I nod as the door opens to reveal two pretty blond boys.

I don't know either of them because our grandparents kept us apart, but because of his mind-reader act, Elliott Blackwell's face is all over town, and the boy beside him looks too much like him to be anyone other than a brother. After they come through the door, another boy steps in. I tighten my grip on Theo's hand.

Because it's Beckett.

"What are you—? I mean, why?" I say, completely confused.

"Lia?" he says, looking as shocked as I am. "You look different."

I guess I do. When we met, I was in a sweatshirt and flip-flops, face tearstained and hair a wind-tangled mess. Now, with my understated makeup, smooth bun, and heels, I probably look like I'm running for office. But my change in appearance hardly seems the most surprising thing. He has no reason to be here.

Unless.

I look over at the younger blond. His cousin.

"No," I say, putting it together. "No, no, no."

Beckett's face closes down, and he shakes his head a little. "I should have known."

The blond boy grins and looks back and forth between us. "This is the girl from the beach? The one you said—"

But I don't get to hear what he said, because Beckett breaks in, saying "Chase" in a warning way. Elliott and Chase Blackwell. The name of the younger brother does ring a bell. But I don't ever remember hearing about Beckett.

Unconcerned, Chase continues. "Oh, this is too, too good." He gestures between us. "Amelia Montgomery, meet Beckett Blackwell."

Elliott, who's picked up a bust of Robert-Houdin to examine, looks over his shoulder at me and says, "Emma's sister?"

"Lia Sawyer," I say to Chase.

"What?" Chase says.

"I go by Lia, and my last name is Sawyer."

"Still," he says. "You're a Montgomery girl underneath."

"What does that mean?"

"Cunning, mercenary." He pauses and snaps his fingers a couple of times. "What's the other one Grandpa says?"

"Manipulative," Beckett says. Theo puts a hand on my back. I can't believe my beautiful, charming, mathy boy is a Blackwell.

Chase is still amused. "A little advice? If a kindly friar offers to help the two of you, turn him down."

The library door opens again, and Henry Blackwell steps inside.

Henry looks about as good as a seventy-year-old man can. His hair is snowy white, his figure trim, and his posture straight. He carries himself like someone who's spent his life onstage.

Elliott turns from the mirror, where he's been examining his carefully styled hair, and says, "Grandpa."

"Elliott." Henry nods to his other grandsons. Beckett picks up a chair to bring over to him, and Henry sits.

Peter comes into the room with an envelope in his hand. "Why doesn't everyone have a seat, and I'll read Matilda's letter."

Chase flops into an armchair, while Beckett and Elliott lean against bookshelves, crossing their arms and looking contemptuous. There's no trace of the boy from the beach in Beckett's face, and I miss him.

Peter decides making them sit isn't worth the effort and opens the envelope. "I promised I would read this as written. 'Thank you for coming, you dear, sweet children. And thank you as well, you insufferable Blackwell boys.'"

Peter stops, shakes his head, and then continues.

"'No, Peter, don't apologize. They are insufferable. Especially that oldest one. Mentalism! It's magic for people with neither skill nor conscience.'"

I can't help glancing at Beckett. He gives Chase a wry smile, which makes my heart do an odd little skip, but when he notices me looking at him, his face goes serious again. Does he think I knew this was coming?

"'I'm proposing a little contest. And I'm inviting you—the youngest descendants of those most intimately involved in our act—to take part. The task is simple: Perform a show to honor the Society's hundredth anniversary using tricks taken from our Vegas act. Here are the rules:

"'One: You may choose partners from those I've invited, but no one else. This way the tricks stay in the family, and darling Henry can't complain.'"

Darling Henry looks like he's about to spontaneously combust, but Peter doesn't give him time to speak.

"'Two: All the resources of the Society are yours—the library, the practice theaters, the props, and the tools. Although you must abide by their rules.

"'Three: Each person who agrees to compete will be given two thousand dollars for the first month, and each team will receive a copy of our 1973 act to study.'"

Well, that takes care of repaying my parents for Solstice. There'll be plenty left for the act, and I won't have to worry about a job.

"'Four: After the first month, you will perform a ten-minute act for three Society members selected by Peter. Only those judged minimally competent at this checkpoint will proceed.

"'Five: Those who go on will receive two thousand dollars to fund a second month of work before the final performance.

"'And here, my dears, is your reward. The winners, as judged by members of the Inner Circle, will be given the Starlight Theater to do with as you please.'"

I snap my head toward Peter. Grandma never told me she owned the theater. I'd assumed that since Henry performed there, it was his. I look around the room. Theo seems equally surprised. The Blackwells do not.

Mercenary, Chase had said. They must have grown up hearing Henry complain. Paying Grandma rent every month—after losing the house to her—must be a constant irritant.

"Seems simple enough," Elliott says with a cocky grin, pushing back his black blazer as he puts his hands in his pockets. His T-shirt says MAGICIANS THINK THEY'RE GODS. GOD THINKS HE'S A MENTALIST.

Elliott is confident. Too confident. Because if he thinks he's walking away with this theater without a fight, he's mistaken. This little contest of Grandma's is exactly the sort of game I love, and Chase is right about one thing—I am a Montgomery girl underneath, and I'm not losing my grandmother's theater to a bunch of Blackwell boys.

Peter looks around. "If you're going to do this, you should decide if you want a partner. And I'll need everyone other than Elliott—since he's already a member—to take the oath before we give you free rein in the library."

I hide my book behind me. "I know Emma's not here, but she'll be back before the checkpoint. Can she count as my partner?"

"Where is she?" Elliott asks. I narrow my eyes at him. It's none of his business.

Peter looks at the letter again. "I guess so. She was invited, after all. That seems to be the only real rule."

"I'll be on my own, then," Theo says.

"What do you say, little brother?" Elliott says to Chase. Before answering, Chase, his expression serious for the first time, meets Beckett's eyes.

Beckett says, "Go ahead. I'm fine alone."

"You can be three," Peter says.

"No," Beckett answers, and gives Elliott a dark look.

"Fine," Chase says, and Elliott leans forward to clap him on the back. Chase doesn't react. Something weird is going down among the Blackwell boys.

Theo says, "If we're performing tricks from their old act, won't Henry help them?"

"I have no interest in revealing my secrets," Henry snaps. "To my grandsons or anyone else. The Society shouldn't be supporting Matilda's little game. It's unethical."

Peter clears his throat. "No secrets are being revealed. It's as common as dirt for magicians to reverse engineer someone else's act."

The two men glare at each other in a way that seems like the continuation of an old argument.

"I suppose," Henry says. "And reclaiming ownership of the theater from my vindictive ex-wife would make all this nonsense worthwhile." One by one, he looks at Elliott, Beckett, and Chase. "I expect you to win."

Four

HENRY SLAMS THE DOOR ON HIS WAY OUT. NONE OF THE BOYS SEEM SUR-
PRISED. THEY MUST BE USED TO HIS TEMPER TANTRUMS.

I guess his reaction explains why Grandma included the
Blackwells in this contest. If they didn't have a shot at the theater, Henry would have put up an even bigger fight. But I can't
understand what she's hoping to get out of this. It's an awfully
big risk. And a lot of pressure to put on me, now that I think
about it.

After a few silent seconds, Elliott asks, "Checks now?"

Theo and I exchange a look.

"Oaths first," Peter says. "I know most of you never planned
to do this full-time or to become members. But this is something
each of your grandparents take seriously, and I'd ask you to do
the same. So, please stand and raise your right hand."

I know this is silly. I can hear Mom saying this oath is the
legacy of old men trying to turn a pastime to amuse children
into something sacred. But even as I tell myself it doesn't matter, the hairs on my arms stand up as I take my place beside
Theo. At some point, my grandmother took this same oath.
And so did Thurston Carter, a magician I've seen on television

and read about in books. This ritual connects me to them and to thousands of other magicians in London and New York and LA. Maybe it's not important to the world, but it feels important to me.

"Repeat after me," Peter says. "On my honor, I vow to keep the secrets of the craft, to respect the art of magic, and to protect the work of my fellow magicians as I would protect my own."

When we say the words together, tears spring up in my eyes, and I blink them away, not wanting to draw attention to myself by wiping at them.

"Does this mean we're members?" I ask.

"Provisionally," Peter says. "Matilda and I recommended each of you. At some point, you'll have to demonstrate your skills for the membership, and we'll take a full vote."

"You really don't know where she is?" I can't help asking, even though I know he would have told us if he did.

He shakes his head. "All I know about her plan was in that envelope."

"Can you tell me the difference between regular members and the Inner Circle?" Maybe the secret behind why Grandma did this lies in the way she set up the contest. Her letter said the Inner Circle would decide who gets the theater. Maybe knowing who they are will help me figure out her endgame. Or at least be prepared to win.

"Anyone who's recommended and has the basic skills can become a member—managers, assistants, store owners, even amateurs. But to be inducted into the Inner Circle, you need to make your living as a magician for five years and prove you can invent as well as perform tricks."

I don't see how any of that helps me understand Grandma's goal—or win this contest.

Peter stands. "It'll take me an hour or so to run by the bank and organize the practice theaters. You'll stay here?"

No one objects. The two-thousand-dollar checks are a pretty powerful incentive.

When the door closes behind him, Chase looks around the room. "Ambitious Card?"

"Yay!" I say. Blackwell boy or not, this is a kindred spirit. I bounce into the chair across from him. He grins, and I look away. Emma might forgive falling for one Blackwell boy accidentally, but two in as many days would be too much.

Even for me.

"Really?" Theo says. "We've seen each other's routines so often we could do them ourselves."

"I've never seen Chase's," I say. Or Beckett's, but I don't say that out loud.

Ambitious Card routines, where the magician repeatedly brings a chosen card to the top of the deck, were invented more than a century ago by a guy who fooled Houdini with the trick. There are hundreds of variations, and anyone who wants to be a magician develops their own little twist, usually one where the card shows up the last time. In Mirror Lake, "Show me your Ambitious Card" is a conversation starter that separates locals from tourists. People mostly don't go out without their materials—in my case, my regular deck, plus a specially prepared card or two.

I'm not sure if Chase is proposing this as a way to kill time or if he's seeking to assess our abilities, but I don't mind playing along. The more I know about their strengths, the better I can plan my own act.

"I suggested it, so I'll go first," Chase says. He pulls cards out of his back pocket, shuffles them, and holds them out to Theo, who makes a choice without being asked.

"Sharpie," Chase says, and Beckett throws one to Theo, who signs the face and hands the card back. Chase slides it into the middle of the deck using a Marlo tilt so beautiful I see no evidence even though I'm looking.

"Call your card."

"Hey, card," Theo says with an ironic grin. They're very casual with each other. I remind myself that Peter was Henry's manager too. Still is, probably. Maybe Theo grew up playing with Chase and Beckett?

Chase twitches as if the deck moved in his hands and turns over the top card to reveal Theo's signature. Classic. Chase loses and finds Theo's card two more times before finally pulling it out of Theo's ear. This routine marks him as someone to watch out for.

Theo uses the same moves as Chase but with much less skill. Plus, he makes everything worse with his terrible patter. He starts with "Here's my routine," which triggers the audience to think about this as something well practiced, and not as, you know, magic. And before he pulls the card to the top for the first time, he says, "And with some luck, this should be your card."

Yikes. He's worse than I remember.

"That was good, Theo," Chase says when he finishes.

My disgust must show up on my face, because Chase says, "What? I'm being nice."

"No. You're being condescending," I say, and then clamp my mouth shut. Chase knows as well as I do that you do not call a card trick a routine, and that suggesting that it's working by luck shouts "I don't know what I'm doing," but the less they think I know, the better.

"You closed your eyes every time you did a sleight," Beckett says. "That's a dead giveaway." This habit is super common among people starting out. It's like when babies hide their faces so their parents won't see them. Beginners think if they don't look at their sleight, the audience won't see it either. I don't understand why Beckett's saying this out loud, though. He has no reason to help a competitor.

"No one ever said anything before." Theo glares at Chase.

"Magic isn't really your thing," Chase says.

"Doesn't mean I want to do it wrong." They must be friends. Strangers don't bicker like this.

"Sorry," Chase says, and then, "Beckett, you're up."

"Fine." Beckett takes Chase's place in the chair across from me. Being this close to him makes my heart rate pick up a little. He's got a quiet confidence that totally gets to me. And while the Blackwell boy thing is complicating, it's not fatal. Forbidden could be fun. With the right boy.

40

"Do you go to school here?" I ask while he shuffles, trying to get back some of that connection we had yesterday.

"No, but I'm here every summer. Like you, I guess."

I nod. He looks up from the cards when I don't speak. "Did you know who I was yesterday?" he asks quietly. Everyone else is watching us. Chase looks curious; Theo, a little hostile. I wonder why. Could Beckett be Emma's Blackwell? I hope not. We do not go out with each other's exes. Not that Beckett and I are going out.

Yet.

Maybe there's another secret Blackwell?

Beckett clears his throat, reminding me he's waiting for an answer. "I had no idea. It's not like you look like a Blackwell." I gesture toward Chase and Elliott.

"Convincing," he says. "But I don't believe you."

"Because I'm cunning, manipulative, and mercenary?" I'm not sure what I've done to justify this hostility. Except be a Montgomery.

"Exactly," he says. "Now, choose a card."

We go through his routine. He brings my card to the top twice, asking me to picture it in my mind each time. His technique is flawless and his pacing perfect—slow and certain—but he lacks the charm Chase brought to his performance. It's strange to see this kind of skill without joy. Especially from someone who I saw laugh so easily yesterday. It would have taken him hours and hours to get this good. Why practice like that if you don't love it?

The third time he loses my card, Beckett tells me to get his backpack, which is sitting across the room.

"Now picture your card again and reach into the small pocket." I do, expecting to find my card, but instead there's a lemon. I pull it out. It's entirely intact. Even the stem is attached.

"Nice flex."

Beckett smirks. "Not me. I asked you to picture a card. You must have lost focus."

I turn the lemon around in my hands and smell it. Real. "I've never seen this done."

"Only child. Lots of time on my hands," he says flatly, and I know for sure that is not the explanation for what's going on here.

He takes a letter opener from the desk, cuts the lemon around the middle, twists it open, and pulls out a card that's been rolled into a tube and stuck inside the fruit.

When he flattens the card on the table and it's mine, I clap. I love it when someone can fool me with a trick I know so well.

"Why lemons?"

Beckett shrugs. "I like lemons."

"And can you do it only once a day?"

"Check the big pocket."

I open the main compartment of the backpack and find two more lemons on the bottom.

"Prepared," I say.

Beckett dips his head modestly. "I have a simpler version for when I'm traveling light." His eyes flick toward Elliott. "But I wanted to be ready for today."

I press the two halves of the lemon back together and study

42

them. "Would you believe this is the second time today I've found a message hidden inside food?"

"In Mirror Lake? Sure." He meets my eyes and we're connected again—knowing we're among the few people in the world who get what it's like to live in this place. But then he shakes his head. "You can bat those big brown eyes at me all you want, but I'm not telling you how it's done."

"We'll see," I say. "You like lemons. I like a challenge."

A smile that echoes the ones I got yesterday flashes across his face, but then Elliott interrupts. "Now me."

Beckett cedes the chair to Elliott, who fans his cards. He doesn't shuffle first, and he's careful not to let us see the faces. He may as well announce he's using a trick deck. "Want to play with me, Lia?"

Oh, ick. I'm not exactly sure how much older Elliott is than me, but it's enough that his tone makes me uncomfortable.

"Be careful, Elliott," Beckett says. "I think you met your match there."

I ignore Beckett and pull a card. Ace of spades. Surprise, surprise. Here's my bet: Elliott's gaffed deck is entirely made up of only three different cards.

"Now, back in," he says. After I slide in my card, Elliott has me clap once. He jumps at the sound. "Uh-oh. Too much power. You made your card fly clear across the room."

What? He didn't even pull my card to the top once. Elliott is not respecting the Ambitious Card, and I'm offended as a magician.

He crosses to the desk and reaches inside the pencil holder, where he must have stuck the ace of spades earlier.

When he produces it, I open my eyes big and say, "Oh my goodness!" No sense in letting him know I'm onto him. People tend to underestimate me, and while that's frustrating a lot of the time, it would be best if all the Blackwells left here believing I wasn't a threat.

The thoughtful way Beckett's regarding me tells me it's too late to play dizzy blonde with him—which I don't think I could bring myself to do anyway—but Elliott's buying it.

"Want me to show you the secret?" he says, sitting next to me.

"Do you think I could learn? I can't imagine how it's done." Beckett snorts, and we exchange a glance to share our mutual contempt for Elliott, but he looks away when I shift my expression toward amusement.

Elliott, expecting the Ambitious Card to come up, hid his cards when he came into the room. That way, no matter which of his three cards was picked, he could "miraculously" produce it in another location. A total mentalist cheat. I bet he's got another card under the statue he was messing with and probably one behind the mirror where he spent so much time checking himself out.

"I could get you to competent with a little private tutoring," Elliott says, and now I'm offended as a girl. "I fill the theater every week doing this stuff."

"You fill that theater making promises you can't keep and preying on people's fear and grief," Beckett says.

Oh, boy.

Cousins or not, Beckett and Elliott are definitely not on the same team. I study Chase, trying to figure out whose side he's on. His whole body relaxes when he interacts with Beckett, and he's anxious around his brother. But when we picked partners, he agreed to work with Elliott.

"You need to chill," Elliott says to Beckett.

"Let's not do this here," Chase adds. Referee, maybe?

Elliott glares at Beckett before turning to me. "Let's see what we're working with, Lia."

Beckett's still glowering at Elliott. "Volunteer?" I ask him, hoping to bring back his good humor. Boys tend to enjoy my Ambitious Card.

He shakes his head.

"Chase?" I say, not wanting to engage with Elliott. I shuffle the cards, making sure to flash the faces of my totally standard deck.

"Sure."

I fan the cards in front of him and tell him to touch the one that's calling out to him. He does. Like Elliott, I use a card force to get my volunteer to choose a preselected card, but I do it with sleight of hand instead of a butchered deck. The way God and Erdnase intended.

Real magicians rely on misdirection, but also an incredible amount of dexterity. A trick like Elliott's requires only knowing the secret and a little charisma to sell it. To do the Ambitious Card the way I do—and, in fairness, the way Beckett and Chase do—requires hours and hours of practice. Grandma says it's a sign of respect for the audience.

Handing Chase his card with the back facing me, I say, "Now, think about how much you love your card." Chase grins, and I stand in front of him.

About half of the success of an Ambitious Card routine is in the patter. You need to give the audience a story, a reason the card is jumping about in the deck; otherwise, there's no tension. This is why Beckett had me picture the card and why Chase had Theo call it.

"If you convince your card you love it, it will always come back to you."

"And how do I do that?"

"You have to kiss it," I say seriously.

"Really?" he asks, one corner of his mouth quirking up.

I nod. This part I vary depending on my volunteer and the audience, but Chase seems up for anything, and I'm irritated with Beckett for refusing to volunteer, so I put the card right up against Chase's mouth, making sure I never see its face, and go up on my toes to kiss the back of the card, keeping my eyes on his. This provides the distraction I need. "Just like that."

Eyes crinkling, Chase quickly kisses the card before sliding it back into the deck I'm holding in front of him. I look up at him sadly. "We might have to work on your technique."

"I do all right."

I pull his card to the top a couple of times, but the last time through, I lose it and tell him to check his back pocket.

He pulls out his card—now with a bright-red lipstick print right where he kissed it.

He laughs. "I love that!"

"You would," Beckett says.

"You know what would make it better?" Chase asks.

I tilt my head.

"If the card had your phone number."

"Sometimes it does. That depends on the quality of my volunteer."

"Harsh," he says, but he's smiling.

Five

PETER COMES BACK AND PASSES OUT CHECKS, FLASH DRIVES WITH VIDEOS OF THE ACT, AND PRACTICE SCHEDULES FOR THE THEATERS, SAYING WE'RE WELCOME TO USE THE LIBRARY WHENEVER WE LIKE.

Then he tells me Aunt Julie's waiting downstairs, so I follow him out, looking back over my shoulder at Beckett, who's in heated conversation with Chase. I want to stay and talk through what it means that he's a Blackwell and I'm a Montgomery and how we can go forward with this contest without giving up on that spark that flared up between us yesterday. But I guess he has other things on his mind.

At home, I put a frozen pizza in the oven for lunch and tell Aunt Julie about my morning.

"Don't underestimate Elliott. He's ruthless, and he draws bigger crowds than Henry now."

I think about Beckett's anger and ask, "Doing what?"

"A lot of it's a traditional mentalist act—drawing duplications, identifying objects in the audience, cold reads of vacation plans and lost loves—but I hear that more and more he's wandering into spiritualism. Not every show, but every now and then, he contacts the dead."

Most people don't see a difference between a magician who tells you the card you're holding and a mentalist who reveals the total you paid for your meal before the show, but the performers orient their audiences in incredibly different ways.

Magicians invite audiences to speculate about how tricks are done. Our skill lies in our ability to fool you even while you know you're being tricked. But mentalists ask audiences to believe, and that's why they're dangerous. Vulnerable people are all too willing to part with money—and lots of it—for a chance at fame, love, or, most heartbreakingly, one last talk with someone they've lost. If this is what Elliott's doing, it's no wonder Beckett doesn't like the act.

"But will Elliott be able to do the magic?" I ask, thinking about the total lack of skill he showed this afternoon. "Henry and Matilda didn't perform as mentalists, did they?"

"Not really. But they did some mental magic, and that uses a lot of the same strategies."

"I want to see the act." I know the television specials by heart, but I didn't realize there was video from their Vegas show. And Grandma never told me about it, so I have no idea what to expect.

The video quality is a little grainy, but it's easy to see and hear. Grandma is so beautiful. Her long blond hair is swept into some complicated updo with red roses tucked into it, and she's wearing a long, sequined silver dress with a slit that goes almost up to her hip. All the better for distraction, I guess.

She begins alone onstage, looking around the curtain at the audience. A young man pushes a broom across the stage toward her and stops, apparently struck by her beauty. He presents her with a paper cone, and she, big-eyed and baffled, tilts it toward the audience, showing it's empty. The stagehand reaches inside and pulls out flowers one after the other, showering her with them, far too many to fit in the cone. She throws her arms around him and kisses him on the lips. At this moment, the back curtain parts, and Henry, splendid in a black tuxedo, appears, folding his arms and scowling. There's a nervous laugh from the audience. And he crosses the stage to Matilda.

She apologizes, and he reaches into the cone and pulls out black and gray flowers, one after the other. Again, far too many to be in the cone, particularly since the ground is still covered with the colored flowers that emerged earlier. The effect is amazing, but also a little dark.

The conceit of the angry husband is carried throughout the show—sometimes it's funny, like when Matilda flirts with audience members as she guesses the cards they're holding and the objects in their laps, or when she yawns, pantomiming boredom during Henry's opening card tricks.

But when they get to the grand illusions, the energy turns even darker. In response to her taunts about being bored, Henry brings out a lion in a cabinet—and because you believe he might be willing to hurt her, there's a little anxiety.

"Are you sure this is safe?" she asks before she climbs in the cabinet.

"Matilda, my job is to worry about the trick. Your job is to look pretty."

He shuts the door and says to the audience, "You'd think she doesn't trust me."

I literally cannot imagine how my grandmother was brave enough to do this. Honestly, dogs, even small ones, make me nervous, and she was getting into a box with a lion? Hard no.

Henry spins the cabinet in a circle. When he opens it again, both the lion and Matilda are gone. He spins it again, and they reappear. This time Matilda hops out and they disappear the lion together.

After the lion trick, Henry, full of taunts, saws Matilda into pieces, crushes her under a cement block, and impales her on spikes. It's horrible.

It reminds me of this old television show we saw in my media studies class when we were covering gender. Whenever the husband and wife would fight, he'd make this fist and say, "One of these days, Alice—POW! Right in the kisser." And they'd play the laugh track.

You'd never see that on television now, but even today, you almost can't imagine magic without violence aimed at women. One of the first magicians to use the sawing in half trick—which got big right around the time women were getting the right to vote—used fake blood, parked an ambulance in front of the theater, and kept asking Christabel Pankhurst—a British suffragist—to let him cut her up in his show. His trick inspired a host of imitators: Crushing a Woman. Stretching a Lady. Destroying a Girl. Audiences loved them all.

Henry and Matilda's final few tricks are less violent but still vaguely disturbing.

First, Henry menaces a dancing Matilda using two floating silver orbs that he seems to control with his hands. Then he hypnotizes her, puts her to sleep on a frilled bed, and levitates her into the air.

Finally, Henry ties Matilda to a post at the top of a wooden tower and pulls a curtain up around her before ascending a matching tower across the stage and raising another curtain around himself. When both curtains drop a moment later, Matilda's tower is empty. She's been teleported into Henry's arms, and he dips her for a theatrical kiss.

It's hard to explain why these last tricks bother me. In terms of magic, all three are nice. Cute little stories and mysterious effects, but in all of them, my lively grandmother is so very passive. This is not how I want to look onstage. Especially in an act I build.

Grandma has always been a force to be reckoned with. Even Mom, who takes people to court for a living, is a little afraid of her. Watching Henry order her about—or use her as a prop, like in the levitation—is messing with my head.

Aunt Julie finds me staring at the frozen screen. "You OK?"

"I'm not doing that routine."

She nods. "Yeah. It's not great. I saw it when I was a little younger than you. It's one of the reasons I never got into magic."

"Why do you think she wants us to build from this?"

Aunt Julie shakes her head. "Not sure. Maybe so you can make it less dated? Whatever it is, I promise you she had a reason."

"I'll talk to Emma about it tonight."

Then I tear upstairs to change into leggings and a long-sleeved T-shirt that says TEAM SPARKLY UNICORN, because it's almost four o'clock, the time Beckett and I agreed to meet. I don't know if he's still planning to come, but it's not going to be me who doesn't show up.

I stop in the kitchen to tell Aunt Julie I'm going for a walk.

I'm almost at the door when she says, "Lia." I turn back. "You're awfully lit up for a solo walk on the beach."

I widen my eyes, trying for innocent.

"Make your aunt happy. Tell me it's Theo Yoon waiting for you down there."

"What? No!" I've been friends with Theo since we were toddlers. I can't imagine getting all glowy about him.

Aunt Julie presses her lips together. "OK, then. At least tell me it's not Elliott Blackwell."

"Ew," I say, flapping my hands in disgust. "Why would you even think that?"

"Well . . ."

Her conflicted expression lets me put together the pieces. "No . . . do you mean . . . Emma and Elliott? That's who . . . Really?" This is the worst thing I've ever heard about my sister. I check the time on my phone. "I need to go, but I want to hear all about this later."

"You should talk to her. And remember, the other two are probably trouble as well. That whole family has a reputation for leaving women worse off than when they find them. Especially Montgomery girls."

I think about Aunt Julie's words on the way down to the lake. Because the thing is, there aren't that many Montgomery girls, so how much history can there be? Grandma and Henry, obviously. And I guess Emma and Elliott. A shudder runs through me just thinking about that. But who else? As far as I know, Aunt Julie's never been interested in boys of any kind, so does that mean . . . Mom?! Against my will, my brain starts directing a movie of her in some torrid summer romance with a mysterious Blackwell (who looks like Camden). And even though it's imaginary, I know I will never be able to unsee this.

Our chairs from yesterday are empty, so I sink into one of them, wrapping my arms around my legs and resting my chin on my knees. The water's calm, barely lapping at the shore.

Beckett's probably smart not to have come. Between the contest and whatever's gone down with our families, nothing between us would be easy, and I'm not really good at complicated.

But my resolve evaporates when Beckett sits beside me and says, "Back in your seduction clothes?"

I look down at my athletic wear. "I don't think that's the word you're looking for."

Although I have to admit, it's hard to imagine a better outfit for Beckett than the T-shirt and jeans he has on right now. The loose button-down he wore this morning made it much harder to appreciate the fabulous shape of him.

"When Elliott gave you the rundown on me, he must have told you about my weakness for casual, beachy girls."

"I met Elliott for the first time today."

Beckett shakes his head. "I don't believe it. Chase would never sell me out."

"Why assume I talked to anyone? It's not the weirdest thing in the world that we'd meet on a beach five minutes from both our houses. It's just our bad luck we have grandparents who hate each other." I am completely willing to give him the benefit of the doubt, but he doesn't seem to want to do the same.

"Meeting? Maybe. But what are the chances I'd find a girl who looks like you, crying over her 'dead' grandparent—and nice move, by the way, letting me think that. Oh, and not only is this girl I stumble across flirty and fun, but she's also ridiculously well-informed on theories of infinity? My grandfather's a magician. I know a setup when I see one."

I'm not even sure what I should be most hurt by here—that I'd use my grandmother to manipulate him or that I couldn't possibly be interested in his book.

"I'd guess those odds are about the same as the chances of me meeting a boy who's willing to admit he's sad he lost his grandfather, likes math as much as I do, and just so happens to do a surprisingly impressive Ambitious Card."

Beckett stares at me, confusion all over his face. "No. I don't buy it. If there's any coincidence at all, it's only that you look so much like her. But clearly, the universe has decided to plague me with blondes."

"Who do I look like?"

After a long moment, he says, "You're very good. And not only with me. I saw you with Theo when I came in, and you gave

Chase one kiss and wrapped him around your little finger. He's a fan."

"I didn't kiss Chase. I kissed the three of clubs."

"Whatever. That's your business. And his. All I know is I'm sick to death of people who will do anything to anyone to get what they want."

There is way too much intensity in his words for him to be talking about me. Montgomery girl or not, we just met. "You mean Elliott."

"Sure. But not only him. It's pretty clear you want that theater, and you think playing mind games with the competition might help your chances."

"I didn't even know about the theater yesterday," I argue.

Beckett looks out at the lake. "Uh-huh," he says, obviously skeptical.

"Why does it matter to you so much?" I ask. "What do you want to do with the theater if you win?"

Beckett turns to me. "Burn it. To. The ground."

Six

"WHY WOULD YOU SAY THAT?" EVEN ALLOWING FOR EXAGGERATION, THE ANGER IN HIS VOICE CHILLS ME.

"Look. Maybe you do love your grandmother. I could be wrong about that being an act."

"Gee, thanks."

He shrugs a little. "Magic wasn't good for her. And it wasn't good for my grandfather. Just because they couldn't recognize that doesn't make it less true. You watched the video?"

I nod.

"Trust me. What Elliott's doing is worse. And this is my family. I have to end it."

"But it doesn't have to be that way. Magic can be beautiful. You know that," I say, thinking about his Ambitious Card. He didn't learn that lemon trick without some kind of passion. "You must have loved it once?"

"When I was younger, I guess. Before I saw what it could do. But now . . . it's a tool. That's all."

I sit back. "What happened? What did Elliott do?"

Beckett looks at me a long time before saying, "I'm telling you so you understand why I'm doing this, not so you can talk me out of it. Because whether I love magic or not, I will get as good as I need to be to get this done."

"OK?"

He draws a deep breath and exhales slowly. "Last summer, I met this girl. Her family was renting a place here for the first time."

"Your blonde?"

"Mine for a while." He looks sad. "I fell pretty hard."

I feel a stab of jealousy. Not so much over the girl, but for that feeling. Because I don't fall hard.

I fall often.

"We were spending all this time together, and her family was really nice to me, so to thank them, I took them to Grandpa's show. And to Elliott's."

He looks away with a little shake of his head, as if he can't believe his stupidity, but I can't yet see where this went wrong.

"Elliott had started doing these bits where he talks to the dead. He keeps it pretty light onstage."

"But?" I say, when he stops.

"But . . . Helen's brother died a few years before. In a swimming accident. And her mom lost it when she saw Elliott. Total break from reality. All she wanted was to hear from Sam, and Elliott does these private readings. By the end of the summer, a good chunk of money was gone, Helen's parents were on the way to divorce, and Helen and I couldn't stand the sight of each other."

I reach over to take his hand. "I'm so sorry."

He shakes his head. "I wasn't the victim. But I won't let him do this to someone else."

Maybe it's insensitive to point this out, but I can't help it. "Even if you take the theater, Elliott could still do this in some other town."

"Sure. But here he benefits from our grandfather's name. And the people who come to Mirror Lake are especially vulnerable to this kind of thing."

"And you can't go to the police?"

"He says it's just for entertainment, and he only takes 'donations.' It's not a crime."

Beckett isn't just beautiful and charming; he's good. And I need to stop holding his hand.

I give his fingers a squeeze and withdraw, thinking about what he said. Mentalism has always made me uncomfortable. Too many mind readers encourage belief in their mystical powers in order to con people.

And sometimes, even when you tell people it's made up, they don't believe you. Grandma Matilda taught me to do cold readings—where you use body language and clever questioning to make people think you're inside their heads—because she wanted me to recognize the tricks if anyone ever tried to use them on me.

But I couldn't help wondering if I could get away with it, so I set up a palmistry booth for our homecoming carnival. Most of what I said could apply to any teenager, anywhere. *You're not sure where your life is going. You're destined for more.*

There are people in your life you can't trust. Mix in a few key questions—*Why do you think I'm sensing this? Have you been thinking about this problem recently?*—and you can be surprisingly effective.

Most people treated it like the joke it was, but a few kids were truly freaked out by my "abilities," so I get what Beckett's saying. This is dangerous stuff, and Elliott needs to be stopped. But we're not talking about magic.

"What if I promise to help with Elliott?"

"It's more than Elliott."

"Well, all the mentalists, then." I'm not exactly sure how we'll go about this. Mirror Lake must have at least a dozen tarot card readers, palmists, crystal healers, and psychics.

Beckett rubs his face with his hands.

"It's not the mentalists, Lia."

"What then?"

"It's Mirror Lake. The whole place is rotten. There's all sorts of ways locals separate summer people from their money."

"More than the shows? The shops?" I don't know what he's getting at. This is a vacation spot. The people here rely on tourists, but it doesn't seem all that nefarious.

Beckett looks at me in silence for a while. "What are you doing tonight?"

I grin. "Nothing."

"Settle down over there," he says. "I'm proposing an educational outing, not a date."

"Because you're not interested?" I'm pretty good at reading signals, and I don't buy it.

"If you weren't a Montgomery, I'd be on my knees begging you to go out with me."

The idea has some appeal, but I tell him, "I wouldn't make you beg."

His smile grows. "I know."

He's pretty sure of himself, but his confidence isn't bothering me. We both felt all that possibility flashing between us yesterday, and it's kind of nice not to pretend.

"But I can't get involved with someone connected to Mirror Lake magic right now," he continues. "Especially someone competing for the theater. I don't trust myself."

"Or me," I say quietly.

"Yeah. Or you."

✦

Dressing is a challenge. By expressing a preference for casual while also insisting this isn't a date, Beckett's left me with few outfits that don't feel like a coded message. In the end, I decide on a T-shirt and jeans but elaborately braid my hair. Because I am not your casual, beachy dream girl, Beckett Blackwell.

Except I totally am.

Emma calls while I'm walking downtown toward the fountain where Beckett and I agreed to meet.

When I answer, she says, "Theo says you're flirting with Blackwell boys."

"Aunt Julie says you went out with Elliott," I respond. Because this time, I'm not the screwup. Or . . . at least not the only one. She's quiet for so long I wonder if I've lost her. I press my advantage. "And how come Theo talks to you more often than I do?"

After some more silence, she says, "Truce?"

"Temporary reprieve," I respond, because I am not letting this go. "But tell me about your trip first."

She's in Prague. Prague! Where dashing Europeans hang out under umbrellas on elaborate bridges. But Emma doesn't mention Euro boys or even bridges. Instead, she describes the quality of her performance that evening in note-by-note detail. I love her, but I'm bored out of my mind.

When she wraps up, she says, "Lia, even if we weren't talking about—and you should picture me rolling my eyes here—Blackwell boys, don't you think it might make sense for you take a boy hiatus? You keep ending up in these completely ridiculous situations with guys who aren't worth your time."

She's not wrong. Before Camden, there was Ethan—also known as Liey McLiarface. That ended after a cheerleader from the opposing team and I bonded during halftime by making lists of all the things our boyfriends loved more than us. We thought it was hilarious that we both included hockey, *Futurama*, and this graphic novel where kids make a time machine out of a microwave and a cell phone. It wasn't until we both added butter pecan frozen custard that we realized "his other girlfriend" needed to be on our lists too.

But all that is immaterial here. "This isn't a date. It's an educational outing."

"I'll bet it is," she says.

It's time to take the focus off me. "Now let's talk about Elliott."

"Tomorrow. I promise. It's past midnight here. I've got to get some sleep."

"You can run, but you can't hide," I say.

"Just be careful, Lia."

✦

In the summer, constantly changing colored lights dance across the fountain at the town center in rhythm with carefully approved magic-themed songs that play through hidden speakers. Three members of the city council lost their seats last year because they voted to put Coldplay and Smash Mouth into the rotation. Tonight, Colbie Caillat's "Magic" is playing when I sit on the edge of the fountain beside Beckett, giving me yet another reason to think about the way he's looking at me with those eyes.

He stands. "Ready for your tour of Mirror Lake's vices?"

"Yes, please," I say, looking up at him through my eyelashes.

"Stop that," he says, but he's amused. "Gleason's first."

On the way there, he tells me this is a fact-finding mission and no matter what I see, I shouldn't interfere. This makes me incredibly curious.

"I feel like I'm in one of those gangster movies."

"I mean it." Beckett stops walking to give me a serious look. "Promise me you won't get involved."

"I won't."

"And try to do something about your face."

"My face?"

"Every thought you have is broadcast on fifty-six frequencies. It could get you in trouble." Then he adds, a little more quietly, "And it's distracting as hell."

So that's hopeful.

Gleason's is this magic shop that's over a century old. There are three stores in Mirror Lake that sell prepackaged tricks and novelties, but Gleason's is where serious magicians go. The front of the store looks much like the others—with magic kits for kids, packages of gum that snap your fingers, and tarot cards— although the dark, glossy wood on the floors and walls gives it a classier feel. There's a back room you get to through a swinging door that looks like it's for employees.

This is where the real stuff is. Invisible wire. Books on card tricks, coin passes, and mirror work. Decks of cards altered in subtle ways to make it possible to find any card by touch. Larger illusions based on trapdoors and revolving floors.

I linger over the drawers of notions, picking up a tiny spring to examine. Inspiration strikes. This will be my first trick for the checkpoint.

Looking over my shoulder, Beckett says, "Thinking of making your own?"

I shouldn't have done this with him here. Beckett is very, very quick.

Sometime in the late 1800s, deKolta invented Henry and Matilda's bit with the flowers by using tissue and springs to make tiny blossoms that burst forth into large flowers when triggered. My guess is that Henry and the stagehand each loaded the cone with flowers from their sleeves before reaching in to release them.

You can buy premade deKolta flowers online, but if Emma and I make our own, it'll show the judges we've come to play.

When I don't say any of this out loud, Beckett shakes his head a little. "Sorry. You don't have to tell me. I wasn't going to do the flowers anyway, and I won't say anything to anyone else."

"Thanks," I say, hoping I can trust him. Making our own will be much less impressive if anyone else does it. "This can't be what you wanted to show me, though." I pick up a text on cup-and-ball tricks and flip it over to look at the price. "Thirty dollars for a book is maybe a little excessive, but hardly sinister."

"This way," he says and goes toward the back wall, which is draped with a shiny purple cloth. He pulls it back to reveal a doorway, and I gape. I thought I was a Mirror Lake local because I knew about the secret room at Gleason's, but it turns out there's a secret, secret room.

"How come I've never seen this?"

"Because you're a girl. And worse than that, a Montgom-ery girl."

"Humph."

"Come on," he says, taking my hand. I look up at Beckett questioningly. "It's cover. Play along."

"If you insist." I lean my head on his shoulder and gaze up at him. He rolls his eyes, but his hand tightens on mine as he pulls me forward.

He leads me down a dark hall to a small room in the back. Around a table, five old white men play cards. Two I recognize from parties at Grandma's—Louis Gleason, the store's owner, and Marty Kessler, who played Atlantic City for years. The third I've seen around. A fourth, although unfamiliar, fits in with the others. But the last is an outsider.

He's the same age but looks different in a dozen little ways. He's wearing a bright-colored, silky polo shirt instead of a pale button-down, his skin is flushed, and he's loud. More subtly, he's not examining me and Beckett the way the others are. Cold readings are a way of life in Mirror Lake.

"Beckett," Marty says. "You got a girl."

"That's not a girl, you idiot. That's Lia. Matilda's grandkid," Louis says. He looks at our clasped hands. "You're going to give your grandfather a heart attack." And to me: "What's going on with Matilda? She OK?"

"We hope so."

Louis's eyes look faraway for a moment. "That pink hair was a treat, but I'm hoping for something better this time."

The outsider at the table pushes his seat back and looks at me. "I thought you couldn't get back here without an Ambitious Card. Or are the entrance requirements different for girls?"

Everyone in the room turns toward him. The men at the table are expressionless, but if this guy knew anything at all, he'd get out of here. Now. I look up at Beckett.

He shrugs. "He saw mine last week."

The guy laughs a little. "Yeah, with the lemon. Maybe you can charm some snakes this time?"

I think I might hate this man.

"Go ahead, Lia," Louis says.

Pulling my cards out of my pocket, I fan them in front of Louis. But before he can choose, Beckett reaches around me to point at one. So, I move to stand right in front of him, enjoying the little rush of heat when I get close.

I can see in his eyes that he's anticipating the card kiss. But instead of pressing the card against his lips, like I did with Chase, I kiss the back of the card to demonstrate and hand it over to him.

Beckett raises an eyebrow.

"It's an educational outing, remember," I whisper, but the card he pulls out of his back pocket later has my phone number under the lipstick print. Beckett can't quite hide his smile when he sees it.

The old guy I don't really know says, "That force was beautiful."

"Dropped your thumb, though," Louis says. "Messes with the side angles."

"Thank you," I say, meaning it. Professionals come to Louis for tune-ups. Getting a critique from him is a gift.

"You want to see mine?" the new guy asks me, all eager. I can tell from the veiled amusement of the other men that I don't, but I nod anyway. It's truly awful. He fumbles the double lift, stops once to readjust, and has no patter, so you just watch him butcher the cards the whole time.

"Nice," I say when he finishes.

"Keep working on it, sweetie," the hack says. "You'll get there."

I can't figure out why they're putting up with this guy.

"Can we hang out a bit?" Beckett asks.

"Sure, just keep quiet," Louis says.

Beckett pulls me over to sit on a stack of cardboard boxes behind the card table, and the poker game starts up again. After a few minutes, I get it. New Guy is a mark. And a good one. The cheating is blatant, but he has no idea. Based on the size of his bets, he must also have deep pockets.

The other four are working together, using middle and bottom deals, palmed cards, and false shuffles to control the play. New Guy thinks he's not the only one having a bad night, but I'm sure the others split the take.

Beckett can't keep still. This is unusual for someone who's grown up around magicians. We're taught to control our bodies young, but every few minutes he's shifting his position, changing where his hand rests on his leg and the way his fingers fall. Only after three hands do I notice his movements coincide with new deals.

Beckett Blackwell is cheating at cards.

Seven

SHOCKED, I TURN TOWARD BECKETT. HE GIVES ME A QUICK SHAKE OF HIS HEAD, HIS EXPRESSION SERIOUS.

"But—" I say.

"Not. Here," he practically growls. "Uncle Louis, we're going to head out."

"Probably a good idea," he says. "You don't want to be here with her when Henry shows up."

"Henry Blackwell?" the mark says. "He's coming here? Can I meet him?"

"Sure," Louis says with a sharklike smile, letting me know he brought Henry up to keep the guy at the table. "Probably be here in an hour or so."

I don't know who I'm most irritated with right now. These four men for using magic in a con. The mark for being so obnoxious and oblivious. Or Beckett for helping with the thing he says he's trying to stop.

Marty winks at me, inviting me in. This focuses my outrage.

"Keep doing that top change when he's looking at the deck, and even this guy's going to catch on," I say, not bothering to lower my voice.

Marty's gaze turns cold. "Better watch out for this one, Beckett. She's a Montgomery, for sure. Pretty enough, but the claws come out when they're angry."

Before I can respond, Beckett yanks me out into the corridor. As soon as we're on the sidewalk, he lets go of my hand.

"What were you doing in there?" I ask. "I thought you were opposed to fleecing the tourists."

"I was seven years old when Louis taught me to signal. When I'm there, he expects the help. Not that he needs it."

"You're a part of all this?" This isn't the person I thought Beckett was. I'm a little disappointed. Maybe everyone's right and I should just stay away from Blackwell boys.

"My family always has been. It wasn't until everything happened with Helen that I realized there was anything wrong with it. Since last summer, I've been trying to figure out how much of this is going on in Mirror Lake. And it's everywhere."

He seems genuinely disturbed, but why hasn't he done anything? I'm ready to report all of them to Peter right now. This definitely violates the oath we took. But if Beckett were trying to keep it a secret, he wouldn't have brought me. I need to figure out what's going on.

Time for a little charm. "Come on," I say, putting my hand on his arm. "Let me buy you an ice cream cone."

"Lia," he says, and takes my hand off. "We've been over this."

"Chill. Consuming a single scoop of frozen custard in my presence is not going to turn you into my boyfriend."

Probably.

I mean . . . two or three times is a pattern, not a universal law.

We walk three blocks off the main street to Duke's. Frozen custard is pretty much the best thing about living in Wisconsin. It tastes like what would happen if Ben & Jerry's made soft serve, and for the life of me I can't understand why they don't sell it all over the country.

Beckett gets chocolate. I ask for the flavor of the day (caramel cookie dough), and we sit at a picnic table out back.

After eating in silence for a minute or two—this ice cream demands respect—I ask, "How much will they take that man for?"

"A thousand last week. Probably five thousand tonight if he doesn't figure out what you said. Maybe twice that next time. Louis selects his victims pretty carefully."

I think back about the man—Piaget watch, Burberry sneakers, manicured nails. "Can he afford it?"

Beckett shrugs, making it clear no one at that table cares.

"And your grandfather is a part of this?"

"Sort of. He doesn't play, but he doesn't try to stop it either. He says it's part of the code." Beckett studies me for a moment. "Peter's the same way."

"No," I say, unwilling to believe this. Grandma says Peter Yoon is the most honest manager in the business.

"In Mirror Lake, protecting magicians' secrets comes first. Always."

I have to admit that makes sense. Magicians are fanatical about secrets. Even with the internet, it's surprisingly difficult to find out how tricks are done. Magic books in libraries and regular bookstores explain only the simplest routines.

Here in Mirror Lake, a semifamous magician once self-published a little book about the tricks in his own act, and the Society tracked down all the copies and destroyed them. Except for one that they keep in their library. A little bubble of excitement rises up when I remember I can read it now.

In part, this secrecy is because it's almost impossible for magicians to protect their tricks. Apply for a patent and you give every magician in the country access to your design. Secrets are kept through shunning and by organizations like the Society of American Conjurers that impose penalties—both social and financial—on members who break the code.

And if the Society is run by this Inner Circle—a small group of old men sworn to keep each other's secrets—it's easy to see how they could justify each other's behavior, taking for granted that all magicians deserve to have their secrets kept, no matter what they are.

As a woman and an assistant, my grandmother would never have been a part of this club—no matter how famous she was. Which explains why I didn't know about any of this until tonight.

"Come on," Beckett says, standing. "Two more stops."

I follow him to the lakefront park, feeling complicit in something I don't totally understand. I've always loved Mirror Lake and magic, and I don't like that the people who introduced me to this world are causing harm.

The whole town seems less friendly. The purple-lit palm-istry parlor, the tall tuxedoed man crossing his arms in front of the bar, and even the juggler with his torches all feel a lit-tle sinister.

Across the street in the park, most of the chess tables beside the beach house are empty. But at one on the end, a crowd surrounds a middle-aged man with a dark beard and a tight T-shirt.

"Watch the lady," the man says to his audience as we approach. It's three-card monte, one of the most commonly weaponized magic tricks in the world. I've seen it on street cor-ners when we visited Chicago and New York, but I had no idea this went on in Mirror Lake.

Beckett and I approach the crowd, standing back a bit. The guy at the table gives Beckett a look of recognition, but it's fast. Usually I feel like an insider in Mirror Lake, but compared to Beckett, I'm another tourist.

Five people crowd around the table—two young white women, squeezed into cheap jeans; an older couple dressed for dinner; and a red-haired college kid in a University of Wis-consin T-shirt.

The older man nudges his wife and whispers, "Got it."

"Where is she?" the monte guy says in response. When the husband points to the center card, the monte guy flips it to reveal the queen. "Good eyes. Double your money?"

"Nah. Dinner reservations." The couple leaves with the money they won.

"What do you say?" the guy asks the pair of women. They look at each other, having some intense silent conversation. Desperation rolls off them, and I shake my head, trying to warn them.

"Lia," Beckett whispers. Right. No interfering. I school my face. The brunette opens her little plastic purse and hands over a twenty.

The guy moves the cards around again, urging her to keep her eyes on the lady. I catch it when he flashes the queen once, and then a second time because the brunette missed it. And even though Beckett cautioned me, he winces at how obvious the second flash is. Not surprisingly, the young woman guesses right.

"Want to go again? Make some real money?" The man behind the table holds out the two twenties, like he doesn't care.

The other woman claps her hands and bounces on her toes. "Katie! Yes!" And her friend puts up two more twenties.

This time the cards fly in a dizzying pattern. I don't see it when the dealer palms the queen. And neither does she.

Katie guesses wrong.

With a little shrug, the monte guy puts her twenties in his pocket, and the college kid says, "Can't win them all, right?" Katie nods, looking poleaxed.

She's lost much less than the poker player at Gleason's, but this money mattered to her. People in trouble are so much more likely to get taken in. They'll latch on to any solution, however improbable.

And this woman had no idea what she walked into. The

older couple was a lure. There to convince her the game was winnable. The young guy is the smoother. His job is to make her feel like it was bad luck, not a con, because then she's much less likely to report it to the police, and that way, they can do it over and over again.

The dealer looks at Katie's friend. "How about you? You saw it, didn't you?" He's flattering her, trying to convince her she can succeed where her friend failed.

"I don't know," she says.

"I'll do it," the college kid offers. And both women look grateful. They want another chance to figure this out, but I can't stand here and let this happen. It isn't right.

"Katie," I say. Surprised, the woman turns toward me. She's already forgotten her friend said her name. Really, some people shouldn't be let out unsupervised.

"What's your sign?" I ask, putting on my best cheerleader voice. "Not Aries, is it?"

"No," she says, puzzled. "Capricorn."

"That's exactly what I thought!" This is classic mind reader patter. You ask the first question in the form of a negative because you get to be right either way. (Although you look like a freaking miracle worker if you happen to nail it right off the bat.) Either way, you act like you knew what they told you all along. This is what they'll remember later.

"I had my fortune told earlier. I'm supposed to watch out for an Aries." I give the monte guy a meaningful look. "But she said if I help another Capricorn, I'll be rewarded." Us and them. We're all wired to trust people we think are like us, and I've got age and gender and now astrological sign going for me. "You needed that money, right?"

She nods. "Bus fare home. I don't know what I was thinking."

The monte guy turns toward me with such a fierce look that I step away. Beckett puts his hand on my back, but the pressure isn't reassurance. It's a warning.

I leave the table. Katie and her friend follow me. I don't think she'll get sucked in again, but to be safe, I want her away before I hand her the money.

She tears up when I press two twenties into her hand.

"You have a special gift," she says. "Don't you think, Allie? That she's open to the spirit world."

I take her hand. "Yes. And I'm getting a strong sense you should go home tomorrow. And maybe don't come back?"

She nods. "You're an angel. Thank you."

Across the courtyard, Beckett seems to be having a very different thought. Leaning against a tree, arms crossed, he glares like an angry prince. When I meet his eyes, he crooks his finger. Commanding. I should be irritated at his imperiousness, but some less sensible part of me likes it.

Not enough to go to him, though.

I turn on my heel. But can't help smiling when I hear his footsteps behind me.

"Lia Montgomery," he says when he catches up.

"Amelia Elizabeth Sawyer," I correct.

"What?" he snaps.

"If you're going to do a full-on rant, you'll want to use my actual name. Otherwise, I might not take it seriously."

He pulls me into a nearby arcade. "Do you take anything seriously?"

I barely know Beckett, so his words shouldn't hurt me, but he sounds so much like my mother. I guess two days is plenty of time to decide I'm frivolous. Still, I want to bring the emotional temperature down some, so I say, "Chocolate, sleight of hand, and nonlinear equations. I think linear equations impose a false sense of simplicity on the world."

Around us, tweens cluster in front of video games, teenagers play Skee-Ball, and a group of slightly older people dominate the pool tables in the back. I pull Beckett toward the corner full of kiddie rides because it's mostly empty this time of night, so we'll be able to hear each other without shouting.

When I stop and look up at him, he says, "You remember what I said about this being a fact-finding mission? Scaring off clients does not count as staying out of it."

"Those women lost the money for their way home, and if the other one had opened her purse, they probably would have lost their food money too."

"And so they would have called someone! What do you think is happening back at that table right now? Do you plan to stand out there all night passing out twenty-dollar bills? And tomorrow and the day after that? You're going to burn through that two thousand dollars pretty fast."

"Well, what's your plan?" I cross my arms in front of my chest.

"Sit around and watch resentfully? Everything with Helen happened last summer, and you've known about the poker game since you were a child. Forgive me, but I'd like to work at a slightly quicker pace."

"And forgive me if I want take thirty seconds between when I feel something and when I act on it."

"It doesn't seem all that complicated. What's there to think about?"

Beckett puts both hands in his hair. "I grew up in this. Do you know how hard it was to see it as wrong? To turn on the people who helped raise me? Much less to figure out something sensible to do about it?"

I believe Beckett wants to take the theater away from Elliott. But I'm not convinced he's willing to take down Louis's card game and the three-card monte players. He's known about this a long time without doing anything.

"So what's your oh-so-carefully considered plan?"

"The Society makes the rules in Mirror Lake. I'm trying to figure out how to get involved so I can steer them toward setting some limits on how magic gets used. This contest is the first real hope I've had. If I own the theater, I can stop Elliott's show and maybe get some of the Inner Circle members to listen to me. But that isn't going to happen if you turn every voting member into an enemy in a single evening."

"The monte guy is Inner Circle?" I ask. That actually makes sense. His card work was fabulous.

"Yeah," Beckett snaps. "And the poker players."

Uh-oh. I'm not sure how big the Inner Circle is, but I've

managed to alienate a fair number of the people who'll vote on this contest in a pretty short period of time.

"Sorry," I say, because I may have also taken Beckett down with me.

He watches my face for a while before saying, "Let me walk you home."

"I thought there were three stops on our tour."

"There were. But I've had enough excitement for the night, so we'll skip the séance. Besides, the medium only charges ten dollars a head, and she's mostly a nice woman." Moving toward the door, he calls back over his shoulder, "I've decided she doesn't deserve the full Lia Sawyer experience."

Eight

IN THE MORNING, I SIT AT THE LITTLE DESK IN MY BEDROOM AND PLAN MY CHECKPOINT PERFORMANCE.

Along with the deKolta flowers, I choose Henry's opening card tricks because I already know two of them. My next best bets are probably Guessing Objects or the Tossed-Out Deck. I'll need a partner for these, but Emma will be back in time, and it'll take me a little while to figure out how they work anyway. I send Emma a link to the show, hoping she'll see something I missed, and bring her up to date on my adventures.

Then I pick up Grandma's postcard to study it again. I'd kind of thought there'd be a donkey or clowns in her act, but I should have known it wouldn't be that easy. I grab another history of magic book from the little shelf in my room, checking the index for animal tricks, but there's no mention of donkeys. I flip to the front. On the first page, the name "Ivey Gregor" is written in black ink, which is strange. Gregor was Grandma Matilda's maiden name. I don't remember her mother, though—she could have been Ivey, I guess.

But what would that mean? That Grandma was at least thinking about magic before she met Henry. Maybe her whole family was. That would explain why she was onstage before her wedding, but I'd always gotten the impression her parents didn't approve of magic.

Although . . . maybe I was just projecting my own life onto Grandma's?

My phone plays Emma's ringtone, and I close the book, wondering when I'm going to start finding answers instead of more questions.

"What are you doing up?" I say.

"It's the middle of the afternoon here."

Right. Time zones. "Well, are you ready to tell all?"

"Ugh," she says. "It's so embarrassing."

I grab my bag so I can walk over to the Society while she's talking. "My boyfriend fell for my mother. I'm pretty sure I win all the prizes for embarrassing."

"I don't know about that. It all happened right after I turned sixteen."

I think about that summer. A girl my age had moved in down the road from Grandma, and Emma and I were going through a couple years where the two-year gap between us seemed to matter more than usual.

"Elliott had just graduated from high school. He was gorgeous, and we had that whole star-crossed lovers, meeting-in-secret thing going on."

"But . . . *Elliott?*" I can't get past this.

A little irritation creeps into Emma's voice. "You're not the only one who's allowed to make disastrous dating choices." I guess that's true. But it seems unfair that everyone knows about mine while Emma's kept hers a secret.

"He was really sweet in the beginning. He told me I was like an undiscovered diamond." That totally sounds like Elliott—he probably said it while pulling some cheap crystal out of one of his pockets—but I can't believe she fell for it. "I was flattered this older guy was interested in me. I'm not like you."

"What do you mean?" I say, surprised.

"You know. Sparkly. Everyone's object of desire."

I shake my head a little, rejecting this, even though she can't see me. I've spent my whole life looking up to Emma, and I can't process her insecurity. She's had only two boyfriends, but both relationships lasted forever because they adored her. I might be sparkly, but guys get over my appeal pretty quickly. If Emma's a hidden gem, I'm more like fool's gold.

When Emma doesn't keep going, my stomach twists. Maybe this is much, much worse than I imagined. "What happened, Em?"

"I let him take these pictures," she whispers. "I don't know how he talked me into it, except that he made me feel so beautiful. He's sort of a genius at playing on insecurities."

"Oh, Emma."

"It all seemed fun at the time, but when I went back to White-fish Bay, he shared them with some friends. And I started getting these really gross emails."

"And you didn't tell Mom?" Or me.

"No! Can you imagine? I'd have been front-page news. Trial of the century. I told Aunt Julie. She sent them and their parents scary emails, and it stopped."

"What did she do to Elliott?"

"Just told him to stay away. And he did. Although he never apologized. Not even a sorry-face text."

I consider that. "So Elliott needs to pay?"

"Oh, Lia. Yes, please."

✦

Theo's working at a table in the Society library when I come in. Seeing him reminds me I still haven't gotten an answer from Emma on what her deal is with him, but that's a conversation for another time. For now, I need to focus on Elliott.

I am for sure taking this theater from him. But that's not all—there will have to be something else too. Something fitting, just for him.

Turning my desire for revenge over to my subconscious, I search for a book on deKolta flowers. The organization of the library is a bit odd, with some books filed by topic and others by last name of the magician who wrote them. Five glassed-in bookshelves hold random collections given by donors. None of the titles are tracked by computer.

Finally, I find an illustrated encyclopedia that shows step by step how to make the flowers. The process is fiddly but not too difficult. I can buy what I need on the way home. The book says deKolta performed the original trick with dozens of blossoms in all different colors. I decide to do red—romantic and dreamy—because that's the way it should have been for Henry and Matilda. The darkness in their show added drama, but if they'd gone for light, they would have had a miracle.

Next up is Tossed-Out Deck and Guessing Objects. Unlike the flower trick, I don't know the history of either of these, so I'm not even sure what book to look for. I put the flash drive into the old desktop computer in the corner. Theo sits next to me, watching as I speed past the flowers and Henry's card tricks.

"Are we supposed to be helping each other?" I ask.

He shrugs. "I don't really care about the theater. My grandpa wants me to do the competition, and it's a lot better than lifeguarding. I just want to make it through the checkpoint so I get paid for the whole summer."

When I get to the trick where Henry's in the audience and Matilda names the things people hold in their laps, Theo says, "I watched that one a dozen times yesterday. It's not a code. He says the exact same thing every time."

I noticed that too. Usually, this trick is done with an elaborate system of memorized prompts. "Don't show it" might mean *purse*, while "Ready?" is *wallet*. But Henry and Matilda found some other way.

"Maybe a hand signal?" a voice behind me says, and I jump. Chase and Beckett are standing behind us. "Her blindfold could be see-through," Chase continues.

"I don't think that's it," Beckett says. "Her vision would be obscured, and he barely moves his hands. Play it again, Lia."

I glare over my shoulder at him, because that whole master-of-the-universe thing isn't working for me today. "We're ready to move to the next trick," I say.

"Fine." He crosses his arms and leans back against the table. Chase grins and looks between us like he's watching a tennis match. Only about half of magic is knowing how to do the tricks. The rest is how you execute it, so figuring this out together is probably better. We'll do it faster and leave more time to work on the act. Stage presence is where I'll beat Beckett anyway.

"Let's try watching the Tossed-Out Deck without sound," I say. "She takes the blindfold off before the trick. It must be so she can see something."

"Makes sense," Chase says, pulling up a chair on my other side.

Opening my notebook so I can record everything, I let it play through the trick. Henry has five people each take a card from the top of the deck and then prompts everyone with black cards to stand. The people with red cards stay in their seats. Why do this? Even if Grandma has the deck memorized, it doesn't tell her which card they have, but somehow, she names all five cards right after the people stand. Biting my thumb, I play it again—this time watching her.

Chase pulls out a deck of cards and starts shuffling, working through a series of passes. He's good. Better than I am. Magicians are always saying it doesn't matter how big your hands are, but obviously it's much easier to palm a card when it fits all the way inside your hand.

"Can you stop that?" I say, unable to concentrate.

"You sound like Aunt Anjali. I'll go back to the table. I'm no help to Beckett on this kind of trick anyway." I look after him curiously. Chase is working with Elliott but helping Beckett?

"I'm out too," Theo says. "This one's too complicated."

I raise my eyebrows at Beckett. He shrugs and takes Chase's

seat. We watch the same four minutes without sound again and again, both of us taking notes.

"She doesn't wait for him to signal," Beckett says, tapping his notebook with his pen. "As soon as she knows the colors, she names the cards."

He's right. "Let's watch with the sound on."

This time I track what's happening in my notebook. As far as I can tell, when Grandma names the cards, all she knows is the color pattern. Then the names of the cards she's saying sink in. I can't believe I didn't notice before.

"I know how she's doing it."

Beckett looks from me to the screen to my notebook, where I've written down the color patterns. His eyes widen. "They're using De Bruijn sequences."

Even though I just gave the secret away, I'm happy to share this discovery with someone who gets it. I don't know another person who would recognize this from these clues. You need to know both math and magic. This is why Grandma said I was made to do this. Emma never would've figured it out, but this boy next to me would have with just a little more time.

I jump up out of my seat with Beckett a few steps behind as we race toward the shelf for books about math, which overlaps with magic more often than you might think.

Chase comes around the corner. "I want to play!"

I pull out the book I'm looking for and check the index. When I find the right page, Chase says, "Equations? You were running because of math?" He sounds deeply disgusted.

"It's math that explains the magic."

Chase looks at the book for a moment. "Not to me."

He goes back to the table, but Beckett steps closer, looking over my shoulder. His soap smells like pine trees, and the scent makes me want to lean back against him. Beckett takes one side of the book from me and rests his other arm on top of the bookshelf, closing me in. This boy is a Blackwell. He should not make me feel safe.

But he does.

"Turn the page," he whispers. This is not the most romantic thing anyone's ever said in my ear, but it's definitely not the least either.

I flip the page, and we study the diagram. If you arrange a deck of cards in De Bruijn sequences, you can name any five-card sequence by color (like, red, black, black, red, red), and know what each card is because the cards will come up in that order only once in the whole deck. The red at the front of that sequence will always be the three of diamonds (or whatever) because that's the only card that can launch that particular color pattern.

Learning to perform this would be bonkers. First, it would take a ridiculously long time to map out De Bruijn sequences for fifty-two cards. Then, you'd have to memorize the order of the cards and the unique color sequence for each card in your deck. It's bananas, but it's possible.

Magic is a sport of endurance. Regular people can't believe how much work magicians are willing to do to fool them. This is actually the thing that bothers Mom most. She'd be OK with magic being frivolous if it didn't suck up so much effort—effort that could be better spent on finding replacements for fossil fuels or whatever.

But this is only for one summer. It's not like I was going to revolutionize wind power in the next two months.

Beckett says, "You think they used a light deck?"

That's clever. If you could get the number of cards you're working with down into the thirties, it'd be easier to find the right sequences and memorize everything you need. Because of Grandma, I know she didn't take this shortcut, but I keep this one little advantage to myself.

Instead, I tell Beckett, "Maybe. Large cards, heavy paper. Most people wouldn't be able to tell the difference."

"Come on," he says, and heads back to the table.

He takes his deck out of his pocket and flips open his notebook. I put out my hand for half the cards, and looking at his notes, we reconstruct the three sequences Matilda recited in the show.

"Halfway to a light deck," Beckett says when we have fifteen cards laid out.

Not me. I know these series of cards. I can recite them in my sleep. This is the deck order Grandma had me memorize over spring break with the haunted house trick. She wasn't just teaching me a strategy. She was preparing me for this trick. Which means she's been planning this for a long time. When I look up, I find Beckett watching me instead of the cards, a little smile on his face.

"You're looking pretty cheerful for someone gazing at a manipulative Montgomery girl."

"You read that infinity book, didn't you?"

"I did," I say, a little bitterness seeping into my voice.

"Sorry I was so obnoxious. I'm working through some stuff."

I get it. If you grow up around so many adults who aren't trustworthy and are betrayed by your cousin, you're going to have some baggage. But I'm tired of this—people believing I don't have a single brain cell in my head because I'm a cheerleader and I paint my nails and I like music people have actually heard of. I get talked over in calculus and asked if I'm in the right place when I show up at math camps and cross-examined about cheating when I ace physics labs.

"It's fine," I say.

Beckett comes around the table to sit next to me. "It's not. Tell me when you fell in love with math."

This is a game math people play—our version of describing a favorite book. I like that Beckett's asking.

"My dad and I used to play chess. We had no other overlapping interests. Still don't, I guess. But on car trips, he'd give me chess problems to do in my head. At first, I loved them, only because I'd finally found something I was better at than Emma. But pretty soon I fell for the puzzles and the patterns for their own sake. I loved the way they claimed all of my attention." I've never really understood how people could find math boring. For me, it's always been this space where my mind quiets down and I lose myself in the challenge of it. "What about you?"

Beckett gives me a sideways look. "There was this girl."

"All your stories start the same way."

"She was beautiful, sophisticated." A pause. "And my babysitter."

"And how did this older woman lure you into math?"

"Her homework. She paid me a quarter a problem to do it for her."

"Now who's mercenary?"

"Once, there was this problem where the design got bigger by four tiles each time, and I loved the idea that you could write an equation to describe what was happening in a picture. Before that, I didn't know you could use numbers to do anything but count."

Watching him remember, I see what he must have looked like as a little boy, and something in my chest tightens. "What do you want to do after college?"

"Not sure. In the fall, I start at Madison in a program that's essentially STEM undecided. What about you?"

"Don't know. I'll probably major in math, I guess . . ."

"So you'll be a teacher?"

"Oh, no. I don't think so. Too many rules and every day the same as the next? I'd be bored silly."

"Then . . ."

I can't help thinking about the theater. I want to win it to beat the Blackwells, and punish Elliott, and show what I can do as a magician, but also I'm starting to wonder if it could be something more.

"Would it be ridiculous to say I want do this?" I gesture at the cards in front of us.

He grimaces. "You mean perform? For a living?"

So I guess that's a yes. The disappointment in his voice deflates something inside me. I thought since he grew up around magic, he might understand. Maybe I should stop answering questions about what I want to do when I grow up or say, "Cure cancer." People would probably like that.

Peter sticks his head through the door. "Lia. Beckett. We need you upstairs. Now."

With a nervous look at Theo, I jump up and head for the door. I'm not actually used to people taking this tone with me. Amused exasperation is usually as bad as it gets.

Walking down the hall, I look up at Beckett. "Last night," he mouths.

Oh.

The third floor is a series of small rooms, which seem to be offices. I had no idea magic required this much paperwork. We go toward the front of the house. Before opening the door, Peter turns to us. "My advice is to say as little as possible." I nod. Beckett looks unconcerned.

Inside, sitting on one side of a large oval table, are Henry Blackwell and Louis Gleason. Beckett pulls out a chair for me before sitting. I'm not sure what to make of this gesture.

Henry and Louis both look angry.

Peter seems more worried. "You want to explain what you were doing last night?"

Beckett stretches his arm out on the chair behind me and grins. "I would have thought that was obvious."

I attempt to look unsurprised.

"You know better, Beckett," Henry says.

"This is what passes for a date nowadays," Louis says. "Watching a poker game and harassing entertainers."

"Entertainers," I scoff.

Beckett squeezes my shoulder, and Peter shakes his head.

"Lia's emotional. She got carried away." Beckett taps my nose with his index finger. "Didn't you, kitten?"

I do not claw his eyes out.

It's a close call, though.

Peter gives me a stern look. "To be clear, the position of the Society is that performers on the lakefront, in the shops, and in private homes are magicians and are therefore entitled to the loyalty and protection of those who have taken our oath."

"But they weren't respecting the art, Uncle Peter. That's part of the oath too."

I look to Beckett for support, but he just crosses his arms over his chest. I can't believe he's not backing me up on this. Cautious is one thing. Cowardly is another. And it's too late to pretend we don't know.

"Lia," Peter says, leaning forward in his seat. "Magic is dying. We're competing with blockbuster movies and video games and reality TV. When's the last time you saw a television special about magic?"

I shrug.

"Magic's still popular in Vegas, but that's about it. A decade ago, we filled the theater here seven days a week. We had outdoor performances and festivals. Now we're lucky to get a full house on the weekends. The people in Mirror Lake have devoted their lives to magic, and they're hanging on any way they can."

"Grandma would hate this. She always says the miracle in magic is that people come in knowing they're going to be fooled, and we get them anyway. But what I saw last night wasn't magic. It was cons."

"Watch yourself, little girl," Henry says. And there's a quiet anger in his voice that alarms me. "Matilda gave up her right to make the rules about magic a long time ago."

Peter puts a hand on Henry's arm. "If both of you want to continue with this contest, we expect you to stay away from the street work. Am I clear?"

Beckett gives a quick nod.

"And don't ever bring her back to the game," Louis says, looking at Beckett.

"Because poker's magic too?" I say, both angry and hurt, because I've become "her" to Louis, who's known me since I was a kid.

"It is in my hands, darling," Louis says.

I push away from the table, unable to look at these men, including Beckett, for one more minute.

On my way downstairs, I make a plan. By the end of this summer, I will claim that theater, end all this petty larceny in Mirror Lake, and make Elliott regret ever looking at my sister, much less taking pictures of her.

The details of my plan are a little fuzzy, but thanks to that meeting, I now have the broad outline. If the Society of American Conjurers is in the business of protecting cons, I'm going to run one.

Nine

AT HOME, I SPREAD OUT MY MATERIALS ON THE KITCHEN TABLE, PUT ON THE FOOD NETWORK, AND GET TO WORK. AFTER A COUPLE OF HOURS, I HAVE A DOZEN FLOWERS. THE FIRST ONES ARE A LITTLE RAGGED, BUT I'M GETTING PRETTY GOOD.

"You've been busy," Aunt Julie says when she comes into the kitchen.

"I'm going to do hundreds. It's the volume that makes it amazing."

"That sounds a little ambitious. This isn't your only trick, right?"

"No." I sigh.

"And your mom's bugging me about making sure you're keeping up with that SAT thing. I can tell her you're doing that, right?"

"Sure," I say. "Tell her that."

Aunt Julie narrows her eyes. "I'll fib, but don't make me a liar."

"I'll start today," I promise.

I can feel my list of tasks growing. In between getting Emma's revenge and cleaning up Mirror Lake and now watching videos about reverse engineering test questions, I've got to master the Tossed-Out Deck, which will be—by far—the hardest trick I've ever learned, even with the head start Grandma gave me.

Because of her, I've already imagined every card as a person and arranged them in my imaginary haunted house to remember the deck order. To keep it simple, I made clubs mathematicians, spades family members, diamonds singers from boy bands, and hearts ex-boyfriends (except for the king of hearts, who is my mystery future soul mate).

Now, I need to turn the card colors into numbers (because that's easier to remember) and attach a pattern to each person. So Niall Horan's now wearing a 2-2-1-1-2 T-shirt, which means he launches the red-red-black-black-red sequence. Niall. Ethan. Pythagoras. Mom. Nick Jonas. Or, king of diamonds, two of hearts, six of clubs, queen of spades, four of diamonds.

Only fifty-one sequences to go.

I put my head on the table.

"You'll get it," Aunt Julie says. The doorbell rings, and she goes to answer it. "Lia, there's a Blackwell boy here to see you."

"Is it Chase?" I call back, although I know it's not.

After a murmured exchanged at the door, she says, "No."

"Then tell him I'm not interested."

"Sorry, my niece isn't at home to callers today," she says, and returns to the kitchen. "I've always wanted to say that. Feels like we're living in an Edith Wharton novel."

Moments later, Beckett comes around back and knocks on the kitchen door.

"If we had a butler, he'd take care of this," I say, getting up.

"Hold firm," Aunt Julie says as she heads toward the bathroom.

I open the door. "I am not speaking to you. You called me 'kitten.' "

Beckett's mouth twitches. "In my defense, I enjoyed it only a tiny bit."

I shut the door. He knocks again. After I make him wait a satisfactory amount of time, I open it.

"I'm sorry." He looks like he might mean it.

"You made me feel ridiculous."

"I only meant to make you *seem* ridiculous." I move to shut the door again, but he puts his foot on the jamb. "Trust me. If you want to stay in this contest, ridiculous is a better option than dangerous."

"Dangerous is more accurate."

"No argument here." He holds up his hands in a placating gesture.

"OK. Come in and tell me everything you know about Elliott. I'm going to end him."

We sit at the table. Beckett triggers one of my red flowers, and it blooms in his hand. "Impressive," he says, and I'm excessively flattered.

Aunt Julie comes in and gives me a shocked look. "You let him in?"

"I'm flipping him," I say in a small voice.

"I don't need to be flipped," Beckett adds. "I have even more reason to hate Elliott than you do."

"I very much doubt that," Aunt Julie says. "And you keep your hands off my niece." She turns to me. "Do not trust him. And for God's sake, no matter what he says, keep your clothes on."

A little panicked, Beckett looks at me. "What?"

"My older sister got involved with Elliott a couple years ago."

He sighs. "I'm sorry."

"Not your fault," I say. "You're not him."

"No," he says fiercely. "I'm not."

"We'll see," Aunt Julie says. "I'll be in the other room. Nearby." She goes into the living room and bangs about aggressively.

"I don't think your aunt likes me," Beckett says.

"You're behind enemy lines, what did you expect?"

"Honestly? Pink silk–draped walls, shrines to Greek goddesses, and the heads of men you've vanquished as trophies on the wall."

I grin. "All that's upstairs. Tell me what Elliott wants." Cons work only if you can hook people with their emotions. You'd think people who run cons would be difficult marks, but truth is, lots of con artists have had their victims turn their scams around on them.

And magic and cons have always been tangled together. Magic brings out a strange sort of faith that's easy to take advantage of if you're the sort of person who's into exploiting people's weaknesses.

When I was doing my palmistry booth for homecoming, I told my friend Sera, who took tickets for me, how every trick was done, but when we were packing up at the end of the night, she said, "But isn't it a little bit real? You must have inherited some kind of psychic power from your grandma?" People want to believe.

"Elliott loves attention," Beckett says. "He wants fame. And money too, but for him, both are mostly proof that people like him. Elliott was happy to take all that money from Helen's mom, but what he loved was being the most important person in her world. And he's good at giving people what they want." Beckett considers me across the table. "Kind of like you."

"Watch it," I say. "You haven't been entirely forgiven for this morning."

"I'm not saying you'd use it against people." Although he's obviously not fully convinced. "But in three days, I've seen you be pretty different things for different people—an avenging angel with those girls at the monte game, a playmate with Chase, and with me . . . this fierce, brilliant girl in a cotton candy package. Granted, I haven't known you for long, but I have no idea who the real Lia is."

He's got a lot of nerve. He was the one making nice with the bad guys.

"You act like 'real' requires being only one thing. Maybe that's how it is for some people, but not for me. Wearing lipstick doesn't actually interfere with my ability to have a complicated thought. I can do both—at the same time. And I didn't give that roomful of dinosaurs what they wanted this morning or that monte guy last night. That was you."

"I know," Beckett says. "That's what makes me think you're different from Elliott."

I'm still figuring out if I should be offended by the comparison when Aunt Julie returns. "What are you planning here, Lia?"

"Vengeance?"

"Is that a good idea? You've got this checkpoint coming up in three weeks, and Emma won't be here to help for a while."

"I have to do this. Emma's heart is more important than magic. You don't let a boy treat your sister like that. Even if it was a few years ago, there's no statute of limitations on revenge." Besides, there are some side benefits. Elliott's my most serious competitor in this contest—card skills or not, he's the only one of us who performs professionally. Plus, he's the primary reason Beckett's so hell-bent on destroying the theater. Wreaking some havoc in his life can't hurt my chances of winning.

"For the record, I'm agreeing because I think protest is futile," Aunt Julie says. "Not because I agree with you."

"Duly noted," I say.

Aunt Julie puts cheese sticks and mini quiches into the oven for dinner. I didn't think I'd ever say this, but I miss Mom's brown rice stir fries. I've been here for three days, and all our meals have been heated, not cooked.

"I need to see Elliott's show," I say. "It's tonight, right?"

"Eight o'clock," Beckett says.

"I'm not going to that," Aunt Julie says. "I don't ever want to see that boy's smug face again."

"I'll take you," Beckett says. "I'm used to his smug face."

"I need Elliott to trust to me. Is seeing me with you going to get in the way of that?"

He shakes his head. "If anything, it'll help. He'll love the idea of taking your attention away from me." His voice turns a little dark when he says this, and I wonder if the whole Helen saga was more complicated than he let on.

I make a salad to go with dinner, because I'm desperate for something crunchy and green. Aunt Julie fills her plate and, on the way out, says, "I need to make some phone calls. Make good choices."

"Always."

Well, sometimes.

Tonight, anyway.

Now that my plans for the checkpoint and Elliott are coming together, I'm ready to turn my attention to the Mirror Lake crime bosses. Like Elliott, they're going to be sorry they messed with a Montgomery girl.

"How come those three guys are running the Society, anyway?" I ask Beckett. "I thought Thurston Carter was president."

Thurston Carter retired from the national stage in 1969—although he performed in the Midwest for a few more years. When he made Mirror Lake his year-round home, he gave his summer house to the Society and bought an even bigger place on the remote end of the lake. He's been president ever since.

"I think Thurston put Peter in charge—he was his manager too. And Louis and Henry are Inner Circle, so they help."

"Well, after we deal with Elliott, we need to take them on," I say. "We can't keep letting magicians use what they know to run cons. People get hurt, and it gives magic a bad name."

Beckett smiles.

"What?" I say.

"Just picturing you with a white hat and a sheriff's badge."

Beckett seems to be enjoying the image, but this isn't actually the look I need. For Elliott, I want innocent but interesting. Leaving Beckett to finish the disappointing mini quiches, I go up to change, selecting a bright-orange sundress, a hot-pink cropped sweater, and a giant flower for my ponytail. I look like a neon light. Even in a crowd, there's no way Elliott won't notice me. Now I need to work on looking impressed, because Beckett's right. My biggest weakness in both magic and cons is how easily people can read my face.

Aunt Julie's waiting by my door when I come out. "You're loaded for bear."

"Relax. They're work clothes."

"Be careful. Elliott's a terrible human being, but he's good at what he does."

"So am I."

Ten

BECKETT TAKES ONE LOOK AT ME AND COVERS HIS FACE. "MY EYES! YOU'RE BURNING MY RETINAS."

This isn't the reaction I hoped for, but I believe boys are trainable.

"No," I say. "Your line is, 'Lia Sawyer, you are always worth the wait.'"

He goes to hold the back door for me. "We haven't known each other long enough to talk about always."

On the way, I ask Beckett if we'll have trouble getting tickets, but he says Elliott reserves a few seats every night in hopes that someday a talent scout will show up and need them.

So Elliott's thirsty. I can work with that.

The Starlight sits three blocks back from the lake on a street that runs directly through the center of town. It's tiny—seventy-five seats squeezed in between an Italian restaurant and a bakery in an old white brick building. The red-trimmed marquee out front advertises WORLD-FAMOUS MAGICIAN HENRY BLACKWELL. Slightly smaller letters underneath say AND INTRODUCING ELLIOTT BLACKWELL, MAN OF MYSTERIES.

On either side of the gold doors are glamour shots of Henry and Elliott—Henry, statesmanlike in his tux, and Elliott, looking like the cover of *Rolling Stone* in his black T-shirt, jeans, and blazer.

Beckett has a quick conversation at the ticket booth, and then we head inside.

Because of Grandma, I've only ever been here to see amateur acts and never thought much of the space, but the little theater, with its red vinyl seats and faded velvet curtains, feels more alluring knowing it could be mine. Trailing my fingers over the smooth wood of the armrests, I imagine the theater full of parents waiting to see their kids perform . . . or tourists waiting to see me.

Our seats are good—on one of the two aisles about halfway up, where the sight lines on tricks will be most impressive. This makes sense if Elliott's hoping to put a scout here. Theaters in big cities sometimes go looking for magicians to replace ones who are retiring or to open for other acts, so it's not an impossible hope. Mirror Lake is somewhere people from Chicago or Milwaukee might look.

The theater's carpet and wall coverings are a little worse for wear, with muted swirls of red and gold, but the lighting up front and behind me is state-of-the-art. Lighting is even more important for magic than for plays. This is how we make things disappear. When I turn back toward the stage, Beckett is watching me.

"Yes?" I say.

"Nothing," he says, shaking his head as his eyes wander over me.

I cannot figure this boy out. He looks for all the world like he wants to wrap me up and take me home, but he's angled away from me in the seat and leaning on the other armrest, so we can't do that accidental getting-up-in-each-other's-spaces thing that as far as I'm concerned is the whole point of theaters.

This thing with Beckett feels like it could be ... *more* ... than anything with anyone before. Camden wanted a girl who'd hang on his every thought. And Ethan was looking for a cheerleader—any cheerleader—to sit on his lap. Beckett, even though he is maybe still a little bit suspicious, seems fully into me as a person. But I'm confused about what he'd like to do about it.

At 8:01, the lights go down, and amid a puff of red smoke, Elliott appears onstage.

He is undeniably gorgeous, if a little too aware of it. "My name is Elliott Blackwell," he begins. "And I'll start with a disclaimer: I come from a long line of magicians, but I have no special powers." He opens his hand to reveal a little bluebird that flies off to the back of the theater. "But by the end of evening, you won't believe that."

His first trick is an old one. A guy in the audience selects a card from a deck. Elliott tears it up and pulls a signed, sealed, and postmarked envelope out of a little mailbox at the front of the theater. The guy opens the envelope to find his card, fully restored. When he holds it up, the gasps are audible.

The audience would be much less impressed if they knew that the little mailbox had fifty-two envelopes, each marked with a tiny code.

Elliott continues on with a series of similar tricks, letting people find cards taped to the bottoms of their chairs, in purses, and once, cleverly, in a woman's complicated hairdo.

Next, he moves on to the communing-with-the-spirits part of his act, which he begins by announcing the birthdays and anniversaries of audience members. This trick relies on assistants who roam the lobby before the show collecting information.

Then it all gets real. Elliott passes out little slips of paper to the spectators in the row across from us, asking them to write down the name of a person who's not with them tonight but who they can picture clearly in their minds. Beckett shifts in his chair and looks away. This must be where it started. Given that command, how could Helen's mother think of anyone but her lost son?

I want to take Beckett's hand, but I have to be careful about what Elliott might read between us. This is literally how he makes his living. So instead, I lean forward a little in my seat, keeping my eyes wide, and I study the people writing on Elliott's bits of paper.

There's a teenage couple—my age or a little younger—and three middle-aged women. To test myself, I guess which one will make the best read. The boy, who's leaning back in his seat with one leg crossed over the other, is smirky. So, no. He probably wrote down a cartoon character and wants to turn the whole thing into a joke.

And the two older women on the end have matching closed body language. From the identical way they cross their arms and their legs, I suspect they're sisters, and neither wants to play.

This leaves the last middle-aged woman and the teenage girl. Both are leaning forward a little, arms at their sides, knees pointed toward Elliott. Open. If it were me, I'd take the older woman, but for Elliott, the girl is the best choice. I'm not surprised when he asks her to come up.

Elliott's been working the apron of the stage, occasionally coming down into the audience. But now the center curtain parts to reveal a small black table, set with two green velvet armchairs, bathed in a pool of light. On the table there's a glass bowl.

Elliott pulls out a chair for the girl and waits for her to sit before he takes the other.

Gallant.

"Now," he says, "we've never met. Is that correct?"

"No. I mean, yes," she says, and giggles. "I mean, we haven't met."

She's delightful. Elliott made the right choice. It's not just about someone you can read, but someone the audience can root for (or against).

"And can you tell the audience your name?" The phrasing is perfect, because it suggests he already knows. The table must be miked, because although her voice is quiet, she's easy to hear.

"Maddie."

"And did you follow the rules, Maddie? Write down the name of someone not with you tonight? Or did you put down the name of the gentleman you're with this evening? I'm sure he's very much on your mind."

Maddie blushes and looks at the table. "I followed the rules," she whispers.

Oh. Elliott's a genius. I'd like to say this is luck, but it's not. He read something in their bodies long before he started this trick. Probably picked that row because of Maddie. This is about to be a great bit of theater, because Maddie put the name of another boy on that paper. As awkward as that is, I'm glad Elliott's doing this tonight. If he'd picked a woman radiating grief—as I'm sure he must have done with Helen's mother—I wouldn't have been able to sit here quietly.

Elliott asks Maddie to fold her paper once and then again before handing it over. Using a center tear, he rips Maddie's paper into little pieces and sprinkles them into the bowl, where he sets them on fire through some unseen means. The middle of the paper, where she wrote the name, will remain intact, and during the distraction of the flames (unnaturally large because of some fuel in the bottom of the bowl), Elliott will peek at it before hiding it away. Even though I know it's happening, I can't spot when he does it.

When the flames die down, Elliott reaches across the table, takes her hands in his, and strokes his thumbs across her wrists. She shivers visibly.

Elliott's card work at the Society didn't do his skills justice.

"You're thinking of someone far away—physically or maybe emotionally?"

"Physically far, yes," Maddie says.

"And he . . . It is a *he*, right?"

She nods. I look over at the no-longer-smirky boy she came with. Ten points to Elliott.

"This boy had a very real connection with you."

"Yes."

"You met . . . it wasn't at summer camp, was it?"

She shakes her head.

"But somewhere like camp." Elliott waits. People don't like silence, so they want to fill it.

"I was an exchange student," Maddie says. "In Spain, last year."

"Yes. And now that he's far away, you wonder if your connection is enough? Or if you should move on with someone new?"

A small nod.

"I know the name of your soul mate. Do you want me to say it out loud or whisper in your ear?"

Maddie, with a glance out at the boy, says, "Whisper it."

Elliott comes around to the other side of the table and crouches down beside her, which gives the audience a fabulous view of her face when her mouth falls open in shock as he whispers the name. Her tears fall, and Elliott hands her a tissue from his pocket, drawing attention to her reaction.

Maddie goes back to her seat in a daze, ignoring the boy next to her. Elliott does similar reads with two more people before moving on to lighter material—levitating furniture with his mind, bending spoons, and reproducing people's drawings onstage.

What he's done here isn't as bad as using grief for financial gain, but looking at Maddie's face, it's easy to see he's altered her life. Probably not for the better. If she thinks this boy across the ocean is her destiny, who knows what she'll give up here? Granted, the smirker is no loss, but that doesn't mean someone better isn't out there. And either way, the decision should be hers, not something she thinks is preordained.

The applause after Elliott's last trick—a levitation of a woman in the audience whose flowy dress means she must be a plant—is thunderous. When it dies down, Elliott thanks the audience and tells us private appointments can be arranged at the ticket booth.

I can only imagine how many people, seeing what he did with Maddie, believe he could help them. Looking over at Beckett, I say, "Take me to see him?"

"If you want." I'm not sure if his disapproval is real or for show, but it doesn't matter. He's playing this exactly right. Elliott's done a good job not making it obvious, but he's been aware of us from the beginning.

In the lobby, I stand in a corner under a soft light and try to look adoring as I watch Elliott accept compliments and sign the postcards in the lobby.

When the crowd clears, Elliott comes over.

"Beckett," he says with a nod. "This is a surprise."

"She insisted," Beckett says, stuffing his hands in his pockets.

"And what did you think?" Elliott asks me.

"It was amazing. Not just the tricks, but your stage presence. I've never seen anyone as good as you are at working the audience." I'm a little worried I'm laying it on too thick, but Elliott laps it up.

"Mentalists don't like to call what we do tricks. It demeans the work."

"Of course. I'm sorry." I look down at the ground.

He touches my arm, and I step a little closer, looking up into his eyes. Then I drop mine. I can't blush on cue, but I bet he'd swear I am. Beckett makes an irritable sound next to me. So helpful. Elliott clearly loves that he's getting to Beckett.

"Do you want some help getting ready for this contest?" Elliott asks. "I mean, I plan to win, but I wouldn't want you to embarrass yourself."

"You would do that?"

"Sure. How about three tomorrow? Beckett can tell you where I live."

I hesitate. I don't want to be alone in Elliott's house. "Maybe the café? I don't think my aunt . . ." I let my voice trail off, and I watch Elliott remember who my aunt is.

"Probably for the best," he agrees. "See you then."

"She's seventeen," Beckett says, his voice cold.

"Relax. We're just talking magic." Elliott smiles at me. "I've always wanted a protégée."

But as Beckett opens the front door for me, Elliott calls out, "Lia!" And I stop. "Out of curiosity, when's your birthday?"

Making my voice as light as I can manage, I say, "October."

"Not so long, then."

When the door closes behind us, I do a little horrified, discovering-a-nest-of-spiders dance, trying to shake off my encounter with Elliott. Thinking about him with Emma makes me sick to my stomach.

Beckett shakes his head. "Well, I'm glad you have some sense."

"I need frozen custard. Or a smoothie. Or frozen custard and a smoothie. Also fudge."

"Fair enough," he says with a little laugh. "You deserve a reward."

Beckett takes me to a little coffee shop right on the lakefront. I've never been here before, so it must be pretty new. A deck hangs out over the water, and Beckett leaves me there while he gets food. I'm grateful. All that time controlling myself in front of Elliott was exhausting.

Beckett returns with a frozen coffee covered in whipped cream, which he puts in front of me, a black coffee for himself, and a giant brownie.

"Thank you," I say.

"Thank you for taking this seriously," he says. "No one else has."

"What about your parents?"

"My dad hated growing up here. Hated being Henry Blackwell's son." I imagine a male version of Emma. Even though she's a performer, she's never liked attention offstage, and any kind of over-the-top drama makes her uncomfortable. Mom's the same way. She couldn't wait to get out of Mirror Lake. "He thinks anyone who spends time or money here deserves what they get. Doesn't see a difference between paying for a show and paying for a séance. So, he doesn't love what Elliott's doing, but he doesn't think it's unique either. And my mom tries to stay out of it. She mostly thinks white people are out of their minds, anyway."

"She's not wrong. So why are you here so much?"

"Chase. He grew up here."

I take a bite of brownie. It's wonderful, but the coffee's plenty sweet on its own, so I push it toward Beckett. He breaks off a piece, puts it in his mouth, and licks the frosting off his finger. I watch the process like I'm about to take an exam on it.

"Do I have chocolate on my face?" he asks.

I shake my head.

"Well, you do."

I go to brush it off, but he shakes his head and says, "Other side. Here." He reaches across the table and brushes his thumb along the corner of my mouth.

Completely mesmerized by the gentleness of his touch, I watch as he slowly draws his hand back. I want him to return it immediately. We stay quiet for a few moments, letting the promise of it all zing back and forth between us.

Then Beckett shakes his head a little. "Sorry. What were we talking about?"

I have no earthly idea. "Chocolate? Maybe?"

"Before that. I think Chase?"

Right. Chase. "Are you two close?" If he starts talking again, maybe I can get it together over here.

"Yeah, we are. You can imagine what growing up with Elliott as a brother was like. Their dad left when they were little, and their mom—Grandpa Henry's daughter—was never all that stable. Chase had a pretty rough time in middle school, and he came to live with us, but we always spend the summers here with Grandpa."

I try to imagine that happy, golden boy having a rough time of it. The girls at my high school would eat him up with a spoon.

"He wasn't always like he is today," Beckett says dryly. "There's been a growth spurt or two. And he got a lot more confident when he wasn't around Elliott all the time."

"You're the same age?"

"He's a year younger. Same as you."

"How did you know how old I was? You told Elliott I was seventeen." Remembering the fierce protectiveness in his voice warms me. I'm not used to people looking out for me like that.

"You haven't internet-stalked me?" Beckett asks with a smile.

I shake my head. It actually didn't occur to me. I sort of figured him being a Blackwell boy was all I needed to know.

He watches me, trying to figure out if I'm telling the truth.

"A little humility would do you no harm," I say.

He grins. "I figured you'd check out the competition. That's all I was doing."

"So you looked up Theo too?"

He opens his mouth to lie but can't bring himself to do it.

"Uh-huh," I say.

We settle into in a comfortable silence, mostly looking out at the water. Every few minutes I study his profile, trying to figure out what he's thinking. He said he wasn't interested, but I think he's changing his mind. Do I bring it up? Or let him?

When he catches me looking, Beckett raises his eyebrows. I freeze, hoping he'll speak. When he doesn't, I look away.

"I'll be right back." I've had a lot more experience being pursued than pursuing. I'm not exactly sure how this is supposed to go.

After using the bathroom, I pick up a fruit cup. When I come back out, Beckett says, "I thought you wanted ice cream and smoothies and chocolate?"

"Turns out I'm more like my mother than I thought."

"What does that mean?"

"When I'm at home, I mostly notice how different I am from everyone else in my family." I give Beckett a look. "You'd like them. They're very consistent."

"Well, I like you too. Inconsistencies and all."

"You do?" I ask, pleased to have this confirmed.

"Yes. But when you're here . . ." he prompts, steering me back to the less interesting conversation.

"When I'm here, I notice how much like my family I am. Aunt Julie eats anything, at all different times, but never sitting down at a table, and I'm pretty sure she goes whole days without vegetables. She's also perfectly happy being alone all day long. And doesn't seem to have any kind of regular schedule. It's not like this when my grandma's here. Grandma Matilda and Mom drive each other wild, but they're a lot alike. Lots of little rules."

"What do you think she's doing? Your grandma?"

I look across the lake at our house. There's only one light on.

"I'm not sure." I haven't said this out loud to anyone, even Emma. But by taking me to see Elliott tonight and talking about his family, Beckett's let me in some, so I return the favor. "She left some little clues for me. I think she wants me to avenge her in some way. Something more than getting that theater. But I don't know why she didn't tell me what she wants. Or why she had to leave."

"Do you think it has something to do with my grandpa?" Beckett asks. "Their act . . ." His face reflects all the distaste I felt watching it.

"I know. It made my skin crawl. It's weird people liked it."

"Different time."

"I guess," I say, thinking about that old television show. Hard to believe threats of domestic violence used to count for humor.

Trying to shake off my discomfort, I focus on my frozen coffee, which has tiny pieces of chocolate in it. It's pretty perfect. Like the view. And the mild summer night. And this boy. I'm finding the way he shifts between playful and serious awfully appealing. Maybe because his range makes me feel like it's OK to be all over the place myself. I've been with boys who like that I can differentiate an equation and boys who like that I bat my eyelashes. But Beckett seems to like both.

After a while, he says, "Grandpa Henry has his issues, but he's not like Elliott. Grandpa treats magic like it's a religion. And he's been really good to Chase and me. I love him. I don't know if I can help with whatever you're working on for your grandma."

"Well, since I don't know what I'm working on yet, that's no big loss."

We throw away our trash and walk back to my house. When we get there, I go up one step and turn to face Beckett, putting myself at a convenient height.

Because I'm considerate like that.

He pulls out his phone. "I'm going to text you. When you meet Elliott tomorrow, I'll be in the bookstore next door. Send an SOS if you need me."

Hearing this unsettles me. "Do you think he's dangerous?"

"No, not like that. But he'll assume he can talk you into whatever he wants. Don't let him."

I nod. "Thank you for coming tonight and for the coffee."

"My pleasure." He puts his phone away and keeps his hands in his pockets but doesn't back away. We're so close I can feel his warmth. I look into his eyes but don't move. I've been pretty clear about what I want. Now it's his turn.

His eyes roam over my face like he's trying to memorize me, and a sort of liquid heat pools at my core.

"You are ridiculously fascinating," he says.

"I am?"

"Yeah. I could make a hobby out of watching you think."

Favorite. Compliment. Ever. So much better than pretty.

"And you're smart and intuitive and funny—and a little frightening."

"Frightening?"

"Just a little," he says, eyes crinkling. "Do you think . . ." His voice trails off.

When he doesn't start again, I prompt him. "Do I think what?"

He draws a long breath and releases it.

Just ask, Beckett. This isn't the labors of Hercules.

"That despite whatever's going on with our families, and this contest, and Elliott . . ."

He stops again, and I lean toward him a little, drawn in equally by his words and his foresty scent.

"Lia . . . do you think we could figure out a way to be actual friends?"

MY IRRITATION IS FRESH WHEN I WAKE THE NEXT MORNING, SO I LACE UP MY RUNNING SHOES AND HEAD OUTSIDE INSTEAD OF LOUNGING ABOUT IN THE KITCHEN DRINKING FLAVORED COFFEE.

Even though the sun's up, the fog is heavy on the ground. I might twist my ankle if I run on the lake path, so instead I head up toward the sidewalk, aiming for a half-mile track that wraps around a park with a playground and a splash pad. Visibility is so bad that running through the empty streets feels eerie. There's only one good breakfast place in Mirror Lake. This is a town that wakes up at night.

I'd been too shocked to speak after Beckett's question, so I'd simply turned and gone inside. But we'd exchanged a series of texts when I calmed down enough to type.

Beckett: I'm sorry! Really. But I don't see how what I said was so terrible that it required a door-slamming temper tantrum.

Lia: 1. Don't apologize and then completely undo your apology in the next sentence. It could be perceived as insincere. 2. Did I miss the part when we were dating? Did Elliott hypnotize me and wipe my memory? Because usually I get to kiss someone at least once before he tells me he's changed his mind and wants to be Just Friends.

Beckett: Look. I am sorry if I hurt your feelings. But I didn't know saying I wanted to be friends was going to be taken as a mortal insult.

Lia: Clearly I misread things.

Beckett: Another time, another place, I'd love to get up to all kinds of things with you, but I'm trying to reduce drama in my life at the moment.

Lia: Yes, well, do forgive me for intruding on your peace and solitude.

Beckett: Lia . . .

Lia: I wish you exceedingly peaceful dreams.

Beckett: I'll still be at the bookstore tomorrow.

Lia: Only if you're up for the excitement.

Although it's early, a few other runners circle the track. I'm not surprised, because the lights and the flat surface make this the only sensible place to run at this time of day. Still, it's a bit of a shock when one of them goes by and says, "Lia?"

"Chase?" He turns around and runs backward in front of me, so I add, "Show-off."

"Want some company?"

"Depends on whether you're willing to slow down."

"No problem," he says. "Soccer isn't for months."

After a couple of silent laps, he says, "So how'd it go with Beckett last night?"

I look over at him to see if he's being sarcastic, but he seems clueless.

"Lovely. He said he wants to be friends," I say.

Chase stumbles, which gives me an excellent excuse to stop running. I walk off into the grass, and he follows.

"I have to say I did not see that coming."

"Thank you for saying so," I say, glad to know I wasn't entirely imagining Beckett's interest.

I walk over to the empty basketball court to stretch, because the grass is too wet to sit down on. When I put my head on the ground between my legs, Chase says, "I can't even touch my toes."

"Your talents probably lie elsewhere."

"Maybe, but they're not helping with all those boxes Elliott keeps cramming me into. I'd feel better about the whole thing if I thought he'd lose any sleep if I end up with nine toes."

I'm a little surprised Elliott's working on one of the big illusions for the checkpoint. It feels like overkill, but maybe he doesn't want to rely on Chase for the card work, and the success of the cutting, crushing, and stretching tricks depends mostly on the dexterity of the assistant and the ingenuity of the apparatus. Whatever Henry said about not wanting to share, maybe he gave Elliott his designs?

This might explain why Elliott wants to meet with me. I bet he'd like an assistant who can curl up for the saw trick and fit into the hidden compartment on the side of the boxes-and-blades cabinet. One look at Chase's shoulders tells me it's not going to be him.

"Why are you working with him?" I now understand all those undercurrents flowing among the three of them when we picked partners. Beckett didn't go into detail, but I'm sure

Chase learned early to fear an older brother with a gift for cold reads and manipulation.

Chase sits down in front of me, bending his legs and wrapping his arms around his knees.

"He's arrogant as hell, so he still trusts me. And if I'm working with him, I can make sure he doesn't win—even if I have to lose a limb to do it."

The look in Chase's eyes is dark, confirming my suspicions. "How bad did it get?"

Chase looks at me for a long time. I can't tell if he's trying to figure out the answer or to decide if he's going to tell me. Then he sighs. "When I was eight, he used this illusion of Grandpa's to make me disappear in front of a mirror. I thought my body vanished. Then he took me downtown and told me to walk out into traffic."

"Chase!"

"I was so surprised when that car hit me. I completely believed him." Chase stands and pulls me up after him. "But that was the last time."

"You were OK, though?"

"Bruised and scraped up. The car wasn't going that fast. I like to think he wasn't actually trying to kill me." He walks back toward town, and I follow.

I think of all the saws and blades in Henry's tricks. "Be careful with the act, OK? Some of this is dangerous."

"I grew up around it too. And I'm not eight years old anymore."

I decide that while Chase is in a sharing mood, I may as well run my plan by him. "What would Elliott do to get on television?"

"Anything," he says. "He'd do anything."

Thought so. "How much does he know about how it works?"

Chase shrugs. "No more than we all do. He started performing right after high school, so he never went to college. He doesn't know anything but Mirror Lake."

"Good."

"What are you up to?"

I bite my finger, studying him. What I'm thinking is big and a little out there. I'm not sure either Beckett or Emma will approve, but Chase seems like he might have enough wild in him to appreciate it.

"A few cons? Magic Wallet. Big Store. Maybe Spanish Prisoner if I get ambitious."

Chase stops walking, and his eyes widen. "What are you going to take him for?"

"The money he took from Helen's family. And the theater. But I'll do that the honest way, through the contest." Also, a little dignity as payback for Emma, but I'm not telling Chase that part.

"And you're roping him with a TV show?"

I nod.

"You're scary."

"That's what Beckett said," I say with a little frown.

Chase smiles. "I like it."

Aunt Julie's in Chicago for the day. I go back and forth about whether to call her, but ultimately I do.

"What do you do when you want to launch a new TV show?" I ask.

She laughs. "Well, I'm not really at the stage where I launch my own new shows, but you'd write something up explaining the premise and introducing the people in it. Make some kind of argument about who the audience would be. Have lots of meetings to talk people into it. Why?"

I explain my plan.

"Oh, Lia," she says. "Are you sure this is a good idea?"

"I don't know. How high a standard is 'sure'?"

"You're lucky you've got a rebellious little sister as an aunt."

"I love you, Aunt Julie."

"Elliott's twenty-one now?" she asks.

"Beckett says he is."

"OK, then. One condition. If you take money from him, he has to get what he's paying for. But I think I know someone who can make that happen for you."

"You're the best."

"If your mother finds out, I will deny everything."

"That doesn't work. Trust me."

I spend the rest of the morning—even though I should be memorizing sequences or, possibly, doing an SAT practice test—at the drugstore printing headshots of me from the fall play and at the library printing color copies of the pages Aunt

Julie sends, which are brilliant. When I get home, I FaceTime with Emma, who needs to OK the plan before I go forward.

When I explain it all, she claps. "That's brilliant, Lia. You're the best sister in the whole world."

"And so next time, you'll tell me right away if some idiot breaks your heart."

"I will. But can you put this off until I get back? I really, really want to be there when you do it."

"Sure. But . . . you're not still hung up on him, are you?"

"No," she says. "I've moved on." Her small smile tells me she's not pretending.

"With who?"

Her smile gets bigger and a little bit sheepish, and somehow that's enough of a clue.

"Theo," I say. "How did this happen?"

"We've been doing all this texting and talking this whole year, and at first, it really was just as friends. But then I realized he's the first person I talk to when I get up and the last person I text at night, and I'm thinking about him all the time in between. I'm traveling with like eight guys on this trip, and I couldn't even tell you what they look like."

"Pity," I say, and she laughs. "Have you told him? Does he feel the same way?"

She shakes her head. "I don't think so. He's still asking for advice about other girls."

"Not a good sign," I agree. "Maybe it's weird for him. You've known each other forever. I don't think I could feel butterflies for a friend. There's no mystery there." I love those early days

123

when you're figuring someone out and it's all kissing and telling stories and doing that twenty questions thing.

"My best relationships started as friends," Emma says. "It's the ones that are all heat and uncertainty you have to watch out for."

"Maybe," I concede. I might have to think more about this, because it is possible that Beckett has a point. Although he is obviously confused about what friendship entails. For example, I'm pretty sure friends do not tell each they are "ridiculously fascinating."

And, if possible, they should try not to smell so good.

After we say goodbye, I pull out the flash cards I made with the photos of family members on the fronts and the matching De Bruijn sequences on the backs. I figured I'd start with spades since people in my family are bound to be the most memorable. After twenty minutes going through them, I master four.

After a quick lunch, I head over to the Society to do some work on my opening card tricks. Beckett, laptop in front of him, is sitting at a table in the corner. No one else is here. He looks at me and back at his screen. Awkward achieved.

I take a seat across the room and pull out my notebook, but before I can start on anything, he slides into the chair across from me.

"Can we talk?"

I look back, expressionless. "Oh good. First we're just friends, and now we get to talk. You sure know how to get right to all the fun parts."

He gives me a quick closed-mouth smile. "Chase says your reaction was not unreasonable."

"Chase is wise."

"Said no one ever. And for the record, I didn't say 'just friends.' I said 'actual friends.'"

"Really? That's the defense you want to go with here—linguistic accuracy? Not an explanation for why you were gazing into my eyes and brushing crumbs off my lips and calling me 'fascinating.'"

He has the good sense to look embarrassed. "Sorry. I shouldn't have led you on. It's just you are . . . even with everything else . . . But I made some bad decisions last year, and I don't want to do it again. For the next few weeks, I need to focus on the theater and Elliott and not get distracted."

This makes some sense. "Fine. But you can't look at me the way you did last night. It's not fair."

"I don't think I can control how I look at you."

"Try."

"Come here," he says, going back to his computer. "I want to show you something."

Looking over his shoulder, I expect to see a video, but it's lines and lines of computer code. "What is this?"

"It's a program. Written in Python. I'm adapting it to find the De Bruijn sequences for thirty-two cards."

I feel a little bit guilty I've been able to skip this step, but it's pretty awesome Beckett's figured this out.

He goes back to typing, and I watch over his shoulder. I've never been all that interested in computers, even with the relationship between math and coding. There are some proofs that have only been solved by machines, but as far as I'm concerned, it doesn't count unless a human's involved.

Beckett looks over his shoulder. "What do you think?"

"You don't have to worry about giving away your secrets. I can't make heads or tails of what you're doing there."

He shakes his head. "I'm not worried. But figuring out the sequences is only the first step. After that, we have to memorize the deck order and the color pattern of each sequence. I was thinking, we could work on it together. Help each other drill?"

I recognize this for the peace offering it is. And it's super sweet. If Grandma Matilda hadn't already taught me the deck order, there's no way I could have figured the sequences out. He's giving up a big advantage.

And I have to return the favor. I pull my cards out of my pocket and put them in front of him. "That's a full deck—already in the order they used in the show."

He gives me a skeptical look and starts flipping cards. When he gets to the first five-card sequence Matilda recited, he says the cards as he flips them, and even though I'm sitting across the table and can't see the faces, I keep naming the cards as he picks them up, going through the whole deck.

Beckett cuts the cards, tells me the first one, and we go through it all again with him flipping and me naming. All kinds of emotions flash across his face. Amazement. Humor. Suspicion.

"Were you pretending yesterday—when you said you figured out how this worked?"

"No. My grandmother had me learn this deck when I visited over spring break, but I thought we were just working on memory. I had no idea this was coming. Or that the order mattered."

Beckett deals the cards out faceup around the perimeter of the table. He goes around the circle, running his finger under groups of five. "All the color combinations are unique?"

I nod. "You'll need to learn the deck first, but then we can make flash cards of the sequences and drill each other."

"Why help me?"

"I do better with company, and . . . you won't really burn the theater down, will you?" If for some reason I don't pull this off, I'd rather have Beckett win than Elliott.

"Of course not. It's right in the middle of a city block. I'll turn it into apartments."

"Still?" I ask, wondering if I've had any effect on him at all these last couple of days.

He gives me a searching look. "Maybe not."

"Then consider this a bribe."

Beckett rejects the haunted house as an organizer in favor of the house he grew up in, because it's vivid in his mind. I concede that this makes sense.

"Why go through all the trouble of turning every card into a person?" he asks. "Wouldn't it be easier to picture the cards in the house and do it that way?"

I shrug. "You can try. But it never worked for me until I did people. You can make it easier by assigning categories to suits. Like spades are people in my family. And clubs are mathematicians.

And once you have that, you can use it to memorize any deck, not just this one."

He sorts his deck by suit, and I open *The Expert at the Card Table* to work on Henry's card tricks. After about a half hour, Beckett hands me a sheet of paper and says, "Test me." He used family for spades (Elliott is nowhere on the list), but I don't recognize any of the names for clubs. When I ask, he says they're teachers. This is boring, but it works since you can assign them by grade to make memorizing easier.

"What did you do for diamonds?" he asks.

"Singers." No need to go into detail. I wouldn't want him jealous over darling Niall.

"And hearts?"

"Ex-boyfriends."

His eyes get big. "There are thirteen?"

"I started with Dylan McAllister, who asked me to marry him with a ring he got at the dentist when we were five."

"Even if I start in kindergarten, I don't have enough exes to fill a suit."

"You could do friends," I say sweetly.

Twelve

BEFORE I MEET ELLIOTT, I GO INTO THE BATHROOM AND WIND MY TWO PIGTAILS INTO TWISTY LITTLE KNOTS AT THE TOP OF MY HEAD, PUT ON DARKER LIPSTICK, AND REPLACE MY CONTACTS WITH BRIGHT-RED GLASSES TO MATCH THE UNIVERSITY OF WISCONSIN HOODIE I'M WEARING WITH MY DENIM SKIRT.

Beckett, waiting at the top of the stairs, shakes his head when he sees me.

"What?" I ask.

"That's a look made for Elliott."

"Yes, it is," I say, and head downstairs.

"You're going to be early," he says, following me.

"That's my goal."

"He'll be late. He likes to make people wait."

On the way downtown, I ask Beckett how much money Elliott took from Helen's family.

"Just over eight thousand."

That's a lot, but I was prepared for worse. Psychics have taken people for hundreds of thousands of dollars. I can do this. After all my reading on magic and cons, I'm excited to have a cause that justifies trying this out. Like with cold reads, once you have the knowledge, it's hard not to want to use it.

"What's your plan today?" Beckett says.

"Roping the mark?" The first step in any con.

Bewildered, Beckett stares at me. Then he shakes his head a little. "Maybe you should focus on the contest and not go tearing off after something that isn't your problem."

"This is my problem," I say sharply.

His confusion clears when he remembers Emma. "Right. Sorry. Again."

I wave his apology away. "Besides, I think it's all wrapped up together—Elliott and the poker games and the monte guys." I bet unraveling all these little Mirror Lake secrets is what Grandma really wants from me. It was never just about magic. It was about something bigger.

We're at the bookstore now, so I tell Beckett to go inside and wait. He makes me promise not to leave with Elliott and says to text if I need him.

In the little café, I choose a booth in the back and pull out the leather portfolio from Aunt Julie's production company that I found in her room. I tuck it between the side of the seat and the wall with the corner sticking out.

I settle myself in the opposite side of the booth, facing the door. When the waitress comes, I ask for a muffin and a glass of iced tea, which I use to make water rings on both sides of the table. After drinking half of it, I pull the muffin into pieces, scattering a few crumbs.

It's three o'clock. I sit up in my seat and look eagerly toward the door every time it opens. Elliott shows up at 3:07. Beckett called it.

"You look different," he says as he sits down. His attention is on me, so he doesn't notice the folder. So far, so good.

"Better or worse?"

"More interesting."

"Thanks for meeting me. I really appreciate someone like you giving me the time. I'm pretty good on the technical stuff. But I've never done magic onstage before. I'm worried I won't be able to pull it off."

"Being comfortable up there is important. You know how sometimes you see an amateur and you're embarrassed to be in the same room with him?"

I nod, not having to act. Performances like that make my teeth hurt.

"Performing alone can be tricky. Confidence is key."

Hearing him say this makes me doubt myself. I push through the feeling, because that's what he intended. I've got to play him, not the other way around. "I want that theater."

"Because you want to do this for a living?"

"Yes." The certainty in my voice comes through a little stronger than I planned, making me realize I might not be pretending about this part, but I stop thinking about it, because I can't afford to work though my feelings in front of Elliott.

"Me too." He sits back in the booth, stretching out his arms. "You know my grandfather was never as successful as he was with your grandmother?"

"Really?" Lay some wisdom on me, Elliott.

"Their chemistry made their act great. Audiences loved it. You and I could do that again. You're not much younger than she was when they started." I work hard to keep my expression interested. Knowing what I know, I could never perform with him—or even let him touch me.

"Most assistants fade into the background," he continues. "They're interchangeable. But audiences want to see someone who fights back. It's more exciting that way. Your grandmother got that."

Maybe. Or maybe she felt like she had no choice. I wonder if she would have kept performing if she'd been able to do another kind of act.

"What if I don't want to be an assistant?" I ask. "What if I want to be the magician?"

He laughs. "That's never going to happen. There will never be a famous female magician."

"Why not?"

"Because men won't pay to be fooled by a woman. And they definitely don't want to see a woman saw a man in half. So, it doesn't really matter what you want."

The scary thing here is I suspect he's right. Proportionally, there are probably more women astronauts than magicians. "Excuse me a minute?"

I get up to go to the bathroom. It's time for Elliott to find my folder, because I can't stand to be around him much longer. Everything I read says this will work. He'll get bored. Investigate his surroundings. But I'm nervous.

I text Beckett to say I'm OK and that I haven't given away my life's savings. He responds by telling me to wrap up, because he's coming to get me in ten minutes. I'm too relieved to argue.

When I sit down again, Elliott studies me thoughtfully. Trust the process, Lia.

"You've been holding out on me," he says.

Bingo.

I open my eyes wide. "What do mean?"

"Who were you meeting with earlier?"

I look away. "No one?"

Elliott gestures to the crumbs and glass marks in front of him and puts the folder on the table. "Whoever it was left this." He flips it open. Inside are my headshots; a doctored business card for Gabrielle Walker, executive producer; and a prospectus for a new reality show tentatively called *Girl Magician*, pitched as *Duck Dynasty* meets *Breaking the Magician's Code*. The show proposes to follow adorable (thanks, Aunt Julie!) teenager Lia Sawyer as she enters her family's magic business. Included in the proposal are descriptions of the quirky setting, my oddball relatives, and Beckett and Chase, my potential love interests (cousins—oh, the drama!).

I open my mouth. Caught.

"I want in," Elliott says.

Shaking my head, I say, "I have no control over it."

"The story's better if it's the two of us. Reuniting our families. Henry and Matilda didn't last because we were meant to be. They'll love it."

Gag.

"Let me get this back to Gabby," I say, reaching for the folder. "I'll talk to her. See what she says."

He pulls the folder back toward him. "There's nothing in here she needs. She must have other copies of all this."

"There are pictures of me!" I say.

"So, send her more."

"Easy for you to say. They were really expensive."

"Where'd you have them done?"

"Talent agency near Chicago. The name's on the back."

He flips it over and studies it a minute. "I'm keeping this."

"Elliott!"

Beckett comes through the front door. "Oh no," I say, standing.

Elliott looks over his shoulder. "Does he know about any of this?"

I shake my head fast.

"He won't like it." He grins. "But you don't need him. Plenty of other love interests around."

Elliott tucks the folder under his arm and leaves, saying, "Cuz," and smacking Beckett on the arm as he goes by.

Beckett watches Elliott walk out the door. "What did you do?"

"Magic Wallet?" Chase seemed to know what I was talking about when I told him, but Beckett looks at me blankly.

"Sit down," I say. "I'll explain."

He picks at the muffin pieces in front of me. In a traditional Magic Wallet, the mark finds a wallet stuffed with money. A bystander who's in on the con tells the mark about the wallet's owner. This leads the mark to a second con artist, who launches the real con seemingly in thanks for the returned wallet. The whole thing works because the mark seeks out the con artist instead of the other way around, plus the fat wallet makes the mark think he's dealing with someone rich.

I explain the standard con as well as my variation. "That can't possibly work," Beckett says. "And why aren't you eating anything?"

"The muffin was mostly a prop. I wanted him to think I was here with someone else first."

Beckett waves at the waitress. "Can I get a Coke, please?" he asks. "And what do you actually want?"

"Something healthy? And vegetarian?"

"We have a hummus plate," the waitress says.

"Yes, please." After she leaves, I look at Beckett. "Thanks. I am hungry. I was too anxious to eat at lunch."

"I'm relieved to hear that. You've got kind of a master criminal vibe going on here."

One of the drugstore phones I bought chimes. Elliott. I hold up a finger to Beckett and listen to the voice mail. I respond by text, saying a full package of headshots runs two thousand dollars (not coincidentally, the exact amount of money Elliott just fell into with this contest—it's easy to let a windfall go), and I'll let him know when we have an opening in the schedule. Elliott asks for something as soon as possible. I tell him there's a rush fee, but that we'll waive it if we can post his photos on our website. I want him feeling grateful.

"Is that a burner phone?" Beckett asks, incredulous.

"Maybe," I say with a little smile. I bought one to be the talent agency and one to be Gabrielle Walker, producer. When you do something like this, you need to commit.

I pass the phone to Beckett. When he finishes listening and reading, he says, "Is this legal?"

"Sure. He's paying for a portfolio of photos. He'll get one."

"And then what?"

"Emma gets copies of the pictures to use however she wants. Because revenge. The money goes to a good cause. And Elliott can send his headshots wherever he likes."

Beckett sits back in the booth and crosses his arms. "I can't tell if you're an evil genius or just evil."

Chase bursts through the door of the café at the same time the waitress returns with my food. He drops to his knees in front of me and bows his head. "Lia Sawyer, I am at your service. Let me do your bidding."

I take a celery stick and knight him before dipping it into hummus. Chase throws himself into the booth next to Beckett. "Elliott is in his room trying out shirtless poses in front of the mirror. He asked me if he should wax his chest."

"Tell him yes. And see if you can get him to do his legs too," I say. "It's unbelievably painful."

"You knew about this?" Beckett asks Chase.

"Lia gave me the outline."

"I want to see what you showed Elliott," Beckett says. On my own phone, I call up the little prospectus Aunt Julie wrote and hand it over to them.

Beckett lifts one eyebrow. "He bought this?"

I open my eyes wide and tilt my head. "Why wouldn't he? I would make a fabulous reality TV star."

Beckett is amused. "You're not nearly as adorable as you think you are."

Feigning hurt, I say, "Chase?"

"You are twice as adorable as you think you are."

I look at Beckett but gesture to Chase. "This, Beckett, is how a gentleman responds."

Chase grins. "The love triangle's going to play."

Thirteen

A WEEK LATER, I'VE SCHEDULED AND CANCELED ELLIOTT'S PHOTO SHOOT TWICE. AUNT JULIE PUT ME IN TOUCH WITH MAURA, AN INTERN AT *SCHOOLED* WHOSE HIGH SCHOOL BOYFRIEND DID HER WRONG AND WHO IS, THEREFORE, EAGER TO HELP EMMA. MAURA SAYS THE *SCHOOLED* OFFICES ARE MOSTLY EMPTY FOR THE SUMMER SO WE CAN USE THEM ANYTIME, BUT I'M DRAGGING THINGS OUT UNTIL EMMA GETS BACK.

This is working pretty well. Elliott's increasingly eager, terrified he's going to miss his chance at stardom, which is creating some interesting opportunities for psychological warfare in between my rounds of practice for the contest.

As we have most days this week, Beckett and I spend the afternoon in one of the spare theaters drilling the De Bruijn sequences. I can't believe how quickly he memorized the deck. What took me a week, he did in three days. But layering the fifty-two unique sequences on top of the memorized deck is hard for both of us. I have no idea how Grandma did this.

Sitting cross-legged facing Beckett on the stage, I ask about it. "Do you think they each memorized only half the sequences? Maybe he signaled to her when it was one of his."

Beckett shakes his head. "I've watched that section thirty times now. And the clips of them on the internet. He doesn't signal. Ever. And truth is, I don't think my grandfather could memorize even half of these. His visual memory is for crap. That's why he stopped doing the trick after she left."

A question that never before crossed my mind occurs to me. "Why does everyone call *her* the assistant?"

Beckett looks at me without speaking, clearly thinking it over. Eventually he says, "Because she was wearing the dress?"

I wonder what Grandma Matilda would have had to do to earn the title magician. To get voted into the Inner Circle.

Before I can say any of this to Beckett, the door opens. Elliott pops in. "Can I talk to Lia a minute?"

Silently, Beckett checks with me.

"It's fine. I have my phone." I give him a look to communicate that this is necessary to my plan.

Beckett hops off the stage. "Leave the door open."

"I don't know what you're trying to suggest, Beck. But there wasn't one thing I did with Helen that she didn't want." There's one hypothesis confirmed.

"Except take her mom's money," Beckett says as he goes out the door, propping it behind him.

"What's up?" I say, drawing Elliott's attention back to me.

"Have you talked to that producer? She won't take my calls."

"You know how it is. Word's getting out and all kinds of people are interested. Anyone in Mirror Lake could be on the show, but the producers will choose who they spend the most time with."

Elliott sits in a chair in the front row and puts his feet up against the stage. This practice theater is very small—just twenty seats. "And they want Beckett?"

"They do." I'm not above using this rivalry.

"Why?"

I shrug. "They think Beckett and I are headed in some interesting directions. And—don't tell him—but I sent some pictures. They like that whole smoldery, smart-guy thing he's got going on." Who wouldn't? "And Gabby said the contrast is nice with Chase as the sweet boy next door."

Elliott snorts, but I continue without letting him speak. He needs to hear this next part. "The producers say even though it's real life, all the characters need to fill a different role."

"Where does that leave me?" Elliott asks.

I study him thoughtfully and sit up as if an idea's just occurred to me. "Maybe you should embrace the bad-boy role? They'd probably like that."

"What would that mean?"

"Well, you're older, so that helps. But you look too much like Chase."

"I could dye my hair?"

"Ooh. That could work. Like really black-black. And you could get a tattoo." I clap my hands, all excited. "Or a whole sleeve."

Elliott blanches. "I hate needles."

"Your choice." Elliott really, really wants this. I feel the smallest flicker of guilt, but I think of Emma opening emails from boys she'd never met who'd seen her in the most intimate way.

"Whatever you decide, you need to do it before you take your pictures. They want people to be their 'real' selves."

He nods. "Thanks."

"Good luck."

When Elliott leaves, I go back to flash cards, but I'm struggling, which I don't enjoy. Maybe I'll go home and make some more flowers. Magic is supposed to be fun.

Beckett comes back into the theater and shuts the door behind him. "How'd it go?" he says, boosting himself back up onto the stage.

"Pretty good. I convinced him to dye his hair and get a tattoo."

"Only you," he says with a little laugh. He lies back on the stage, covering his face with one arm. "He makes me completely irrational."

Deciding not to worry about getting my bright-yellow top dirty, I lie back too, although I keep my eyes open. There are only three can lights on the track up above. If we do the trial in here, we aren't going to be able to make anything disappear with lighting. "You want to tell me the whole story?"

"I'm sure you figured it out. After Elliott started reading for her mother, Helen hooked up with him. We were still together, but I had no idea. Until it all went to hell."

"How could she have done that? He was taking their money." And she had Beckett. This girl must have been out of her mind. I don't understand her decision from either end. Elliott is horrible, and Helen must have known that even better than I do, given what he was doing to her family. Plus, she actually got Beckett to fall for her. This smart, kind, gorgeous boy. And she couldn't stay interested? It makes no sense.

"Helen felt like her mom gave up on everything after Sam," Beckett says. "Like she wasn't important enough to live for. I didn't see it at the time, but she might have liked that Elliott was taking advantage of her mom." Beckett puts both his hands on his face. "Honestly, looking back, I think she was feeding him information. He knew way too much."

"Maybe he tricked it out of her? He's super good at cold reads."

"Maybe. I don't know. Helen was dealing with a lot. And sometimes not doing a great job of it. And I was drawn in by that. Not sure what that says about me."

It doesn't escape me that I was crying when Beckett approached me for the first time. If fragile and damaged is what he's into, it's no wonder he lost interest in me. I might be lacking in substance, but I don't need to be rescued.

Still, I feel sorry for him, and I don't want him to feel all alone in his messed-up romantic choices, so I say, "My last boyfriend had a crush on my mom."

Beckett turns his head to look at me. "Was he insane?"

I smile. "No. He was a Serious Person, who thought about Important Things. He found me trivial." I sigh. "Part of me doesn't blame him. He always wanted to talk about the effects of redistricting or the fate of the Paris Agreement, but I was more interested in how David Blaine levitates, and the way quantum mechanics changes the rules of multiplication."

Beckett sits up. "Lia, you think about important things."

Still lying on my back, I shake my head. "No. The math stuff sounds serious, but it's no more important than magic. It has almost no bearing on the real world. I just like it . . . and it makes my parents happy."

"But you think about people, and it doesn't get more serious than that. You want this theater, but instead of practicing, you're spending all this time tormenting Elliott. Because of me and Emma and Chase. And you stood up to Louis. And you leaped in to stop those women from getting taken for everything they had by the monte guy."

"I thought you were angry about that," I say, sitting up so I can look at him.

"Well, it wasn't the wisest move ever. But it wasn't trivial."

Hearing Beckett say this makes me strangely emotional. Out of the blue, I remember Dad reading me and Emma *The Ant and the Grasshopper* when we were little. He exchanged this look with Mom over our heads that said as clearly as words that he thought this was a parable about their kids— their hardworking daughter and their flighty one. Every single thing Emma and I have ever said or done has etched this more deeply.

Beckett seems like he might see my story differently, and I love the way he's looking at me. Not like I am a girl he wants to kiss, but like I am a person he wants to know.

"I'm sorry I flipped out that night after Elliott's show," I say. "I'm happy to be your friend." I almost turned Beckett into every boy I ever dated. Maybe it's a good thing he didn't let that happen.

"Thanks," he says. "Sorry for all the mixed signals. I'm trying to get my head on straight, but you make that challenging."

I raise my eyebrows.

He grins. "Sorry. I'm doing it again."

"It's OK. I'm still figuring all this out too."

He picks up the pile of flash cards between us. "Again?"

I shake my head. I like where we are. I don't want to stay here and screw it up. This being-friends-with-someone-you-want-to-kiss thing is still pretty new to me.

"I've had it for the day," I say. "I'm going to go home and send Elliott designs for tattoos."

"You take your revenge pretty seriously," Beckett says.

"It's not revenge," I say, hopping down from the stage. "It's a service project."

✦

As soon as Emma texts that her plane's landed, I confirm Elliott's appointment with his photographer. Emma spends one night at home and drives up to Mirror Lake, much to Mom and Dad's dismay. That night, as we lie on the twin beds in our room, I ask, "Are you nervous about tomorrow?"

She's been pretty quiet all evening, and I haven't been able to tell if it's because she's exhausted or worried.

"A little. I haven't seen him—up close—since everything happened."

"You won't have to talk to him. He won't even know you're there."

"Good."

"He's why you stopped wanting to come to Mirror Lake, isn't he?" I finally figured out that it wasn't the mimes or the jugglers that soured Emma on our summer trips.

"Yeah. When I see his face on billboards, I feel so stupid."

"You can't blame yourself. You're two years younger than Elliott, and you trusted him."

"Still, it's like the first thing everyone tells you not to do with a cell phone."

"Well. Not the first thing," I say with a smile. Channeling Dad, Emma and I shout, "Away from your ear! You'll get the brain cancer!"

Dad gave us that speech the day we got our cell phones. Mom's talk about pictures for boys came a little later. Emma's super careful about using headsets and the speakerphone. I don't worry about that so much. But I've never even been tempted to break Mom's rule.

We're quiet a little while. And it's partly because I'm not sure she's still awake that I'm brave enough to ask what I'm wondering. "I get I was young when it happened and that Mom's, well, Mom, but I can't help thinking part of the reason you didn't tell anyone was that you wanted to keep being the perfect one. Like it's OK if I mess up, but not you?"

Emma's quiet for so long, I decide she's asleep. But as I'm turning on my side to drift off myself, she says, "Don't you think Mom and Dad want us both to be perfect? I never really understood how you could be brave enough to ignore what they want."

Now I'm quiet as I think that over. "It's not really bravery. It's more when you know you're bound to disappoint them, it's less painful if you don't even try."

"Oh, Lia," she says. "It's not easy for anyone, is it?"

✦

In the morning, we head off to enjoy Elliott's photo shoot from behind a one-way mirror in the *Schooled* offices. Emma's driving the four of us in Aunt Julie's car. In the back seat, Chase bounces up and down with manic glee, while Beckett gives off the air of someone who is enjoying himself but knows he shouldn't be.

I turn around to look at Chase. "You have to tell us. What did he get?"

Chase shakes his head. "You have to see for yourself."

"Just tell me whether it was one of the designs I sent. The skull with the top hat? The scorpion with the magic wand?"

"Turn around," Emma snaps at me.

"You're going to go through the windshield if she stops," Beckett adds.

I flop back around for a minute, but then I lean toward the middle to look over the armrest, making sure to stay under the shoulder strap.

"How does his hair look?"

"Awful. Grandpa Henry had a total meltdown. Said Elliott dishonored the family name. In the beginning, it was just this

146

dead black color, but now I'm almost sure the roots are turning green."

"He looks like a zombie dealing with a stomach virus," Beckett says, and presses his lips together, as if he knows he shouldn't encourage us.

When we get to the offices, located in a converted bungalow in one of the northern suburbs of Chicago, Maura, dressed in black with one of those fancy cameras around her neck, greets us at the front door.

"Nice to finally meet you in person," she says with a big smile. When she turns her attention to Emma, her expression goes serious. "Did Lia tell you? Someone did this to me too?"

Emma nods.

"I recovered. And so will you. But today, let's make him pay."

Maura puts us all in a little room with six folding chairs that face a picture window looking out into a studio. "The window looks like a mirror from the other side, but this room isn't sound-proof, so keep quiet," Maura warns. "Headphones in the corner if you want to hear what's going on."

"Got it," I say.

She shuts the door and heads out to the studio, which is decorated with big lights, colored screens, a rack of costumes, and a box of props. Minutes later, the doorbell rings.

Maura answers. "Elliott, come in, come in. Sorry it took so long to work you in. This month's been bananas." She gestures toward a side table covered in photographs of some pretty well-known television stars.

Once they enter the studio, we can no longer hear them, but Elliott's giving Maura that crooked little smile he uses to charm girls. It's much less effective with this new hair, which definitely has a greenish tinge.

When Emma sees Elliott, she makes a squealy noise and claps her hands over her mouth. She throws her arms around me and whispers, "He looks awful. Thank you. Thank you." I pull her back from the window into the corner.

"Are you going to be OK? You don't have to stay here."

"I'm good."

Emma looks over at Beckett and Chase, who are standing right up by the window. Chase whispers something in Beckett's ear, and in response, Beckett messes with Chase's hair. I like the way they play with each other. Like puppies.

"They're really different from him, aren't they?" she says.

"They are."

Emma shoves me with her shoulder. "Grandma Matilda would have a conniption if she could see your face right now."

"Oh, but she'd be thrilled with you." Emma looks at her shoes, making me feel guilty for teasing her. "Let's go listen."

She and I each put an ear against one side of the headphones. Maura's saying, "You're very photogenic. Those were some nice standard poses."

Elliott's checking out the room. "What are all the costumes for?"

"Oh, you know. People go up for all different kinds of roles. They want headshots that play to type."

Intrigued, Elliott walks over to the rack of costumes. "What if I wanted a bad-boy look?"

"Really?" Maura says, pulling back a little. "I don't know if that's your thing." She's good.

"Why not?" he says, clearly offended.

"Well, you need kind of a sexy, animalistic energy for that to work." She looks at him doubtfully.

Elliott flips through the costumes, and I see what Maura primed him for before he does. If I ever do this again, Maura goes on payroll.

And sure enough, Elliott pulls out this leopard-print caveman toga thing.

Chase looks up at the ceiling and clasps his hands. "God, I will do literally anything if you let this happen." Beckett puts his hand over Chase's mouth to keep him quiet.

"I don't know," Maura says. "Not many guys can pull that off."

"Where's the harm?" Elliott asks. "If I don't like the pictures, I won't use them."

Elliott heads into the bathroom to change, and I relinquish the headphones to Emma so she can immerse herself in the experience.

Chase and Beckett make room for me at the window. Chase bounces on his toes. The door opens, and Elliott steps out.

It's a horror show.

"Why is his chest all red like that?" Beckett whispers.

"The waxing," Chase answers. "You were out when he did it

this morning, but he screamed like a wounded animal for almost twenty minutes straight."

Elliott really is attractive—or at least he used to be, with his blond hair and his clothes on. But his legs—which looked great in slim-cut jeans—resemble a chicken's with nothing on. Especially with this midthigh leopard toga. With his dark hair, his skin looks even paler. And not in a hot vampire way.

"He betrayed my sister, and he let you get hit by a car," I say. Because I'm feeling sorry for the guy.

"And he essentially stole eight thousand dollars from a grieving mother," Beckett adds.

"And no one told him to do this. You just opened the door," Chase says.

Elliott does muscleman poses while Maura dutifully snaps away. I don't know how she's keeping a straight face. Elliott turns his back toward us.

There's a tattoo on his shoulder, but I'm kind of disappointed by it. It's just a circle with a slash through it and an attached arrow.

I look at Chase. "I thought you said the tattoo was good?"

"Oh, it is. I told him it's the Chinese word for magic."

"What is it really?" I ask, because whatever that thing is, it's not a Chinese character. For anything.

The smile Chase gives us is wicked. "It's the symbol vets tattoo on dogs to show they've been neutered."

Beckett puts his hands in his pockets and rocks back on his heels. "Nice work."

"You're scary too," I say, and then I go to tell Emma.

By the time Maura finishes with Elliott, he's done a leather vest (without a shirt), a police uniform, and a crawling-on-all-fours-across-a-fuzzy-pink-rug pose that's so cringeworthy I have to hide my face against Beckett's chest. (As a friend.) I'd feel worse about the whole thing if Elliott didn't seem to be enjoying it so much. And if Emma weren't glowing.

After he leaves, we all go out to the studio with Maura, who asks what she should do with the money and the photographs.

I look at Beckett. "What's Helen's mother's name? Maura will write a check."

"Lia?" he says, surprised.

"It's a start."

Beckett gives Maura the name, and she hands him the check.

"Thank you," he says to me. The sincerity in his voice makes the words mean more.

To Maura, I say, "Send the digital portfolio to Elliott. But Emma gets copies too." I look at her. "Whatever you decide to do with them, I'll back you up."

She shakes her head. "I got everything I need out of this. Although I might put one of those leopard-print ones on my phone to cheer me up on the dark days." She pulls me close to whisper in my ear. "I can't thank you enough. I have a shot at getting over this now. Being the better person wasn't getting it done."

Squeezing her back, I say, "I probably enjoyed it more than I should have."

This is what I think Mom doesn't understand. Sometimes

doing good in the world is more about taking toga pictures than suing the robber barons.

"Remind me not to make you angry," Beckett says as we head out the door.

I look up at him, thinking about his total failure to kiss me after spending that whole night giving me every sign in the world that he wanted to, but I don't say anything. We're supposed be past all that.

Even so, he reads my thoughts in my face. "Again," he says with a rueful smile. "Remind me not to make you angry again."

Fourteen

THE DAY AFTER OUR CHICAGO TRIP, I'M SITTING AT THE KITCHEN TABLE FINDING PHOTOS ONLINE TO USE FOR MY DIAMONDS FLASH CARDS, WHICH IS THE ONLY SUIT I HAVEN'T WORKED ON. I AM—PERHAPS—SPENDING A LITTLE MORE TIME THAN IS STRICTLY NECESSARY FINDING THE PERFECT PICTURE OF HARRY STYLES, BUT I FEEL GRANDMA DESERVES MY VERY BEST EFFORT.

At ten, Emma twirls into the kitchen and kisses the top of my head. "Good morning, very best sister."

Laughing, I say, "You're in a good mood."

"I am. And it's because of you. Let me take you out for a pedicure to celebrate."

I gesture at the computer. "I don't know, Em . . . these sequences aren't sticking, and I've only got a week to the checkpoint. Might be time to put some hours in."

She rests her chin on my head. "I know. But we went a whole year without seeing each other, and I was gone for the first part of summer, and we'll be in different places again in August, and I really, really do want to thank you."

I have missed her, and someday in not so long, we won't even be coming back to the same house for the summer. And even if I don't have the sleights 100 percent down for the checkpoint,

I can probably achieve minimally competent through sparkle alone. It's magic, not rocket science.

"Well . . . I do need to print these pictures somewhere before I can make my last set of flash cards," I say.

She claps. "Yay! Go get cleaned up and we'll go."

✦

We don't get back to the house until just before dinner, because pedicures turned into lunch and lunch turned into shopping, but it was pretty wonderful to spend the day with Emma, and I did get my pictures printed, so as soon as we get home, I shut myself in my room to work on my diamonds sequences. I make some progress, but after an hour or so, I hear laughter downstairs and I'm too distracted to concentrate.

In the kitchen, I find Emma sitting across the kitchen table from Theo.

"Again!" he says.

She chucks a piece of popcorn, and he catches it in his mouth. "Twenty-seven!" Emma says.

"A serious improvement from three weeks ago," Theo responds. "Forget piano. We're going to the show with this."

Three weeks ago? Emma saw Theo when she was dropping me off. That's why she didn't stay to hang out with me and Aunt Julie. "He's why you were in such a hurry—"

Emma gives me the stop-talking-now death glare. As a sister, I am morally obligated to shut my mouth. But I give her a huge grin.

"Shut up," she says.

"I'm not saying anything. Theo, did you hear me say anything?"

"Sorry," he says, looking up from his phone. "Gotta go."

"You don't want to break our record?" Emma asks, sounding so forlorn my grin slips away.

What is wrong with Theo? Can't he see how she feels about him?

He ruffles her hair and says, "Rain check. See you, Lia."

The screen door slams behind him.

"Not a word," Emma says.

"Is there a reason you're not telling him? Or at least flirting a little more aggressively? He can't read your mind."

"He shouldn't have to. He should decide he wants me all on his own."

Well, yes, ideally, that would be how it goes. But that doesn't seem to work in Mirror Lake. Maybe the town is some kind of attraction black hole that only affects boys.

Before I can propose this theory to Emma, she leaps up. "I think I'm going to distract myself with the piano." She looks at my face. "Unless . . . Do you need something?"

I shake my head. I'd love to have her drill me, but I feel silly asking her to put off her practice so she can help with mine. Instead, I'll work on the opening down here, where at least I can hear her play.

After another hour, my deKolta flower routine is like breathing—automatic and satisfying. I pop into the living room to ask Emma if she wants to walk down to the beach, but she shakes her head without even slowing her fingers on the keys, so I tuck one of my practice decks into my back pocket and head out on my own.

When I hit the sand, Grandma's neighbor, white hair bundled under a pink bandanna, waves me over to where she's sitting in a lounge chair watching her grandkids play in the lake.

"Is Matilda back?"

"No," I say, taking the chair next to her. "She didn't say anything to you, did she?" Mr. and Mrs. Kowalski have lived next to Grandma as long as I've been alive.

Mrs. Kowalski shakes her head. "She was fussing about all the things she wasn't allowed to pack for this trip of hers, but she wouldn't tell me where she was going."

"Thanks anyway," I say, glad to at least have further evidence that Grandma left with a plan.

She stands. "Since you're here, can I ask a favor?"

"Sure."

"Keep Mae company a bit." She gestures to her granddaughter on the beach. "The boys are in the water, and they're not always the best about listening to their thirteen-year-old sister."

"No problem," I say, and head over to the beach blanket where Mae's stretched out with a book.

"Hey," I say, sitting down. I don't know her super well, but Mae and her brothers usually spend a few weeks here each summer with their grandparents, and I've babysat a couple of times. "You're not swimming?"

"Didn't feel like it." She puts her book down and sits up. "Besides, I'll be here until August, so I can wait to swim until the monsters leave. They're going home tomorrow."

Mae seems less than thrilled about escaping her younger siblings. "You're not looking forward to spending the summer with your grandparents?"

She looks at me a long time. "Can I ask you something?"

I nod.

"Do you have a boyfriend—or a girlfriend?"

"No," I say, wondering where she's going with this.

"Do you want one?" she asks.

I smile. "I'm trying not to."

"Well, I did. Have one, I mean." She's quiet a moment. "And want one too, I guess."

"But you broke up?"

"Sort of."

"How do you sort of break up?" I've had pretty much the full range of endings, everything from ugly shouting to mutual moving on, but I can't ever remember being in doubt over whether it happened or not.

"Our parents thought we were too young to be so serious. They want us to take a break, so she's at some summer camp and I'm here. They hope we'll be over it by the time we get back."

"Will you?"

"I won't," she says, and she's so calm I believe her. This isn't a hysterical teen acting out. This is someone doing her best to deal with something hard.

"What did they mean . . . too serious?"

"I don't even know . . . It's not like we . . . I mean, we haven't done anything but hold hands and kiss a little, but we were together a lot, and I told her I loved her."

I feel my eyes get big. "You did? How did you know?" This thirteen-year-old is making me feel like a child.

Mae laughs a little. "Aren't you going to tell me it's just puppy love?"

"How would I know what it is?"

She lifts a shoulder. "Everyone else seems to think they do. Even Grandma, and she usually takes my side."

I'm not sure I have any wisdom to offer here. If it were me, I'd be excited about new possibilities in Mirror Lake, but Mae seems like a different kind of girl. "You want to think about something else for a little bit?"

"Like what?" she asks suspiciously, making me suspect that she's been getting a lot of life lessons in disguise, but lucky for her, I have only the frivolous to offer.

I pull out my deck. "Well, if you're going to spend the summer in Mirror Lake, you should have an Ambitious Card."

Her eyes light up. "Really? I've always wanted to learn, but Grandma and Grandpa don't really go for all the magic stuff. They only moved here because they wanted a lake house."

"OK," I say, feeling grateful I found a way to make her sadness fade a little. "First, I'm going to show you how to shuffle. You need to be able to do it without looking down. So practice, OK?"

She nods eagerly. "I will. I promise."

✦

After making plans to meet Mae on the beach the next day, I go back in to find Emma making grilled cheese and tomato soup for dinner. I clean up the kitchen and then cajole Emma into watching me practice my checkpoint card tricks.

"Not there yet," Emma says when I finish.

"No," I agree. "I've been spending too much time on the flowers. They're my favorite."

"Well, you can really buckle down on the card stuff the next couple days. Make up for lost time."

"Mostly, yeah."

She raises her eyebrows, and I tell her about my promise to work with Mae. "She's sad, and she needs someone to talk to."

Emma smiles. "Maybe you should become a therapist."

I shake my head. "I don't think there's insurance codes for running cons and teaching magic tricks."

My phone chimes with a text from Chase.

Chase: There's something you need to see. Right now!

Lia: What?

Chase: Not telling. Meet me downtown?

I want to ask if Beckett will be there, but I can't think of a way of doing it without sounding like I don't want to see Chase.

Lia: Can Emma come?

Chase: Sure. The more the merrier. Half an hour at the fountain?

Lia: We'll be there.

But when I ask Emma, she says she's going to stay home.

"Why?" She already put in at least two hours on the piano.

Looking embarrassed, she shrugs. "Just in case . . ."

"In case . . ." And then I get it. In case Theo shows up. I guess Emma's like Mae—committed even when odds are against her. I can respect that, but it seems like you miss out on a lot of fun that way.

The sun's almost down, but it's light enough that I feel comfortable walking around on my own. Chase is at the fountain doing card tricks for a group of kids. Beckett's nowhere to be seen. Which is fine.

When I catch his eye, Chase puts his deck away, and the kids scatter.

"Well?" I say.

"This way." He gestures toward the downtown.

As we walk, I let the setting sun and tourists and the smell of fudge and Chase's uncomplicated company take my mind off the vague dissatisfaction I picked up this afternoon. Something about both Mae's and Emma's steadiness makes me feel more defensive about my choices than any of Mom's overt attacks.

"Where's Beckett tonight?" I ask.

"Dinner with his parents. They're here for a couple days."

"You didn't want to go?" I'd gotten the impression that Beckett's family had pretty much adopted Chase.

"They're great, but when I can, I like to give them some time to hang out as their actual family."

Chase doesn't seem particularly sad as he says this, but it must be hard to always feel like an outsider.

"Will it be weird next year? When Beckett's gone?"

"A little. Yeah. I think Aunt Anjali and Uncle Max are looking forward to being empty nesters."

"What about your parents?"

"My dad's not in the picture at all. And my mom kind of floats in and out. When I'm here, Grandpa Henry is pretty much my parent."

It's clear we didn't get the whole story on Henry Blackwell from Grandma. Or from the video of their act. People are never one thing.

When we turn toward the Starlight, I look up at Chase curiously.

"Close your eyes," he says.

"I don't want to twist my ankle less than a week before the checkpoint."

"I won't let you fall." He puts his hands on my shoulders and pushes me forward slowly. We get one irritable "watch out," but I don't peek. I like surprises.

He stops, turns me, and says, "Open."

I'm facing the glamour shot of Elliott outside the theater, only he's not in the black blazer anymore. He's rocking the leopard toga, showing way too much skin and looking more angry than mysterious. In the upper right corner of the poster is a sort of ghostly image of him snarling at us from the pink carpet.

"No," I say. Because it's too awful. "Did Emma do this?" I'm willing to defend her, but this is pretty harsh.

But Chase shakes his head. "Elliott," he says. "He did it himself. Brought us all down for the unveiling. I thought Beckett was going to have an aneurysm trying to keep from laughing."

I'm surprised he tried to hide it. Chase, who must see what I'm thinking, says, "He didn't want to do anything that might make Elliott take it down."

I shake my head a little, because the only thing worse than seeing this picture here is knowing that Elliott liked it enough to put it up.

"It has not been easy having Elliott as a brother," Chase says. "But in the last week, it's started to pay off. Let me take you for ice cream?"

Chase and I sit together on top of one of the picnic tables at Duke's, eating our mint Oreo cones and talking about the first magic tricks we ever learned. Chase tells me about the top hat and cape he wore to perform at children's birthday parties until he was fourteen. I tell him about getting taken to the hospital because I tried to disappear a coin up my nose. (Nailed it.)

Then his knee presses against mine.

Accident?

He doesn't move away.

When I look up, Chase gives me a smile that's part invitation, part dare. A little flicker of interest springs up inside me. I'm trying to make sense of this when he says, "Probably this is a terrible idea."

"The worst," I agree, but looking at Chase's playful expression, I'm having a hard time remembering why. Beckett wants to be my friend. And I am not Emma or Mae. I don't think I have it in me to pine.

So there's no reason not to do this. If I want to.

Chase drops his eyes to my lips.

Oh, I might.

Maybe this would work better for everyone. I can go out with Chase and be real friends with Beckett, and Chase and I won't break each other's hearts when we say goodbye at the end of the summer.

Chase tucks a strand of my hair behind my ear. "For what it's worth, he seems really committed to the friend thing."

I sit back a little. "Did you talk to him about this?" I hate the idea of these two boys sitting around negotiating access to me.

"No. I didn't come out tonight with a plan. But you're fun. And he keeps saying he doesn't want more. But maybe I do?"

"What if we try once?" I suggest. "Just to see."

"Like an experiment?"

I nod.

He grins. "In the name of science, then." Chase slides his hand around to the back of my neck, pulls me closer, and kisses me. He tastes like mint ice cream, and the whole thing is lovely in the way it is with sweet boys who know what they're doing. As he's ending it, I take his bottom lip with mine for a second, because I read somewhere that boys like that, and I want to keep my end up.

"You're good at this," he whispers. But I hear the hesitation in his voice.

"You too," I say.

Chase drops his hand and sits back. "It's like with magic. There's no substitute for putting in the time."

But this isn't going to work. The kiss was nice, but it had none of the heat and longing that would make me want to do it again. Even just for fun.

"That was it, though, right?" I ask.

"Yeah, I think so." He scoots back a little, looking confused. "I like you, Lia. But you don't feel girlfriend-shaped."

I give him a startled look, and he shoves my shoulder with his.

"That's not what I meant, and you know it. I'm a huge fan of your shape. But I don't think this is what we're supposed to be."

We look at each other and think about why, and both of us wince at the same time, which makes me laugh.

"Who's going to tell him?" he asks.

I like that Chase doesn't suggest keeping this a secret. I'm under no obligation to Beckett, but keeping this from him would put him on the outside of Chase and me in a way I don't want.

"We both have to. It means different things coming from each of us." I sigh. It's possible I should have thought this through a bit more before I acted.

"Do they do that growth mindset stuff at your high school?" Chase asks.

They do, but I'm not sure where he's going with this. Until I remember my calculus teacher, and say, "Mistakes make your brain grow?"

"Exactly," he says.

"No wonder I'm in all the advanced classes."

Walking back home with Chase is surprisingly easy. On the way, I ask if he or Elliott have figured out any of Henry and Matilda's big illusions.

"Only the common ones—sawing, stretching, blades and boxes. Grandpa has a workshop in the basement, so making the stuff isn't so hard, although none of it looks as good when it's modified for my frame. The hiding places are too big. And we tried to figure out the lion thing, but not only are the angles on the mirrors hard, but we don't know how the stupid animal disappeared after your grandmother climbed out."

"Maybe it was trained. Like a circus lion?"

"To do what? Let down the latch on a mirror? Step out on a ledge and hide behind the cabinet? Nothing makes sense with an animal instead of a person."

"I know," I say, frustrated. I've been trying not to worry about what happens after the checkpoint, but Emma and I are going to have to figure out some of the big tricks. Especially if we don't want to do the violent ones.

When Chase and I get back to the picket fence that runs behind Grandma's house, he unlatches the gate for me and steps aside. "That was fun."

"It was."

"And even though I don't think we should be kissing anymore, we could still hang out sometimes."

"OK." I press my lips together, considering the irony of what I'm about to say.

"What?"

"You might be mad?"

"Unlikely."

"I was just wondering . . . do you want to be friends?"

He laughs. "Partners in crime, more like."

Fifteen

THE KITCHEN IS DARK AND QUIET WHEN I COME IN, ALTHOUGH IT'S NOT LATE. I WANDER THROUGH THE HOUSE LOOKING FOR SIGNS OF LIFE AND FINALLY HEAR CLASSICAL MUSIC COMING FROM THE DINING ROOM.

An elaborate china tea set, pale white with pink flowers and gilded edges, fills the table. Piles of cookies, doughnuts, and muffins are arranged on platters. And at one end sits Emma, a giant teapot beside her. Which is odd.

"Is there an enchanted rose somewhere in the house I don't know about? Do I need to figure out all the magic tricks before the last petal falls?"

Emma doesn't even smile.

"What's the deal with you and Angela Lansbury here?" I say, gesturing at the teapot.

She gives me a baffled look but says, "I was feeling sorry for myself."

Something about this isn't right. Unlike me, Emma loves being alone. I sit next to her. "Because?"

Emma blinks away tears. "Theo's out with some girl. He posted pictures. That's probably the text he got when he left this afternoon."

"Oh, Emma." I move my chair over so I can put my hand on her back. She rests her forehead on the table. Whenever Mom says dating was easier when they were young because they didn't have social media, I think she's out of her mind. How could you possibly have known what was going on? But I guess that's her point. Sometimes the not knowing is better.

"Who was it?"

Without lifting her head, Emma says, "Some summer girl."

"They're the worst. Flouncing in, breaking rules, kissing locals in ice cream shops."

"They weren't at the ice cream shop," Emma says with a frown. "They were at the arcade. And they weren't kissing. Yet." She gives me a bleak look. "But I bet they will."

"You need to tell him what you want."

She shakes her head. "No. It's too embarrassing. He keeps saying what a great friend I am. I thought once we were together in person, everything would change."

"Maybe it will."

"No. He doesn't care about me. Not like that."

"You don't know for sure."

"I think I do." She holds up her phone. "If I mattered to him, why would he be doing this?"

"I don't know. I mean, she's cute, obviously, so it's not really shocking he might want to go out with her," I say, trying not to take Emma's accusing tone personally. "And maybe because he thinks of you as a friend, it hasn't occurred to him that you two could be anything else." Emma looks trembly, so I go on. "Or maybe he's scared because he knows this thing between you could be big, and it makes him nervous, especially since you go to school hundreds of miles apart. Or it could be something else altogether." Like he thought this girl might be fun. As a for instance.

"Do you really think he might feel something for me?"

"Sure," I say, because I can't imagine anyone who knows her not falling for my sweet sister. "But it doesn't matter what I think. There's only one person who knows, and you're not going to find your answer by asking me or looking at the pictures he posts. You've got to talk to Theo."

"Easy for you to say."

I shake my head. "Not really. I need to have a conversation of my own."

"With who? About what?" Her curiosity chases away some of her misery.

"I may have made a small error in judgment this evening."

"What did you do?" she asks.

"Kissed a Blackwell boy."

She gives me a skeptical look. "I don't think that counts as a mistake. It seems more like the culmination of your long-term plan."

"Only . . . it was Chase," I say.

"Why would you do that?" Emma looks far more horrified than the situation calls for. This isn't the most sensible thing I've ever done, but it isn't like I was out drowning kittens.

"I don't know," I say, trying to repress the guilt that keeps rising up despite how frequently I tell myself that I am free to kiss whoever I like. "Chase is sweet, and I thought maybe Beckett was right and he and I should just be friends. So when Chase suggested it, I thought, *Why not*? But it didn't really do anything for me."

"Is Chase mad? Or sad?"

"No. He wasn't feeling it either."

"Then why was it a mistake?"

However unreasonable it might be, there's no getting around this bit. I'm a little sick about it all. "Beckett might be hurt when he finds out. We didn't make any promises, and he said he didn't want to start anything, but I wouldn't like it if I heard he was kissing someone else." Although, let's not forget, I was willing. He said no.

Thinking about why he said no makes me remember Helen. But I don't have the right to talk about this with Emma, so instead, I help her move the dishes to the kitchen and head upstairs, keeping my thoughts to myself. Lying in bed, I chase the same ideas around and around in circles. Last year, Beckett's girlfriend cheated on him with his cousin. And even though I am not his girlfriend—I'm not even a girl he's kissed—that's going to get all muddled up in this for him. But he's going to have to see that this isn't the same thing. I can't break a promise he never asked me to make. And I need him to get that, because if he doesn't, then maybe we won't even be friends anymore. Or worse, maybe he'll think I'm not even the kind of person who's worth being friends with. I remember how I felt sitting with him in that practice theater when he told me that I cared about important things. I'd like to feel that way again.

So I hope I didn't make that impossible.

In the morning, Emma walks into the kitchen while I'm surveying the wreckage of her tea party and says, "Oh."

"Come on," I tell her. "Let's go out to breakfast. Then we'll clean up together." I leave Aunt Julie a note, saying not to bother with the dishes. We'll do them when we get back.

Because there's only one decent restaurant that opens for breakfast, it's pretty busy. All the booths are full, but a few little tables crammed together in the middle are open, and we grab one of them. Emma pulls out the volume of poetry she brought while I spend some time checking in with friends from home on my phone. When the waitress returns with my parfait and Emma's bacon, eggs, and toast, she puts her book away.

Looking at her plate, I say, "That's new."

"You'll see next year. It's almost impossible to say no to bacon when you eat in a dining hall."

"But pigs are almost as smart as people."

"Maybe," she says. "But they don't make bacon out of people." Seems like she's doing better today.

I'm about to ask if Mom knows about Emma's lapsed vegetarianism when Chase and two people I don't know—although I can take a pretty good guess—walk through the door. As soon as Chase sees me, he face-palms, and the two grown-ups look at him.

He gestures toward us, saying something quietly, and they all approach our table. Emma and I stand.

"It's nice to meet you, Mr. and Mrs. Blackwell," I say. And it is. Although in my ideal world, I wouldn't be meeting Beckett's parents the morning after kissing their nephew.

Beckett's mom smiles. She has the same eyes as him. "It's Ms. Awasty, actually. I kept my name. But please call me Anjali."

"And Max," Beckett's dad says, taking a seat at the table next to us. Chase gives me a wild-eyed look while Max continues, "You both look so much like her."

"Grandma Matilda?" Emma says. "We hear that a lot."

"Actually, I meant Kristen. Tell her I said hello. If it comes from you, she might not even throw anything." Then he focuses on his tablet. I can see Emma's thinking the same thing I am: Mom threw things?

"We've heard a lot about you," Anjali says.

I can't help looking toward the door.

She laughs. "Oh, not from Beckett. If I had to rely on him for information, I couldn't be certain he's in the room, even when he's right in front of me." She rubs Chase's shoulder. "This one's more forthcoming."

Worried, I turn to Chase, but he gives me an of-course-not look. Even so, guilt and anxiety nearly swamp me. There's no way I can eat. I push my parfait toward Emma, but she shakes her head rapidly back and forth and says, "You know I don't even like looking at yogurt. Especially *used* yogurt."

When Beckett comes in, Emma looks from him to me to Chase with a fascinated expression. It's too bad we aren't doing *Girl Magician* for real, because we'd definitely bring in some ratings with this.

Beckett's face is shuttered, but he's polite enough, saying, "Emma. Lia" as he sits down. He puts a newspaper in front of his mother. "As requested."

"I love these little local papers," she says to me and Emma. "Did you know they print the flavor of the day for all three frozen custard shops? Who does that?"

She opens the pages and scans the text. "We definitely have to go today. It's mint Oreo at Duke's."

"That was yesterday," Chase and I say together. We grimace at each other and finally turn away before we can commit more synchronized cuteness in front of Beckett's entire family.

"Was it good?" Anjali asks.

I look back up. Chase turns from me to Beckett, clearly struggling for some kind of acceptable answer.

"It was all right." He looks at me. "I mean, really great in a lot of ways." He shakes his head a little. "Although, even though I enjoyed it, I guess if I had it to do over, I'd probably . . . order something else?" He looks at me helplessly.

Beckett rolls his eyes.

Anjali studies Chase, clear now that this is not about ice cream. Emma covers her mouth with her hands like she's watching a car crash. Enough of this.

I look to Beckett. "Can I talk to you out back for a minute?"

He shakes his head. "I haven't even had coffee yet."

I hold my cup out to him.

He takes a sip and winces. "Is there more sugar or coffee in here?" I look over at Emma's cup, because she's drinking it straight up today, probably because of her sugar hangover from last night. She wraps her hands protectively around her mug.

"Cope," I tell him, and get up without checking to see if he's following. When the queen of England sits, she expects a chair to be waiting.

We go out back into the little courtyard behind the restaurant. He takes another sip of my coffee and grimaces again. "So talk."

"I guess Chase told you what happened."

"'What happened.'" He snorts. "It wasn't a natural disaster. Human actors were involved."

"I'm aware. But I wasn't really thinking about—"

He cuts me off. "Swept up in the moment?"

"I don't know. I guess. But it was a onetime thing. It doesn't have to affect . . . us."

He gives me an incredulous look. "Oh, absolutely. Why should the fact that you'll apparently kiss anyone—"

"Hey!" I say. I'm trying to be a grown-up here, but I'm not required to justify myself to someone who keeps saying he doesn't want me.

He steps back. "I'm just glad I found out before I got too involved this time. And I guess I'm grateful that you chose Chase instead of Elliott. At least it shows some taste."

The anger that bubbled up a moment ago spills over. "No. This is not like Helen. I didn't betray you. You said you didn't want this." I gesture between us. "You said you wanted to be friends."

"I didn't say I didn't want this. I said I didn't want this *now*. I didn't realize your interest in me was a limited-time offer. And

I can't believe Chase. Hundreds of girls in Mirror Lake and he kisses you." Beckett's entering dangerous ground here.

"I am a human being. You don't get to call dibs and put a cone of silence around me until you decide you're ready."

He opens his mouth to argue and shuts it again. Smart boy. He stays quiet for a minute, and his shoulders come down some. "I wasn't imagining a cone of silence," he says with a small smile. "More like a no-fly zone."

I take a deep breath, trying to settle myself as well. "If you're actually wanting this to go somewhere, we don't have to be done. It was just a kiss."

"And it meant nothing?"

"Honestly? It didn't mean much."

Beckett shoves his hands in his pockets and looks at me like I just told him the truth about Santa Claus. "It would have to me."

Then he goes back into the restaurant.

I lean against the wall and sink to the ground, resting my forehead on my knees. My righteous anger vanished with that last look of his. All that's left is a lost sort of wonder at how I could have treated something that could have been so unbelievably precious as if it were disposable. For a kiss that turned out to matter so little.

I usually cry easily, but I feel too numb for tears right now. And a little like I don't deserve them. When you date guys who don't take you seriously, endings are easy. Not only is there not much to miss, but you get all the fun of being the ill-used heroine of the story. Being the villain isn't as enjoyable.

The door opens and I turn to look, although I don't pick my head up off my knees. Emma crouches down beside me.

"I'm OK," I say. "You can finish your breakfast."

"You've been out here twenty minutes."

"Oh."

"I guess things didn't go so great?"

I shake my head. "You might want to ignore any advice I gave you yesterday. My credibility's shot to hell."

"Are you kidding? You're my hero. I would have jumped up and run away as soon as Chase came through the door, and I definitely wouldn't have ordered Beckett to come out here and talk to me. You're very mature."

I raise my eyebrows.

"I mean, except for the obvious."

Sixteen

I SPEND THE NEXT FOUR DAYS WRITING APOLOGIES AND EXPLANATIONS IN MY HEAD, BUT I DON'T TEXT ANY OF THEM TO BECKETT.

Instead, I try to be the kind of person who would not kiss someone on a whim, but who would instead patiently wait for the boy who mattered to figure out his mess. I feel like I've spent so much of my life chasing fun that I couldn't even recognize something important when it was right in front of me.

My biggest act of repentance is my now-daily work on Mom's SAT class. After ignoring it for almost a month, I watch video after video, take two practice tests, and don't object when Aunt Julie takes credit for my efforts with Mom. I'm going to be a serious person if it kills me.

I also make time every day for Mae, because her grand-mother says she smiles only when she's with me, which makes me feel like I'm not a completely terrible person. By the end of the week, Mae can do a simple Ambitious Card, losing and find-ing any card chosen by her grandparents. More complicated routines, like mine, require a force to get the person to choose the card you want, so when I leave Thursday after lunch, I prom-ise we'll work on that next week.

When I report Mae's progress to Emma, she presses her lips together.

"What?" I ask. I thought she'd be happy I was spending all this time taking tests and cheering up a brokenhearted girl.

"I mean . . . shouldn't you be working on your checkpoint tricks instead of spending all this time with Mae and on the computer?"

"I'm close," I say, although this is maybe stretching the truth a little. "I'll finish the SAT stuff early today and work on sequences."

"Are you OK?" Emma says. "You don't seem like yourself."

"Maybe that's a good thing?"

"What do you mean?"

"It's just . . . maybe if I was in the habit of paying attention to things that mattered, I wouldn't have fallen into that kiss with Chase and I wouldn't have hurt Beckett." Mom's right. I'm almost grown-up. I can't be spending all my time on magic tricks and cons. "I don't . . . I don't want to be frivolous. The SAT matters and Mae matters and I can still be plenty charming onstage. It'll be enough."

Emma pulls me into her arms and holds me tight. "I can't tell you what's right for you. But I can tell you that it's OK to care about what you care about."

Maybe. But I'd do anything to stop seeing Beckett's look on that patio or to no longer hear him say "it would have to me" every time I close my eyes. So if that means I need to shed my cotton-candy coating, then so be it.

"Well," Emma says doubtfully, "do you want to run over to

the practice theaters? You should get familiar with the stage before the checkpoint."

"I can't," I say.

I do plan to practice some this afternoon, and obviously, I can see how doing the show in the theater would help, but I cannot stand the thought of running into Beckett. Looking back, I can see that kissing Chase wasn't about whether I was *allowed*. Of course I was allowed, and Beckett knew it. He was sad because he thought better of me. I'm not ready to see that disappointment in his eyes again.

"I get it," Emma says sympathetically. "But we'd better try tomorrow. You don't want to be working out the kinks in the middle of your show."

"No, I know." But if we go only once, that will make it much less likely that I'd see him. "I still don't have all the sequences down anyway. No point in going to the theater until I know those."

"OK. Well, good luck. Let me know if I can help with any of that." Emma goes back to the piano.

I drill sequences for a while, but it's even tougher than it was before. Getting good at this stuff used to make me so happy. Chasing that rush pushed me to keep going even when practice was hard . . . or boring. But now, I keep asking myself why it even matters.

I wish I could talk to Grandma. She must have felt like this sometimes.

Trying to feel closer to her, I go up to her room, with its dusky lavender walls, four-poster bed with white linen, and wall of framed pictures, some of family, but mostly from her act.

Aunt Julie sticks her head in. "What's up, kiddo? You seem kind of mopey lately."

"I don't know . . . I just feel like I'm not making a lot of progress, and I can't figure out what I should spend my time on. I don't know what's going on with Grandma. And all these old men are still out here running cons, and I haven't done a single thing about that."

Aunt Julie startles. "Were you supposed to?"

"I sort of said I would."

"Sure you did. Seems like a totally doable summer project for a seventeen-year-old girl."

"It seemed more achievable a few weeks ago. Before I got distracted."

"What did you get distracted by?" she says a little pointedly.

I blow out a breath. "Take a guess."

"Beckett or Chase?"

"Both," I admit.

"Do you need me to send some threatening emails?"

I shake my head. "No. This one's on me."

"You'll figure it out." She ruffles my hair and leaves.

I peek in the walk-in closet, searching for I don't know what. I unzip a garment bag in back to find a pair of sequined silver evening gowns. Grandma wore these for her Vegas act. In the bottom of the bag are her silver heels. The straps on top are delicate, but the bottom soles are thick black rubber, designed to be both sturdy and silent. Brilliant.

They're a little tight, but I get them on my feet. For the big performance, I'll have some made in my size. I try on one of the gowns, thinking it would be nice to perform in Grandma's clothes. But not only is it a little tight (assuming I'll need to breathe at some point in the show), but the plunging neckline and silver sequins are too much, both because I'm younger than she was and because Mirror Lake isn't Vegas.

I thought wearing her clothes would make me feel closer to her, but the opposite is true. I never knew this version of my grandmother. The Matilda from the stage show is still a mystery. But even though this dress isn't quite right, I can picture myself in something equally sparkly under a spotlight, and I grin, even though I'm supposed to be thinking about bigger things.

Wearing the dress and heels, I wander over to the wall of pictures, looking for other ideas about what to wear.

When I see the picture up in the corner, I scream. Emma and Aunt Julie come running. I climb on a chair, still in Grandma's dress and heels, to grab the photo.

"Have you lost your mind?" Emma says.

"No. Look!"

I turn the photo around, revealing a very young—as young as me—Matilda in a white evening gown, holding the reins for a donkey.

"It started with this," Emma says. "That's what was on the postcard she sent! With that donkey." She takes the picture from me, and I climb off the chair.

"I mean . . . it probably wasn't *that* donkey," I say. I turn to Aunt Julie. "But this picture has to be a clue." This photo is what Grandma was pointing me toward. She'd be furious if she knew it took me this long to figure it out.

"Are there clowns too?" Aunt Julie asks, clearly remembering the eggs Grandma left.

"I don't know. Good question." We examine all forty pictures but find nothing.

I open the frame of the donkey picture to see if anything's written on the back. In sharp, angular writing, it says *Ivey and Steve, 1969.*

I turn the picture back over. "Wait. Who is Ivey?"

Aunt Julie says, "Your grandmother."

"What do you mean?"

"Matilda was her stage name. She took it after she started performing with Henry, and she kept it."

Oh my gosh. That magic book in my room was hers. This must have been taken in those years before she married Henry.

"Did she perform on her own—or with someone else?"

Aunt Julie shrugs. "Don't know. But it would have been in Mirror Lake. It's the only place she ever performed as Ivey. You could check the old papers at the library, maybe."

"That's a good idea."

I run back to the closet to change. When I pull off the dress, my fingernail catches on something in the back, and I turn it over. There are six tiny metal hoops sewn about three inches apart all the way across the back of the dress. Running my hands along the straps, I find two more right at the top of the shoulders. They're too ugly to be decoration, but I have no idea what purpose they serve, and I can't think about it right now.

As soon as I'm back in my regular clothes, I dash downstairs for my running shoes. I want to get to the library as fast as I can.

As I'm opening the door, Emma puts her hand on my arm. "Do you want—"

"No!" I shout. "I'm good."

And I fling open the door and run.

✦

The librarian apologizes because the old papers haven't been converted to digital files yet, but she hands me a giant bound book. I start in January 1965, looking at each page. It's July 1969 when I find what I'm looking for.

I see the picture first: Grandma in the same dress as the photo standing next to a man in a top hat beside a big black cabinet. In the cabinet is the donkey, with a clown perched on top. The headline says MAGICIAN THURSTON CARTER SHARES HIS SECRETS. Wow. Grandma began her career in magic with Thurston Carter.

The story is about a workshop for magicians at the Society. Reporters were let in for Thurston's explanation of a single trick—the disappearing donkey. The story reports Thurston's demonstration of swinging mirrored panels inside a large cabinet. When in position, the mirrors reflected the painted sides of the cabinet, so it appeared empty. For Thurston's trick, the clown led the donkey into the cabinet, and while the cabinet doors were closed, the clown hid with the donkey behind the mirrors. After they reappeared, the clown hopped out and left the stage. Thurston closed the doors, and the donkey disappeared—only this time without a clown inside to help.

Then Thurston closed the cabinet doors one more time, and when he reopened them, the donkey reappeared, the clown on its back again.

Thurston refused to tell the reporters how the clown got back inside the cabinet or how the donkey could disappear on its own. This is a common tease for magicians. Show people just enough of the trick to make them think they understand it—like with the mirrored panels—but then leave them with something more mysterious: a donkey that disappears on its own and a reappearing clown.

The mystery of how this was done is exactly what Chase was talking about with the lion. With a person inside, it's easy to see how someone could coax the donkey behind the mirror. I mean—not someone like me, but the sort of someone who wasn't afraid to share a tiny box with an animal that could breathe on them . . . or lick them. Shudder.

Grandma definitely leveled up with the lion, but the trick would have worked the same way. She would (somehow?!) have gotten the lion behind the mirror and hidden there too. But when the animal (whatever it is) is alone in the box, I don't know how it could get behind the mirror on its own. Plus, in Thurston's trick, the clown left the box, went backstage, and then ended up back in the cabinet. How would that work?

If Grandma were here, she could tell me.

And then I realize, she did.

There were two clowns.

The donkey didn't disappear on its own—and neither did the lion. Thurston's audience thought there was one clown—and

Henry's thought there was one assistant—but really there were two. One who climbed out of the cabinet and one who stayed, only hidden behind the mirror so no one knew they were there. This is the part of the trick Thurston kept hidden from the newspaper reporters. Even though he showed them how the donkey and clown disappeared the first time, he let them think that the animal did it all by itself the second time.

Emma and I can do this for the real show. Chase might be having a hard time with the mirrors, but that's just geometry. I can figure it out. Maybe there's no big mystery to Grandma's clues. Maybe she just wants me to win.

But then I finish the story. The end is mostly people saying how amazing Thurston is, but the last quote is from him. It says, "I must credit my beautiful assistant for this trick. She hated hiding in that box with Steve, so first I got a clown to take her place, but then she one-upped me by teaching the donkey to disappear on his own."

Fireworks go off in my brain.

I know what Grandma wants. Credit for her work. And not just this trick. All of it. She memorized the deck and the sequences. And she used her strength, flexibility, and dexterity for the levitation, and the cutting in half, and the crushing. She designed the donkey trick—or at least she borrowed the design of the cabinet from Thurston and created the bit with the two clowns. Then later, she taught the trick to Henry.

In at least half of the tricks in their act, Grandma Matilda was the magician and Henry was the assistant. But he never acknowledged that. And because of that secrecy agreement, she couldn't tell anyone. This is why she needed me to figure it out on my own. Why she was willing to risk the theater.

By getting me to do this, she gets credit for her work, and she keeps the house because she won't reveal Henry's secrets. I will. The Society will have to admit her to the Inner Circle when she comes home.

I have to pass this checkpoint. Because it turns out it matters after all.

✦

Lost in my thoughts, I almost run smack into Chase as I go by the fountain.

He puts his hands on my shoulders to steady me. Then he looks around, alarmed, and hides his hands behind his back.

"How long is this going to be awkward?" I ask.

"When we're alone, another couple days. In front of Beckett, I'm going to go with the rest of our lives."

"How are you two doing?"

"Getting there. Whatever you said the other day helped."

That's something, anyway. Even if Beckett and I don't recover, he and Chase should.

"What are you doing here?" I ask.

"Working with the kids." He gestures toward the fountain with his head. "They're great to practice in front of. They have no idea what they're supposed to see, so they watch everything. If you can fool an eight-year-old, you can fool anyone. You want to play?"

185

"I don't have my deck," I say, embarrassed to be caught without it.

But Chase just shrugs. "It's not like I take mine when I'm running." He grins. "Besides, you probably don't need to teach your lipstick-print variation to the impressionable youth."

He reaches into his pocket and tosses me a quarter. "We're working on palming. Come help."

And even though I need to get home and start practicing for real, I follow him. Working with Mae has given me a taste for teaching, and it wouldn't hurt to get my confidence up a little before I start the sequences again.

Four kids—who look like siblings—run up to Chase when we move back toward the fountain. Their arms are dripping wet, and they're all holding coins in their hands.

"You had them stealing from the fountain?" I say.

"Borrowing. We're going to put them back, right, guys?"

"Unless you can teach us to make them disappear," one of the boys says.

The one girl in the group approaches me. "Can you show me too?" she asks quietly, and I nod, thinking that she probably would have just hung back behind her brothers if I hadn't been here. Something about that makes my chest hurt.

She's the youngest and the smallest of the four kids, but this is actually an advantage with palming coins. Adults usually learn with silver dollars because it's a little easier to cup a bigger coin in your palm while making sure your hand looks natural, but the quarter is the perfect size for this girl, who says her name is Abby.

When Chase calls us back together after about twenty minutes and tells the kids to show what they can do, Abby is the only one who doesn't drop her coin.

"That was good, Abbs," her oldest brother says, respect in his voice.

"Will you show me?" another brother asks.

Abby grins at me and nods.

Chase makes them toss the coins back in the fountain, and they wave before running back to their parents.

"I've never taught anyone magic before this week," I say. "But it's kind of the best."

"You see it with new eyes," Chase agrees.

I think about the excitement I saw from both Mae and Abby when they pulled off a trick. There should be a way of making that happen that doesn't depend on who lives next door or whether you run into the right guy at the fountain.

Really, there should be a place in Mirror Lake where both grown-ups and kids can learn magic. Even people who are just visiting. "Does the Society run camps for kids in the summer? Or trainings for adults?"

"Like the Magic and Mystery School, you mean?"

"Exactly." The Magic and Mystery School in Las Vegas runs classes on cards, coins, big illusions, and mentalism. People fly in from all over the country and pay hundreds of dollars for the privilege. We'd draw more regionally here, but with Thurston Carter, and Henry—and even Louis, who was never a big performer but is famous among magicians for tricks he's created—we could probably bring in a good number of people. And if magicians could make money this way, maybe there would be fewer poker games and street betting.

Maybe Chase—who's really good at this—and I could put together a summer camp or an after-school program or both.

Chase tilts his head. "What are you thinking?"

I explain my idea.

"That's good. Grandpa would love it. I don't know why they've never thought of it before."

I shake my head. "Probably because of the whole culture of secrecy. They don't want to let anyone in. But this is how you keep Mirror Lake magic from dying."

"I'll talk it up when I get home," Chase says. "Are you ready for Saturday?"

"I don't know. Is Elliott?"

"Yeah, but don't worry, I'll make sure he doesn't win the big one."

"We'll be at the theater tomorrow to practice."

Chase hears what I'm not asking. "Beckett too." He squeezes my arm briefly and smiles. "Don't worry. He's stubborn, but he's going to get there."

Seventeen

GIANT PREHISTORIC BUTTERFLIES FLAP AROUND IN MY STOMACH WHILE I WAIT OUT IN THE HALL FOR CHASE AND ELLIOTT TO FINISH THEIR CHECK-POINT PERFORMANCE.

Beckett's sitting across from me, watching his hands as he shuffles. This is building a bad habit, but I guess he'd rather do that than look at me. We ran into each other once yesterday, and he gave me a quick, expressionless "hello" before ducking back into his practice theater.

I've spent almost all my time since the library drilling sequences, but I put off practicing for too long, and there are just too many to hold in my head all at once. So I've put the ones I don't know at the bottom of the deck. Most of the time when someone cuts a deck, they aim for roughly the middle, so it's unlikely we'll get a deep cut.

Emma and I sit shoulder to shoulder against the wall. She's—understandably—freaked out about being in the same place as Elliott, and I can tell she's worried about me too.

When I draw in a deep breath, she says, "Just . . . however it goes, don't beat yourself up. It's not wrong that you put all that energy into the SAT and Mae . . . and me. Sometimes less important things have to take a back seat . . . and just because magic was Grandma's whole life doesn't mean it has to be yours. She shouldn't have expected that of you."

I know she's trying to make me feel better, but it's not working. When I told Aunt Julie and Emma what I learned at the library, they were outraged that Grandma put all this pressure on me, but the thing is, I get where she was coming from. Only I can't quite figure out how to explain it to Emma and Aunt Julie when they're both so aggressively taking my side.

The door to the theater slams open. Elliott claps once and does a strange sort of hoot. Chase rolls his eyes and tells Theo, "You're up."

Meanwhile, Elliott's eyes focus on Emma, and a very un-Elliott-like joy flashes across his face before it's replaced with his usual arrogant smirk. "Emma," he says. "College agrees with you."

Emma looks lost, but before I can get to my feet, Theo takes her hand to pull her up and draw her toward him. He says to Elliott, "No. You don't speak to her. Ever again."

Wow.

Emma, looking a little swoony, smiles at Theo. She goes up on her toes to kiss his cheek and whispers, "Good luck." The surprise on Theo's face is almost comic. He shakes his head a little and goes into the theater. Emma's eyes stay on the door even after it closes. Elliott's still watching her.

I cross to him and whisper, "Walk. Away."

Realization creeps over his face. "Guess it's not a secret anymore."

"Nope."

He shrugs. "It was a long time ago." I wonder if he thinks this is an apology. He gives me a once-over. "That isn't a flattering look on you, Lia."

Getting fashion advice from someone with green hair feels on point for today. I opted for an *Alice in Wonderland*–inspired costume—light-blue pinafore dress over a white blouse—to play up the sweetness of the flower routine. My hair is held back with a thick blue headband. I'm hoping looking young will make the magic seem more impressive.

"Can we talk?" He gestures, and I follow him to the end of the hall, feeling Beckett's eyes on me. "Any word on the show?"

I shake my head. I'm not sure if I have more plans for Elliott. I'd like to see him pay back a little more of the money he took, but I'm not sure how to get that done. Still, I don't see what I gain by letting him know there is no television show.

He nods. "These things take time, I guess. I just wanted to say that if it doesn't go well for you in there, you could be my assistant when I perform in August."

"What about Chase?"

"Not pretty enough," he says. Nice to know what he thinks my talents are. "And you and me would be a great opening for the TV show. They could cut our act with scenes of Henry and Matilda."

That's actually not a bad idea. If there was a show. And if I could stand Elliott.

"I'm not performing as anyone's assistant," I say.

"Well, yeah, not in that dress."

OK, we're done here. "Congratulations on the checkpoint. I need to get ready."

"Think about it, Lia," he says as I walk back to Emma. "The judges said even if you don't move forward today, I can use you in the final performance. The theater would still be mine, but I'd pay you or something."

Use me is about right. For Elliott, I'm another prop.

Emma gives me a curious look when I come back.

"I don't think he'll bother you again, but I wouldn't count on getting an apology either."

She shakes her phone a little. "This does compensate some for that."

We smile at each other.

"I love you," she says. "Whatever happens in there."

It's a nice thought, but I kind of wish she hadn't added that second part.

The auditorium door flies open. Looking shell-shocked, Theo steps out. Emma leaps to her feet. "What happened?"

He shakes his head. "I froze. It was awful."

"Are you going to be OK?"

He looks at her blankly, but after a while he says, "Sure. It's not like I really wanted this. It was pretty embarrassing, though. And they weren't nice. Not even Grandpa."

Emma looks at me over her shoulder, her eyes big.

"We'll be OK," I mouth. I might not be as ready as I could be. But it's still a stage. That's my happy place.

Theo whispers, "Come by later so I can cry on your shoulder?"

Emma nods.

"OK, then. I'm going to get out of here. I want to put off talking to Grandpa as long as I can." He squeezes her hand and goes.

Beckett stands. Emma and I drew last position.

"Good luck," I say to him.

He looks down at me for a moment, and I can't tell what he's thinking. Finally, he responds, "You too."

The verdict on Beckett is also positive, although he's much less exuberant about the result than Elliott.

When Emma and I enter the theater, Peter and the three judges turn toward us. Next to Peter is Louis Gleason and then some guy I don't know. Finally, and distressingly, Marty from the poker game, who gives me a vicious little smile when I meet his eyes.

Oh no. Peter refused to tell us who he'd picked, and this is just about my nightmare scenario. The only person missing is the monte guy. Small favors, I guess.

I glance at Emma, but she shrugs. I never told her about my encounter at the poker game, so she has no reason to be particularly concerned.

The judges sit together in the center of the theater with clipboards on their laps. This is a little awkward, because I need to approach them for the "pick your card" tricks. But since no one else is in the audience, I guess I'll move into the row in front of them. I wish now that I'd spent a little more time in this theater. I was so focused on the tricks yesterday, I never got to the point of picturing the audience.

"Do you need to set up? We can close the curtain," Peter says.

"No, we're light on props today." My tissue flowers are in my sleeves, and my cards are in the giant pockets in the front of my dress—one deck for the first set of tricks, another for the Tossed-Out Deck.

I leap up onto the stage but sit with my legs hanging off—playing up the little girl thing. "Emma's mostly here for moral support," I say. "She won't be performing."

"That's fine," Peter says.

Louis and Marty don't react.

My hands start to sweat, and my throat is drying out. I wish I'd brought water with me. All the patter we wrote is flying right out of my head. I'm not ready. And it's far too late to change that.

Peter silently checks in with the judges and nods to me. "When you're ready. You have ten minutes from when you start."

Looking down at my toes, I take a deep breath and think of my grandmother, who never got credit for the tricks she created. I need to protect her theater and create a chance for me to show everyone what she did.

I lift my head and give the judges a look of wide-eyed surprise. "Oops!" I say, and hop down from the stage. "I forgot something. Can I borrow a piece of paper?"

Peter tears a sheet off his legal pad and offers it to me. This was Emma's idea. To make the flowers more impressive by making it clear that there is nothing special about the paper used to make the cone.

I thank Peter, roll the paper into a cone, and say, "I want to thank you all for having me today." And I pull my beautiful deKolta flowers out of the cone, handing an improbably large number of them to the judges, saying, "For you and for you and for you. Oh! And there's more" in that ditzy, glamour-girl voice my grandmother did so well.

When their laps are full, I drop the paper, making it look like an accident, but my goal is to show there's nothing hidden inside. Then I pick it up and return to the stage. I roll it again, reload, and look into it with surprise, exclaiming, "Oh! I forgot some!" Finally, I drop them around the aisles and in Emma's lap.

Peter is smiling, and even Louis nods in a sort of satisfied way. This gives me the confidence to move into the card tricks. The first two go pretty well, but I have to really focus on the last one, which I learned just for the checkpoint. I smile when I get it right, but when I look over at Emma for approval, she mouths, "Talk!" and I realize I've completely dropped my patter because I was focusing so hard on the moves.

Definitely not good. But *minimally competent*?

Maybe.

And it's time for the Tossed-Out Deck. I hand the deck to Peter and walk back to the stage. This trick is impressive in part because of the distance between the magician and the cards, so I hop back onstage, sitting as I was at the start of the show.

But I have a problem: I need five cards to know a sequence, but I have only three judges plus Peter. I can't believe we didn't think about this.

Panicked, I look at Emma. She's figured this out too and looks equally alarmed but offers no suggestions. I tilt my head and give her a look. After a moment, she gets it and moves into the judges' row, a couple seats over from Peter. Louis looks over at her irritably.

I ask Louis to cut the cards and—praise be—he does a shallow cut. At my direction, they each take a card from the top.

"If you have a red card, will you stand?"

Peter and the guy I don't know stand.

Black. Red. Black. Red. Black. This one's easy. Dad, Aiden (the sweetest of my exes), Aunt Julie, Jimin, Emmy Noether.

I go down the line, pointing. "King of spades. Ten of hearts. Eight of spades. Five of diamonds. Queen of clubs." Emma smiles, visibly relieved.

Louis gives me a little "not bad" nod. He held the deck, so he knows it's got all fifty-two cards. I'm hoping the difficulty of the trick makes up for some of my lack of finesse. I try to decide what to do here. I have two minutes left on the timer and we're supposed to do this twice, but it felt so much more difficult than I anticipated. Maybe I should take the win? Finish with my Ambitious Card instead of one from Henry and Matilda's show?

But what if that disqualifies me?

And I've had a few serious mistakes. The drop of patter with the earlier card trick, and my obvious panic at the beginning of this one. I need a strong finish.

"Emma?" I say.

She gives me a look to let me know she thinks this is A Bad Idea™, but she collects everyone's cards, returns them to the bottom of the deck, and hands the deck to Marty, asking him to cut the cards again. He does.

With a deep cut.

But not so deep that we're back in those last five cards I know. As they all take another card, I recite the deck to myself, hoping to calm my mind. But my problem isn't knowing the order. It's the sequences. And no amount of calm is going to help with that.

I meet Emma's eyes, and her mouth drops open as she realizes I'm in trouble.

My heart pounds and sweat pricks out on my forehead and palms. In a state of total panic, I ask everyone with red cards to stand. Only Emma and Marty do. Red. Black. Black. Black. Red.

Oh God. No.

I have no idea what this sequence is.

Absolutely none.

In my mind, I'm racing through people in the haunted house, hoping to hit on the pattern by accident, although some part of me knows I'll never figure it out this way.

Hallway? No.

Living room? No.

Kitchen? Staircase? Library? Attic? No, no, no, no.

I'm failing. And I have no idea what to do to recover. I never let myself imagine an escape plan. I always assumed that, one way or another, I'd pull this off. Because that's what I do.

I can't believe I let this happen. That I threw away this chance to make magic my life.

Because it *does* matter.

To Grandma, sure. But also to me.

I can feel that certainty in my bones. No matter how silly Mom or Dad or Emma think magic is, *I* care about it. And that should've been enough. But instead, I told myself I had to fit it in around everything I did to make other people happy. As if not practicing magic would make me a serious person. As if it was wrong to care because other people didn't feel the same way.

I burst into tears. To the horror of everyone in the room.

"It's OK, Lia. It's OK," Peter says. "Deep breaths. Let's take a minute here. Emma, can you—?"

She comes to sit next to me and puts her arm around me, but she's stiff. I think maybe she's in shock. Emma routinely battles stage fright, but she's never had a performance this disastrous. She hands me a tissue, and I press it to my eyes. I'm as embarrassed about my reaction as my performance. This isn't how grown-ups handle bad news.

Taking shallow breaths over and over—deep breaths feel too close to sobs—I meet Peter's eyes. His face is filled with pity, which makes me want to cry even more, so I look over at Louis. He seems smug. This ignites a welcome flash of anger.

"How about we start with the good news?" the man I don't know says. "The flower routine was nice. The blossoms were beautiful and the execution flawless. Dropping the paper was a nice touch."

"The card tricks were less successful, though," Louis says, jumping in. "You had the moves down, but you were so worried about doing it right, you made the audience anxious. You need to keep talking. I think you found out the difference today between doing this professionally and doing a trick or two in front of friends. You should be grateful you learned you weren't cut out for this before we put you in front of a crowd."

Hearing those words turns me inside out. *Not cut out for this.* Until I heard this judgment, I hadn't realized how much I want this. And not just winning the contest. I want the theater. I want to start a school. I want magic and a life in Mirror Lake.

Marty jumps in. "And, as you obviously realized, your Tossed-Out Deck was a mess. You came up with the cards in the first cycle, but the second time was a disaster."

Louis adds, "Being able to do a Tossed-Out Deck with fifty-two cards is a rare accomplishment. And frankly, not one suited to the fairer sex."

"I'm sorry?" I say, shocked out of my silence. "Are you saying I couldn't do this because I'm a girl?"

"I'm saying that's one reason. Now, I know it's not politically correct, but let's face it. You're sitting here crying because you made a mistake. And really, how many successful women magicians have there been? I can think of one. Adelaide Herrmann. And that's because she trained with her husband for decades. Magic isn't just about charisma and dexterity. There's a good bit of visual and spatial reasoning involved."

My cheeks flush. I'm angry and embarrassed and flustered, and in no position to launch a defense, given my disastrous performance. But I won't believe this. I refuse to. I failed today because I tricked myself into thinking that not taking practicing tricks seriously would make Mom—and Beckett—think I was another kind of person. But it is not because I'm a girl.

"We're not saying you can't be involved in magic somehow," Louis says. "Arthur's right. The bit with the flowers was lovely. And so are you. But tricks like the Tossed-Out Deck require an almost photographic memory. And, sweetheart, that's probably not something someone like you is going to develop."

Sweetheart.

Someone like me.

"I'm sorry, Lia," Peter says, his voice sad. "But we can't pass you on."

"But Elliott says he'd like to have you as an assistant," Marty says. "That might be better suited to your abilities."

Eighteen

SOMEHOW I GET OUT OF THE ROOM WITHOUT CRYING AGAIN. WHEN I GO THROUGH THE DOOR, I REGISTER CHASE'S ALARM AND BECKETT'S CONCERN, BUT I SHRUG THEM OFF, NOT WANTING TO TALK TO ANYONE.

Emma and I walk back home in silence, my mind playing a constant high-definition replay of my ten minutes in that practice theater. When we get home, I sit on the porch swing, pulling my legs up and wrapping my arms around my knees.

Emma sits next to me, and we look out on the lake for a little bit.

"Here's what I don't get," she finally says. "If you cared this much about it, why didn't you spend more time on it? Are you upset just because of what you found out about Grandma?"

"No," I say. "I mean . . . for sure that makes it much, much worse. But I think I would have felt awful anyway."

"Then why . . ."

Of course she doesn't get this. Emma has never had any trouble turning down invitations or part-time jobs that would get in the way of piano. And as far as I know, she's never even felt guilty about it. Her GPA was a good bit lower than mine because she never let studying take time away from her practice. But I've never known how to be that sure of myself.

"Magic always seemed like it wasn't important enough to spend a lot of time on. It was one thing when it didn't get in the way of anything else, but when the tricks got hard and I had to say no to other things to practice, it felt wrong."

"Why?"

"It's like Mom says—when I grow up, I should want to do something worthy. And when all that happened with Beckett and Chase, I felt so terrible. I didn't want to keep being the kind of person who does things just because they're fun."

"Lia. Beckett was upset because you kissed his cousin, not because you cared more about the Tossed-Out Deck than your SAT scores. From what you said, he was as excited about all that sequence stuff as you were."

"I don't know . . . maybe. Mostly, he's doing this because he doesn't want Elliott to hurt anyone else."

"Look. I know it's not the same. Because classical music is . . . a whole thing. But really, what I do isn't saving babies, or ending hunger, or teaching kids to read. I play songs." She puts her hands on either side of my face and turns me toward her. "You're not a bad person if you spend time on things other people think are silly. And devoting your life to something a little bit frivolous doesn't also mean that you're going to kiss someone every time you're tempted."

Despite everything, I let out a puff of air that's almost a laugh. "Are you sure?"

"I really am."

"How does it feel to be so innately sensible?"

"I wouldn't know," she says, standing. "My next stop is to go cheer up the boy I'm pining for, presumably so he can enjoy his date with someone else."

"Does that mean I can give you advice now?"

"Seems fair."

"Tell him."

"You think?"

I nod. "Go get 'em, tiger."

✦

I stay in the swing until it's dark. Despite Emma's comforting words, my stomach's still too sick to be hungry, so I make a mug of tea and take it to the office, where I sit on the love seat, look out into the night, and hear the judges' words swirl around in my head.

A little after midnight, the door creaks open. I turn, expecting Emma, but it's Aunt Julie.

When she sits beside me and pulls me against her, tears pour out of my eyes. Unlike earlier, there's no sobs or ragged breathing, just water streaming down my face. Like I'm one of those Virgin Mary miracle statues.

"Let me tell you something about my mother, Lia. She always plays the long game. She wouldn't have risked that theater if she wasn't willing to lose it."

I wipe my face with my sleeves. "If I'd done everything I could to win this, that would probably make me feel better." My voice breaks a little, and I draw a shuddering breath. "But I didn't."

"Well, I guess that means you start now."

"How? It's all over."

Aunt Julie shrugs this off. "There's still time to figure out what you want—and how to go about getting it."

"Thanks, Aunt Julie," I say as she stands.

She touches my face. "I know you've had to fend for yourself a bit more than you're used to here. I'm more of a big-picture kind of grown-up."

I smile. "Turns out that's what I need."

Something eases inside me after Aunt Julie leaves. I'm nowhere near sleep, but I'm calm enough to think. What do I want?

I want to stay and fix this, but I don't know how. If I'm serious about magic—and maybe this school idea—I can go forward from here. Sure, it would have been amazing to start with that theater, but it's not the only way. I just need to admit—to myself and to Mom—that magic is more than a hobby to me.

But that's not my only problem. It's not even my most pressing one. I have to get some kind of justice for Grandma. After the way Marty and Louis talked to me, I want that more than ever. My plan had been to perform Grandma's tricks in front of the Inner Circle and reveal her role in crafting them during the show, but I don't know how to make that happen if I'm not doing the final performance. Just telling them isn't going to work.

I'm lying back on the couch, looking at the ceiling, when the answer hits me: Her tricks can still be performed and her role revealed. Just not by me. As I let go of the fantasy of doing her tricks on that stage while wearing a glittery dress, sadness settles like a weight around my heart, but I know this is my way forward.

When the sun comes up, I'm less sad, but twice as anxious. No part of me wants to have the conversation I need to have. Not yet ready to see anyone, I creep into the kitchen, make a giant cup of coffee, and take it out to the front porch.

Beckett's sitting on the stairs.

Perfect.

I can only imagine what I look like. I've thrown an ancient sweatshirt over my flannel pants, haven't brushed my hair, and I'm pretty sure the smudges under my eyes look like I'm suiting up for football. I sort of thought I'd have some time to put myself together before my big ask. Looking like this, I'm not giving him a lot of reasons to say yes.

Meanwhile, Beckett, alert and freshly showered, looks like a magazine ad for morning. "I didn't want to wake anyone," he says. "But I wanted to see how you're doing."

I sit down next to him. "I've been better."

He nods. "What happened in there?"

I go through the story, although I don't tell him everything they said afterward. I don't want to taste those words in my mouth.

"Did you do the Tossed-Out Deck?" I ask when I finish.

He nods. "But I used a light deck. They told me to nix the shortcuts for the final performance, but . . ."

But they passed him. I should have done the same thing. On top of everything else, I was arrogant. "How did you get around four audience members?"

"I had Peter hold a card in each hand and raise them for the colors." Another good idea.

"I bet you thought of that ahead of time."

He shrugs. "I'm a planner."

We sit quietly, looking out at the lake. I'm trying to figure out how to convince Beckett to use his act to tell the real story of Henry and Matilda, revealing enough behind the tricks to make my grandmother's role clear. In some ways, it will be better coming from him. The Inner Circle will be more likely to listen.

But I'm not sure what to say. Beckett cares about what's right, but he also loves his grandfather. He told me before that he didn't know if he could help with what I was planning, and he won't want to believe Henry took credit for tricks that weren't his. It's one thing to think that maybe he's letting tourists get scammed, but it's something else to think he might have betrayed another magician.

And, despite Beckett showing up here this morning, it's not like I'm his favorite person right now either.

"Do the show with me in August," Beckett says into the silence. I turn toward him, feeling like someone hit a pause button in my brain. All my plans fly apart.

But before I get too far down this path, I tell Beckett what I told Elliott. "I don't want to be someone's assistant." I'm certain my grandmother would rather lose the theater and keep her secrets than see that happen. I know I would. I'm almost sure I'm right about this—that I don't want to do it because it's wrong and not just because it would be embarrassing.

Beckett shakes his head. "Not as my assistant. As my partner. We won't be able to tell them, because Peter says official partners need to have made it through the checkpoint together. But we'll plan it together, both do tricks, and if we win, I'll give you half the theater."

Lack of sleep is making me slow. I need to make sense of this new possibility and what it means for me and for Grandma Matilda. And—this is terrible—but I'm not sure if I should trust him. All my instincts say yes, but after the last twenty-four hours, I don't trust my judgment.

"Why would you do that?"

"First, I can't let Elliott win, and we have a better chance together. Not just because you're good, but you make me remember why I liked magic in the first place."

"I do?" I say, feeling hopeful . . . maybe about more than just the show.

He smiles. "And second, I'm grateful for what you did. I sent Helen's mom the money from Elliott and the first check from your grandmother. That's half of what he took. I can look at myself in the mirror for the first time in a year. Because of you. And third, I never would have figured out the Tossed-Out Deck on my own. You're really good at this, Lia. Don't let whatever happened yesterday convince you otherwise."

I look away and wipe at my eyes. I hadn't realized how much I needed to hear someone say that until he did. Something moves behind me, and I turn. Beckett's hand is hovering uncertainly in the air about six inches from my shoulder.

I look back at his face.

Embarrassed, he says, "I can't decide if putting my arm around you would be comforting or confusing."

"For me or for you?"

"For you," he says. "For me, it's definitely both."

In response, I lean into him. He settles his hand on my shoulder and pulls me toward him. I press my face into his chest, breathing him in.

"You'd really split the theater?" I ask.

He rests his chin on my head. "Yes. And I'll even let you decide what to do with it as long as you rein Elliott in. Which you are shockingly good at."

"Unlike magic," I say, sitting back.

He drops his arm and takes me by the shoulders. "Hey. It was a bad performance. Not a referendum on who you are."

"They said I was 'lovely.'" In some ways this compliment hurts more than their insults. As if my looks are all I have to offer.

"You are lovely," Beckett says. And grins. "I mean, maybe not so much at the moment, but in general. But that's not all you are."

I wipe away the new tears at the corners of my eyes. "Will you sign something? About the theater? I'd feel better if we did it that way."

It's not so much that I think Beckett won't keep his word, but this morning I need to try out being the kind of person who likes magic but who also makes responsible decisions.

"Of course—although will it be legit on your end? You're a minor."

"My mom's a lawyer. She'll figure something out." I study Beckett's face. He looks entirely sincere. And I have very little to lose. "Thank you. For this."

He nods.

"I have some ideas about the show," I start, thinking I should tell him about what I want to do for Grandma, but a giant yawn stops me.

Beckett laughs. "How about we start tomorrow?"

"Sounds good." I'm beyond exhausted, and I need a little time to put together my best case about Grandma. If he really hates the idea, I'll figure something else out.

He stands, looks down at me for a minute, and kisses the top of my head. "Looking forward to it."

✦

As soon as he leaves—even though I don't want to—I call Mom.

"Hi," I say, my voice trembling again.

"Emma told me," she says quickly. "I'm sorry it didn't work out. Do you want to come home? You don't have to feel guilty. I can handle my mother."

It's obvious nothing would make her happier, but I say, "Actually . . . I'm going to stay? Only I think I need a lawyer?"

"Just what every mother longs to hear from her child," she says.

I explain Beckett's and my plan.

"And this is what you want?"

"Yes." I tell her what I learned about Grandma and why she set up the contest in the first place, but I can't quite bring myself to tell her that I want this for myself too.

"Well, Aunt Julie says you're making good progress on the SAT course, so no harm done there, I guess."

"No, no harm." I do not share that going forward, my study plans do not include parsing the intentions of unknown narrators. One step at a time.

"All right. Just don't get too hung up on this. In the grand scheme of things, it's not a big deal."

"I know. But I want to do it anyway."

✦

I make banana muffins for breakfast—the kitchen is better stocked since I've taken over shopping—and cut up a bowl of strawberries.

Aunt Julie grabs a muffin on the way out the door, saying, "You'd better go back to bed. Teenagers aren't supposed to look that tired—even after a night of crying and no sleep."

"As always, thanks for your support, Aunt Julie," I say, pushing some sarcasm into my voice. But I let my eyes show that I mean it.

When Emma comes in, she pours a cup of coffee, takes a muffin, and sits down at the table. "You look awful."

"That seems to be the consensus," I say. "I have a plan, though." I explain about Beckett and our agreement.

"What's Grandma going to think about that?" Emma asks.

"Don't know. But it's my only option. Unfortunately, I have not, as Aunt Julie would say, made good choices."

"They haven't all been bad. I know it took a lot of time, but I'm glad you tortured Elliott. Just knowing I have those pictures on my phone makes me feel different. More equal, I guess. And Mrs. Kowalski stopped by to drop off cookies to say thank you for spending time with Mae." She pauses and smiles a little. "And maybe you screwed up your own love life, but you were dead-on about mine."

"I was? What happened?"

Emma bobs her head a little. "I told him what I wanted. And he said he needed time. That he's not sure he can feel that way about someone he played in the sandbox with. But I did it." Emma grins. "Because of you."

A little more of the tension in my stomach eases.

"Beckett and I are going to plan the act tomorrow. Will you help?"

"This matters to you?" Emma asks. "For real."

"It does. I know it's not—"

She cuts me off. "No. Don't apologize. If you care about it, that's all I need to know. But you need to put the time in, or the result won't be any different."

"I will. I promise. I'm going to take a nap, because otherwise I might die, but I'll spend the afternoon drilling sequences and working on a design for the donkey cabinet."

"The what?" Emma says, wrinkling her nose.

"I'll explain later."

The next day, Beckett, Emma, and I watch the act again and again so we can design our show. When we get to Guessing Objects the third time, Emma hits pause.

"I know how this works," she says.

Shocked, I turn to her. "You do?" I'm going to be mad if Emma's better than me at magic now too.

"It's like music," she says. "Half the meaning's in the silence." Emma opens a metronome app on her phone, and when it begins ticking, she hits play again.

Music isn't my thing, but I try to follow along.

First up is a woman with a black purse in her lap. "Got it?" Henry says. *Tick. Tick. Tick.* "Good." *Tick. Tick.* "Don't show it now."

Onstage, Matilda says, "I'm sensing a purse? Is it black?"

Then the next person. "Got it?" *Tick. Tick. Tick. Tick. Tick.* "Good." *Tick. Tick. Tick.* "Don't show it now."

"Something you write with? A pencil . . . no, a pen. A blue one."

And the third. "Got it?" *Tick.* "Good." *Tick. Tick. Tick. Tick. Tick. Tick.* "Don't show it now."

"No way!" Beckett says and looks at me.

His recognition triggers mine. "It's the pauses. That's the signal."

Emma claps her hands. "You got it. But it's still tricky; you have to be totally in sync for it to work. Count in your head in the same rhythm. The person on the floor and the person onstage."

"We can practice with the metronome. Play it all the time. Until it's habit."

"We'll only need a few codes," Beckett says. "Purse. Phone. Wallet. Sweater. Then the colors. Things we're most likely to see, and I can choose people based on what they have."

Next, I explain how the trick with the lion was done, describe the donkey variation (if I ever start a band, that'll be our name), and talk Beckett through the drawings I made yesterday afternoon.

"These are good," he says. "Have you taken a drafting class?"

"No, but it's just about the angle of reflection. Essentially, it's a physics problem. I'm a little fuzzy on the applied part, though. Do you think you can build this?"

"With Chase's help . . . yes. We used to do this stuff with Grandpa all the time. But I have no idea where to get an animal."

I am trying not to think about this part of the trick. I'm resolved to do whatever we need to do to win this, but when I picture climbing into a box with a donkey, my nerve falters.

"Maybe we could ask Thurston Carter where he got Steve?" I say. Ever since I saw that newspaper story, I've been wanting to talk to him about Grandma. This would give me the excuse. "He might have some other pointers."

"OK. Field trip tomorrow. I'll see if Grandpa can get us in the door." He stands. "Time for a walk?"

Committed to taking my promise to practice seriously, I look over at Emma.

"Go ahead. You've earned a break. But sequences and metronome when you get back."

We go down to the path around the lake, walking in the opposite direction from town. Beckett seems on edge. I wonder if he regrets signing that agreement this morning. I don't think I would have performed without it, but I would've helped him think through his act. I don't want Elliott to win either.

After a good five minutes of silence, I say, "Just tell me."

He stops and faces me, looking unsure. I am both confused and curious.

"I want to apologize. About the Chase thing. You had no reason to be thinking about me. I told you I wanted to be friends. But . . . that wasn't true." This isn't where I thought we were going, but I like it.

"In fairness, I did suspect that."

"But you shouldn't have had to guess. Last summer, everything happened so fast. By the time I realized what Elliott was doing . . ." He sighs. "And what Helen was doing. With Elliott. I was too far gone to act rationally. I broke it all to her mother in the worst possible way, and I'll feel terrible about that for the rest of my life."

I take his hand. I'd probably feel guilty too, but there is no good way to find out someone you trust has been preying on your grief while also seducing your daughter. I can't imagine the way the message was delivered mattered much.

"And now there's you." When he smiles down at me, a light flares up in his dark eyes. "But we're caught up in this contest, and whatever's happening with our families, and Elliott. I don't want us to be broken before we start. And—if I'm honest—I don't want to find out I'm wrong again. If we got more involved, and I found out you were using me for the theater, it would wreck me."

I let go of his hand. Is this what he thinks of me? Because I'm used to being thought of as flighty, but no one—and especially no one who has known me even a little bit—has ever thought I was cruel . . . or dishonest. This is too much.

He takes my shoulders and turns me back toward him. "I'm sorry. It's not really about you. It's just, it would be so easy to fall into something too fast again."

"I haven't noticed you having any trouble with slow," I say, a little grumpily.

Beckett cups my cheek with his hand and tilts my face up toward his. "If that's what you think, you're not paying attention."

Closing my eyes and pressing my cheek against his hand, I try to trust this connection between us. All the feelings hit at once. Hope and desire and joy and hurt and injured pride. If Beckett didn't care about me, he never would have agreed to split the theater. But I don't like that he's suspicious of my motives.

I take a step back and turn toward our house. "What are you saying? Exactly?"

"Well. I want to spend time with you. And I don't want to see anyone else. And I get I have no say about this, but, in the interest of full disclosure, I don't want you to see anyone else either. And when the contest is over, we can start up for real. When we know each other better and we don't have anything hanging over our heads."

I stop again and study his face as if I'm going to find a sensible translation of what he said written across his forehead. It's

215

the "for real" bit that's tripping me up. I'm reminded of my SAT prep: "for real" in this sentence likely means . . .

"Are you saying you want to date? Only without the kissing parts? Is that what you mean?" It can't possibly be what he means.

He laughs. "I hadn't thought about it like that, but I guess so, yeah."

"You're an unusual boy, Beckett Blackwell." Then something occurs to me that makes me suspicious. "Is this a test?" I get he was hurt by Helen, but I won't be happy if he wants to see if I can be faithful before he fully commits.

"No. This is me telling you what I want, because me not being clear about that didn't go so great."

This is a strange idea, but it could be right for me too. I've now known Beckett for almost five weeks. In that same time span, most of my previous relationships came into being, lived out their natural lives, and died fiery deaths. Maybe if I'd gone slower, they'd have lasted longer. Or in some cases, not started at all. Which would have been for the best.

Maybe this is what it means for someone to take me seriously.

"But why is this what you want?" I ask, because I still don't totally understand what he's trying to get out of this.

"Part of the reason things were so awful last summer was that everything with Helen got really intense, really fast." He gives me a questioning look, trying to figure out if I know what he's saying. I'm guessing that he's trying to tell me he slept with her, but I don't actually want the details.

"OK?"

"Because I was so completely cught up in her, I overlooked a lot of things I should have paid attention to. Which I'd done before. You remember the day we met on the beach?"

"Regularly," I say, and he smiles.

"I thought you were this smart, beautiful girl who was unafraid of being entirely open about who you are and what you want. That was new for me, and I really liked it."

His words and the heat in his eyes warm me, but I know he's not done. "But then?" I ask, a little afraid of what he might say next.

"But then I saw you at the Society. And I thought something else."

I knew this, but his words still hurt. "Do you still not trust me?"

He opens his mouth and then closes it and looks away. After a few more painful seconds, he says, "I don't not trust you. But you're sort of a hard person to get to know. I'm never sure who's going to show up—the math-y girl in T-shirts, the focused magician dressed like Alice, or the flirty con artist with red lipstick and a plan for revenge."

"It's all me," I say, because this isn't something I am apologizing for. I hate the idea that because I'm more than one thing, some of it must be an act. And this is exactly how I got into trouble last time—thinking being serious meant giving up the part of me that likes wearing red lipstick. I want to find a way to be both a committed girlfriend and a lover of all things sparkly, and I need someone who's going to be OK with that.

217

He smiles. "I know. And to be clear, I like every version I've seen. I just want a little more time to wrap my mind around it all."

Hard to argue with that. And we're only talking about a couple of weeks here. If I could go back in time and have spent a little while hanging out with Ethan before I kissed him, I'd do it in a heartbeat. It might not have been as serious as what happened with Beckett and Helen, but I know how being physically involved with someone sometimes makes you committed to seeing the best in them. Even if they don't deserve it.

"So, should I get a book on courting from the 1850s or something?" I ask.

"I'm open to ideas," he says. "But I was thinking more, we'd work on the show. I'll take you to dinner sometime. And—if it's not too much to ask—you could maybe not kiss Chase?"

"The sacrifices I make." But I give him a look that lets him know I'd give up a lot more for a chance at whatever this could be.

Nineteen

I WORK ON THE SEQUENCES BEFORE BED AND AGAIN IN THE MORNING. BECK-ETT RECOMMENDED TEN MINUTES ON AND TEN MINUTES OFF, A RHYTHM THAT HUGELY IMPROVES MY CONCENTRATION. I'M A LITTLE STUNNED BY THIS. FOR SO LONG, I THOUGHT THAT NOT BEING ABLE TO BINGE-PRACTICE LIKE EMMA MEANT I COULDN'T PRACTICE AT ALL.

During my breaks, I try out patter, tell stories about ex-boyfriends, and offer to braid Emma's hair. But when I ask if she wants to learn to juggle, Emma says, "You don't have to entertain me."

"I don't want you to be bored."

Emma gets out of her chair and sits right in front of me. "I'm here because I'm your sister. You don't have to earn it."

I press my lips together to stop them from trembling. Emma's known me since the day I was born, so I should not be surprised she gets what I'm doing. But everything since the checkpoint feels risky. Living up to Grandma's expectations. Letting Beck-ett know me—without the incentive of kissing. Putting all I am into this show. Knowing that eventually, I'm going to have to tell Mom that magic isn't just a summer project, but my whole life. Charm feels like my only advantage.

"If I'm really boring to hang out with, won't you just want to be with Theo or your friends at home?" I ask.

Emma drops her hands. "No." Then she smiles. "I mean, to be honest, I pretty much always want to be with Theo. But how boring you are isn't part of that equation."

"OK," I say.

"Ready to get back to work?"

"Yes. No. What if Beckett and I spend all this time together and he decides he doesn't want to date me after all? Because I'm immature and silly."

"Then you'll be grateful you found out before things got more serious."

I nod. And then I ask what I'm really worried about. "What if I work really hard on all these tricks and I'm still not good enough?"

"If it matters to you, then you'll pick yourself up. Like you did the first time." She goes back to her chair. "Do you think I never worry about this stuff? About what Mom and Dad would have said if I didn't get into a music program after all that time and money? About what they'll say in a few years if I get a music degree but never play professionally? All the effort I put into piano is a huge risk."

It has literally never occurred to me that Emma worried like this. She's always seemed so confident. "Why do it, then?"

"Because I want it."

I've never given anyone or anything the power to break my heart. Even magic. But if Beckett walks away or if the judges say I'm not cut out for magic after I give it everything, that's what's going to happen.

Maybe my problem hasn't been that what I care about is trivial. Maybe it's that I haven't really cared about anything. I cried for like three minutes after I broke up with Camden and mostly because it was embarrassing. And the reason I didn't learn those sequences for the Tossed-Out Deck wasn't because it was hard: It was because I didn't really think it mattered. If I'm honest, I figured I could get through that checkpoint with a hair flip and a smile.

It's scary to decide something's important.

My phone chimes. It's Chase asking me to come to the Society to talk about my school idea, and it feels like a pop quiz.

I stare at the phone a long time, thinking about what Emma will say if I tell her I'm going to abandon my practicing to go off on another adventure. But then I decide it doesn't matter what she thinks. This is like when I went to the library to uncover Grandma's secret and not when I left my sequences to take practice SATs. Our final performance is important to Grandma, but the possibility of a school for magic matters to me.

Taking a deep breath, I tell Emma what I'm going to do.

She smiles. "Sounds good."

✦

When I meet Chase on the Society's porch, he says, "I think they're going to do this."

"Why do they want to talk to us?"

"I don't know, maybe because I told them we wanted to start a summer camp?"

Thinking about walking through the door of this building makes my stomach churn. But unless I'm ready to say this is the end of my magic career (and I'm not), I have to get over it.

"Who's going to be there?"

"Peter and Grandpa, definitely. Maybe Louis."

I take a step back. "I don't think I'm ready." The embarrassment of looking these men in the face again is almost more than I can take.

Chase opens the door. "Decisions get made by people who show up."

"All right. But if I cry again, I want you to push me out a window."

As Chase predicted, Peter and Henry are sitting in the library. Louis, thankfully, is nowhere to be seen, so I only have to face one actual witness to my total breakdown.

"Chase," Henry says when we sit. "Do you want to tell Peter your idea?"

Chase leans forward. "I was thinking—"

I kick him in the ankle.

"Ow," he says, and glares at me. I raise my eyebrows, and the side of his mouth quirks up.

"Maybe Lia should tell you. It was really her idea."

I explain my thinking about the school as a way of drawing more people into Mirror Lake and creating another source of (honest) income for the magicians here.

"Would young people come? We're worried about sinking resources into a school and having no one show up," Peter says.

Chase and I look at each other and shrug. We're hardly the best representatives of the general public.

"The problem," Henry says, "is serious magicians, even serious amateurs, are going to go to the established schools in Los Angeles and Las Vegas. We need a way of attracting novices."

"You could put out ads," Chase says. "TV? Online?"

"That's a whole other expense," Peter says.

As they talk about other possibilities for getting the word out, I think about advertising. It would still cost something to place the ads, but I bet it would be a lot cheaper if we had someone who knew about taking and editing videos to make the ads for free.

"Are we boring you, Lia?" Henry says.

"Only a little."

Chase makes an amused sound that he quickly stifles.

"Actually, I have an idea about advertising, but I need to check something," I say, and pull out my phone.

"Sure, go ahead," Henry says. "Don't mind us."

I ignore him and press the call button. "Hey, Aunt Julie."

"Lia. Why are you calling me in the middle of the day? Are you in trouble?"

"No."

"Are you staying away from Blackwell boys?"

"Um," I say, looking at Chase and then the floor. "That depends on what you mean by 'away.'"

She tsks but says, "You can't help it. They're like catnip for Montgomery girls."

My cheeks warm, and I glance at Chase again, who gives me a puzzled look.

"Can we talk about that part later?" I say. "I've got company."

Chase snorts, clearly having figured out where the conversation's going. He's not the only one. Across the table, Peter also looks amused. I turn away from everyone and explain what I'm thinking. Aunt Julie asks if this is important to me. When I say it is, she says she'll make it happen. I tell her I love her and sign off.

"She'll make the ads for us," I tell everyone. "For the school."

"That's fabulous, Lia. I'm sure the Society can pull together money to get them out there," Peter says.

"She has some conditions, though," I say, although she didn't. "You have to let me and Chase try out a summer camp. We want to bring in kids a few mornings a week to teach magic."

"Sure," Henry says, waving a hand. "Sounds like a good project for you two. We can work out the details when we get further along."

"Of course," I say with a smile. "But also . . . you can't let Elliott have anything to do with the school. Even with the adults."

"That's ridiculous," Henry says.

I ignore him and look at Peter. "People shouldn't be learning to do what he does."

"Might even be a liability issue," Chase adds. "Especially if it comes out that we warned you."

"Chase!" Henry says.

But Chase doesn't back down. "You know what he's like, Grandpa. What he did."

224

Henry looks at his grandson for a long moment, but then he drops his eyes. "OK. I'll take care of it."

Peter rubs his hands together. "OK, kids. We have some things to take care of on the business end, but we'll be in touch soon. Nice work."

As Chase and I are leaving, Henry calls my name, and I look back at him.

"You're an awful lot like your grandmother," he says.

But not like it's a bad thing.

✦

At home, I spend another couple hours drilling sequences with Emma before Beckett shows up to walk over to Thurston's. We put in our earbuds on the way and use the metronome app to practice counting in rhythm. This is the tricky part. We can work on what the pauses mean later.

At Thurston's house, an enormous but surprisingly sedate gray Victorian, I ask, "Does he know we're coming?"

"Yeah. I had Grandpa call him. He was pretty fired up when he came home from that meeting today."

"He did seem less unreasonably angry when I left."

Beckett, who'd been about to ring the bell, stops. "He's really irrational about your grandmother. Do you know what went down between them? Seems like it must be more than a forty-year-old divorce. They didn't even have kids."

Maybe this is the time to tell Beckett everything, but for him, it's not just learning to see my grandmother as a magician instead of as an assistant. He also has to see his grandfather as someone who would take advantage of his own wife, which I suspect will go down easier if he figures it out on his own, and I think talking with Thurston might help him to do that. If it doesn't come up during our visit, I'll tell him on the way home.

So I say, "Let's go talk to Thurston. He knew them when they were young."

"OK," Beckett says slowly, but I can tell he knows there's more I'm not saying.

A woman in nurse's clothes leads us through the house to the screen porch, which looks out over the lake. Thurston, now half the size of the man I saw in the photograph, is sitting in a chair with a book, a mug beside him.

We sit on the love seat facing him. Thurston asks Beckett about his grandfather, and then Beckett introduces me.

"Your grandmother looked just like you when we met," he says. His voice is low and rumbly. I'm pretty sure it could still fill a theater. "Showed up at my door and asked me to take her on for the summer. Her Ambitious Card was something else."

I modeled my routine on Grandma's. Only she used to have her participant blow a kiss that she caught in the air and pressed onto the card.

"That's what we're here about." I hand him my phone to show him the picture from the newspaper. "Do you remember this?"

"Steve," he says with a laugh. "I hated that donkey. Your grandma did too."

"Where'd you get it?" Beckett asks.

"Petting zoo. They're pretty smart. But you need them quiet. I used to give it a shot of vodka before the show."

I look at Beckett in alarm. I am not getting an animal drunk. Not for Beckett or my grandma or the future of magic. He pats my leg and whispers, "We'll find another way."

"And my grandmother came up with the idea for the clowns?" I ask.

"She did. I used to do it where the assistant stayed behind the mirrors and put the donkey out so it reappeared by itself. But it was better with the two clowns. I did the same trick after she left, only with twins."

"Did my grandma design any of the other tricks she did with you?"

"One other big one that summer. She taught herself David Abbott's floating orb routine. It was gorgeous." His voice is far away.

Beckett leans forward. "That was her routine?" He's thinking about Henry levitating those silver orbs around Matilda toward the end of the act. Beckett just realized Henry wasn't the one controlling the strings.

"Yeah. It was lovely, but pretty quiet. I was never all that interested. Still, I was impressed when she added that second orb with Henry. I've never seen anyone else do that."

Beckett shakes his head a little. "But everyone—even other magicians—thinks my grandfather did it. He got a little write-up in *Genii* when he added the second sphere."

Thurston shrugs. "That's the act, isn't it? And it's more impressive that way. If you know how it's done at all and you watch his hands, it's breathtaking. You can't imagine how he's doing it."

"Because he's not," Beckett says.

"Well, no. But she was his assistant. So . . ." Thurston takes a sip of coffee and shouts, "Tara!" Beckett and I jump. The nurse sticks her head into the room. "Can you set the projector up in the library? And find the box for 1969?" He turns to us. "You want to see her do it? I have all my old practice reels."

"I'd love that," I say.

Beckett is silent.

"Give us a minute to set up." Using his cane, Thurston struggles to his feet and shuffles out of the room. I look out at the lake, because it feels both rude and strangely intimate to watch his efforts. After he leaves, I turn toward Beckett, who looks sick.

"The Tossed-Out Deck, the donkey, the orbs. She did all of it. How can he call it his act?" Beckett says.

"He did the card tricks," I offer. "And she might have designed the effects, but he built them. And he's really charismatic onstage. He sells the story."

"Distraction," Beckett says, a little bitterly. "I even understand why they performed it the way they did. At the time. But afterward, why make such a big deal of her being the assistant? I never heard him give her credit for a single trick. Even in private. Not once."

Maybe this is piling on, but I have to tell him. "He made her sign a nondisclosure agreement as part of the divorce. She couldn't tell anyone what she'd done, or she'd lose the house.

She never got to join the Inner Circle because she couldn't admit to either inventing or performing an original magic trick."

Beckett takes my hand. "I'd like to fix this, but I'm not sure how. I don't think just talking to Grandpa Henry is going to work."

It's time to tell Beckett what I've been thinking. I hope he can hear it without getting defensive.

"We can make this the story behind our act," I say. "The assistant as magician." Not only does each trick need a narrative arc, but the show does as well. And this one will be a lot more fun than Henry and Matilda's jealous-husband shtick.

"So we reveal a bit about how the tricks are done? Like Penn and Teller?" Beckett's thoughtful, not resistant.

"Right." Penn and Teller do these tricks where they show some of the secret, and the rest of their act becomes even more incredible because you know just enough to see how hard what they're doing is.

Some of the tension leaves Beckett's body. "That's good. For the show, and for your grandma. And honestly, for Grandpa too, although he won't see it that way."

I love that Beckett's excited about this. He has such a good heart. When he meets my eyes, I can see him playing with the possibilities, and I have to forcefully remind myself that he isn't interested in being kissed.

Yet.

I'm pretty tempted, though.

He gives me a slow smile, which does nothing to reduce the temptation. "Whatever you're thinking," he says, "I like it."

Thurston's nurse clears her throat, and we jump apart. She brings us into the library, where the shades have been drawn and an old-fashioned movie projector is set up in the middle of the room.

"We used to have to wait a week to get these back after we shot them," Thurston, who's sitting at a chair at his desk, says to us. "Everything was harder then."

Beckett and I lean back against the bookshelves and face the little portable screen. The film opens with a black-and-white image of my grandmother standing onstage in a simple dress, her hair wound into a low bun. She's sitting on a wooden bench, a sparkly ball on the opposite end. When she crooks her finger, the ball rolls toward her. As she gestures with her hands, the ball leaps around, obeying her commands.

Without the stage lighting, you can see the threads—coming out of the ball in four directions and running all over the place, including through loops on the back of her dress (oh!), up to the ceiling, and around her fingers.

The film runs out. "You need to record yourselves. It's the only way to get better. And it's so easy now, there's no excuse."

Beckett and I nod.

"Do you know about the show we have coming up?" I ask Thurston.

"I'll be there."

"Can I borrow the film? I'd like to do this trick."

"You can have it. Probably means more to you," he says. He turns to Beckett. "Take care of her. A good assistant is worth her weight in gold."

Beckett winces, caught between wanting to be polite to an old man who's been generous with his time and wanting to support me. I shake my head a little to show it's OK, but he says, "Lia's not my assistant. She's designing tricks as well as performing them."

"Sure," Thurston says with a smile. "But what are you going to call her? A magicianette?"

Beckett takes my hand. "We prefer 'magician.'"

Twenty

THURSTON'S FINAL COMMENT KEEPS ME GOING OVER THE NEXT WEEK AS
I RUN SEQUENCES, DO CARD TRICKS BLINDFOLDED, AND RIG THE PRACTICE
THEATER FOR THE SPHERES ROUTINE.

I see Beckett only twice outside of our daily practice sessions, and I tell Mae I can't work with her again until after the show. When Aunt Julie asks me about SAT prep, I give her a look and she walks away, although I hear her whisper "your funeral" under her breath.

When we're apart, Beckett and Chase build the cabinet from my drawings, and Beckett visits farms searching for a donkey suited by age or temperament to standing quietly in the dark.

Once we figure out the logistics on the sphere trick, Emma watches me run it and blows an airhorn every time I hit a thread with the hoop, which makes all the rigging shake. A career breaking into those laser-protected vaults might be an option after this.

On Friday, Emma announces it's time for the costume, so we drive to Madison to go shoe shopping and to find someone to make me a dress. The seamstress suggests a floaty silver fabric instead of the sequins, and a draped neckline with narrow shoulder straps instead of the almost-belly-button-baring version Grandma wore. She is puzzled but willing when we tell her to sew the little metal hoops in the back.

We ask a cobbler to put a thick layer of rubber on the bottom of the rhinestone heels we find at a bridal store, which will allow me to cross the stage in silence. On the way home, we pick up dinner and invite Beckett over to decide on the last big illusions.

Once we rule out the sawing, slicing, stretching, and impaling, we're left with the levitation and the tower teleportation.

"I don't think they did the levitation the way Elliott does it," Beckett says after we watch it twice.

"That's good. With the floating orb, we don't need any more strings running through the air. That's a recipe for disaster."

"The easy way is a forklift," Beckett says. "The machine's behind the curtain, and you cover the lift with the same material as the bedspread. With your dress draped over it, the audience won't see it when it goes up. And everything we need is there. Grandpa Henry still does this trick."

I share a look with Emma.

"What?" Beckett says.

"We don't love the sleeping levitation," I say.

"It turns Lia into an object," Emma adds.

Beckett doesn't argue. Give the boy a gold star. "You could levitate me?" he suggests.

I could. But that goes less well with the story we're writing for the act, and I'm not sure that turning the tables is the right idea.

"What if it's not levitation? But flight?" Emma says.

Both of us turn to her.

"So, she'd stand on the lift," Beckett says slowly.

"And I'd do that trying-to-keep-your-balance pose Blaine did with the street levitation," I say. "My foot will block the stand."

"Could be dangerous," Beckett says. "The platform would have to be really small to do it that way. And it's moving."

"We'll use a brace," I say. "Hidden under my dress. I can do it."

"OK. So is that it?" Beckett asks.

"Let's see the towers one more time," Emma says.

Henry ties Matilda to a pole at the top of one tower, raises the curtains around her, descends, and climbs the other tower across the stage before pulling the curtains up around himself. After a brief pause, both curtains drop. Matilda's platform is empty, and Henry's bending her back over his arm, consuming her with his kiss.

Beckett gives me a speculative look.

"Not going to happen," I say. Whatever my private plans for Beckett, I am not doing this onstage.

He smiles. "A boy can dream."

And I'm caught. Lost in the idea of Beckett imagining me in his arms.

Emma snaps her fingers between us. "Do this part later. After I leave."

I shake my head a little, bringing my imagination back from the lovely little trip it spun off on. "What if we combined this with the donkey trick? Like the two clowns?"

Beckett says, "That's good. You climb the tower and reappear in the box with Steve."

"But how would that work? Isn't this trick done with look-alikes?" Emma asks. "One on the tower, one in the box? You're not thinking about some kind of secret tunnel, are you? That's a huge project."

Beckett and I both look at her in silence, waiting for her to get it.

"What?" she says.

I shrug. "A trip to the salon? Heels a little shorter than mine?"

Understanding followed by alarm spreads across Emma's face.

"It would work," Beckett says. "It's not like your grandmother was a twin. No one noticed."

"People didn't notice because your grandfather was eating the face off that look-alike."

Oh. I hadn't really processed that until now. But Emma's right. It wasn't even Grandma Henry was kissing. I can see how it made the trick convincing, but there's no way I would have been OK with that.

"We'll figure out something else to distract the audience," I say. "Put your back to the theater and get you offstage pretty fast. With the matching clothes and the same hair, we can sell it."

Emma's hands go to her braid. "But we don't have the same hair."

"But we could," I say. My color comes out of a bottle, and Emma could stand to lose a few inches.

"I don't do magic," she says. "You want music for the show, I'm there. With my regular hair and a plain black dress."

"I won't make you," I tell her. "But you'd be onstage for less than a minute. Grandma would be really proud. And a bright new hair color might be good for you." I add the kicker. "Maybe it will make certain people see you in a different way than they ever have before?"

Emma watches me, blinking her eyes and thinking it through. Beckett has the sense to stay quiet. We don't need to do this, but bringing in Emma could take this from a good trick to a great one.

"OK," she says.

I clap my hands. "That's the show."

Beckett says that the cabinet is almost done, he has a lead on a donkey he's checking out tomorrow, and the pieces of the tower are already backstage at the Starlight. We agree to spend the weekend on the last bits of background preparation and to start running the show on Monday.

I walk Beckett out to the porch. When I gesture to the swing, he nods. We sit next to each other, his arm stretched out behind me. Despite the heat, I shiver a little when his fingers trace a pattern on my bare shoulder. He gives the swing a little push, and I turn toward him, pulling my feet up.

"How are we doing?" he asks.

"Really well. Thanks to you," I say. "How come you're so willing to help my grandma?" I'd expected him to fight me on this—both because of his relationship with his grandfather and because, well, he's a boy. Most of the guys I go to school with seem to think sexism is so last decade.

He shrugs. "I mean, if you're not white, it's not exactly news that people make assumptions based on what you look like. Plus, my mom's a programmer. She's the only woman on her team a lot, and she lives with three guys. I've had more than the average number of conversations about mansplaining." He gives my ponytail a little tug. "And I think you're brilliant. I'd hate to see you treated like your grandmother was . . . I mean, *is*, I guess."

As I think that over, I realize I'm kind of liking this waiting more than I thought I would. First, living with the anticipation is so fun. And then there are all these moments we would have lost if we'd spent them kissing instead of talking.

Which isn't to say I'm not willing to make that sacrifice later.

But for now, I say, "I'm glad we're starting as friends."

"Me too. You want to do dinner tomorrow, though? Just us?"

"Yes."

We agree to meet at the fountain, and he leaves, giving my hand a little squeeze. I wonder if he's still afraid I could be using him for the theater. It seems impossible. But I'm sure he never imagined Helen was cheating on him. Or working with Elliott. Either way, the show will be here soon enough. With my history, the first kiss always feels like the beginning of the end, and I'm nowhere near ready to start saying goodbye.

When I go back inside, Aunt Julie's waiting, arms crossed, eyebrows raised. "Were you on the porch making out with a Blackwell boy?"

"Aunt Julie, would I do such a thing?"

Her eyebrows creep higher.

"You must know I wasn't, since I'm sure you were looking out the window."

"I may have glanced, and it was heading in that direction."

I consider what to tell her and decide to go with the truth. "I like him. A lot."

Her face softens as she watches me. "OK, I'm reserving judgment on that one. But know that I am fully prepared to lock you in your room if it comes to that."

I scoff. "I'm a magician. You'll have to do better than that."

Twenty-One

A WEEK LATER, EMMA AND I GO TO CUT AND COLOR OUR HAIR. EMMA COMPLAINS MORE IN THOSE THREE HOURS THAN IN THE REST OF HER LIFE PUT TOGETHER, BUT ON THE WAY HOME, I HAVE TO MAKE HER PULL OVER SO I CAN DRIVE BECAUSE SHE KEEPS GETTING MESMERIZED BY HER IMAGE IN THE REARVIEW MIRROR. NOT ONLY IS THE COLOR MUCH MORE VIBRANT, BUT THE SLIGHTLY SHORTER LENGTH, BLOW-DRIED INTO SHINY SMOOTH-NESS, MAKES EMMA LOOK GLAMOROUS. SHE LIKES IT FAR MORE THAN SHE'LL ADMIT.

My hair is up in a bun because I didn't want us to be too twin-sie. Both because that's silly and because the less people think about how similar we look in the weeks leading up to the show, the better. Fortunately, Emma spends most of her time at the piano. We'll have to get her a baseball cap for when she goes out in public—but that can wait until tomorrow. She deserves one fabulous night with her new hair.

At home, we change for our evenings out. Emma's arranged to meet Theo at the café, while Beckett and I are starting at the fountain. Tonight is the first really hot evening in a summer that's been unusually cool. The air is heavy, promising a thun-derstorm before morning. I leave my hair up so it's off my neck, put on a light-pink sundress with a bell-like skirt, and go into the bathroom to do my makeup.

When I return, our room's been turned inside out. I didn't even know we had this many clothes. A little dazed, I turn slowly in between our beds.

"I borrowed some things from you," Emma says forlornly.

"But none of them are on you." Emma's sitting on her bed wearing nothing but an oversize gray T-shirt with a neon image of Beethoven. I will wrestle her to the ground before I let her leave the house in this.

"Everything either looks too much like me or not like me at all."

I flip through the clothes on the bed until I come to a long, stretchy black skirt of hers. I throw this at Emma before moving to the floor to keep digging. I pull out a silky emerald-green tank top of mine. "This," I say. "And these." I hold up high-heeled strappy black sandals.

Emma takes the shoes. "Are you sure? This doesn't look like what you're wearing."

"You and I are doing different things."

"We are?" Emma says, pulling on the skirt.

"Yes," I say, pleased to be the one giving Emma directions for a change. "You and Theo know each other, but you need to figure out if there are fireworks. That's a light-the-match outfit." If Theo doesn't realize what he's missing with Emma when he sees her in this, there's nothing I can do.

"But you and Beckett?"

"Are not worried about fireworks," I say. "For now, we're trying to be friends."

"So, you dressed as a Disney princess?"

Suddenly uncertain, I look down at my dress. "I guess so."

When we get downtown, Emma, who has a little more time than I do, goes off to sit on a bench by the lake, leaving me alone to wait for Beckett. But when someone says my name, it's Theo.

"Hey, how's Team Beckett doing?"

I shake my head a little, objecting to the name. "We're working together. We'll co-own the theater if we win."

Theo looks skeptical. "His grandfather agreed to that?"

"He doesn't have a choice. Beckett signed the paper."

Theo opens his mouth to respond and stops. He's looking right at Emma's back, but it's clear he doesn't recognize her. "Things sure do get more interesting around here in the summer."

"You should go say hi."

"Not worth it. That is a girl with a boyfriend." He looks at his phone. "And I'm meeting Emma soon."

"Still, nothing ventured . . ."

Theo looks at me and at Emma's back again. "Fine, but when I crash and burn, that's on you."

"I can live with the responsibility."

When Theo comes up beside the bench, Emma turns toward him, and Theo freezes. Emma stands and says something. Theo nods. Then he pushes his hands into Emma's new blond hair, pulls her close, and kisses her. Even from here, you can tell it's fireworks.

"You look like a director getting ready to yell 'Cut,'" Beckett says, putting his hand on my back.

"Not me. I always think they end the kissing scenes way too soon."

"But you orchestrated this?"

"I played a small role in moving it along."

"Is there anyone who doesn't bend to your will?"

I raise my eyebrows. "Occasionally, someone tries to resist, but I'm usually victorious in the end."

"Counting on it," he says, and takes my hand.

For dinner, we go to a little Chinese restaurant where they have this eggplant thing I love, and we don't talk magic. I learn Beckett plays lacrosse (which is, apparently, the one with the little nets on sticks), took French but didn't like it, and broke his arm when he was seven because he fell off a plank bridge he and Chase made between two trees in his grandfather's back-yard. I tell him I had to get stitches after a performance of *The Nerd* because of a terrible onstage teacup accident and that my mother refused to let Grandma Matilda babysit for almost a year because I broke my ankle when she let me do a Mary Poppins–style leap off the back deck.

When we leave the restaurant, Beckett takes my hand again, lacing his fingers through mine. This isn't the way he held my hand when we saw Louis's poker game. This is what he does when he means it.

"I have a surprise for you," he says. "Want to see?"

"Obviously." I'm grateful for the idea. I'm not ready to say good night, but the logical next step of going for ice cream is not, I think, an option. Eventually we're going to have to put that behind us, though. I'm not cutting frozen custard out of my life.

We wander into the heavily treed neighborhood behind the downtown. Most of the houses are Victorians, like those on the lake, just a little smaller. The wind tosses the tree branches around. Not much longer before it rains.

Beckett stops in front of a three-story gray house with a fieldstone tower. "Grandpa's," he says. At some point, I'm sure Grandma pointed this out to me, but I'd forgotten.

"Is your grandma still alive?" I ask as he leads me into the backyard.

"She is. She's in Florida. We see her a couple of times a year. She was wife two of four, so it's all a little weird."

"I guess none of us have storybook grandparents."

"Depends on the story."

Beckett takes me to the back corner of the yard, which has been staked off and wrapped in green plastic netting. Standing in the center of the enclosure, head down in a pile of hay, is a giant gray donkey. He smells horrible and makes terrible chomping, swallowing sounds. I didn't know it was possible to make this much noise while chewing.

"Meet Steve II," Beckett says, making a little ta-da motion with his hands.

"Why does he smell like that?" The donkey in Grandma's movie seemed so clean.

"Because he's an animal. Here." Beckett reaches into a bucket at his feet and pulls out a carrot. "We're training him to move when you hold out a carrot. You should be able to get him in and out of the cabinet that way."

Instead of taking the carrot, I put my hands behind my back, step away from the pen, and shake my head back and forth.

"You're a vegetarian," Beckett says. "I thought you liked animals."

"I do like animals. That's why I don't eat them. Or like to think about them being kept in tiny cages. I like them roaming the countryside. Freely. Far, far away from me."

Beckett is oh so amused. "You need to make friends with Steve. You're the one who has to get in the box with him."

I narrow my eyes at him. "We could use clowns."

He shrugs. "Fine by me. You want to tell Emma she needs to wear a wig and a red nose instead of her pretty new hair?"

We stare at each other in silence, and his smile grows bigger as every second passes. "Fine," I say, snatching the carrot out of his hand. "Introduce me."

Beckett opens the pen and gestures me inside, but I dig in my heels on this. I am not stepping into the mud and who knows what else in my little white flats. So, he takes another carrot and waves it in front of Steve, who trots over to us. He's so big up close. Much, much bigger than a dog. I step back against Beckett, who grabs my hand that has the carrot and holds it out in front of me. Steve lunges for it. His hot breath blows over my arm while chunks of carrot drop down onto me. When his slobbery wet lips touch my skin, I scream and press farther back into Beckett, who laughs and pushes me behind him.

Peering around Beckett, I see Steve looking at me sadly, although I'm not sure if this is because he's offended or because he wants more carrot. Beckett scratches Steve between the ears.

"Not much of a country girl, are you?"

"No. I am city streets and manicures and graph paper. Not slobber and work boots and donkeys."

"And no pets growing up, I'm guessing?"

"I had a betta fish for a few years. Her name was Adelaide Herrmann." Louis was right about one thing—she was the first truly great woman magician.

"Well, we've got to get you comfortable. That space behind the mirror is small, and both you and Emma have to fit back there with Steve. He's a little bigger than we hoped, but he's super calm, and his owner was willing."

Beckett fastens the door to the pen. "We've got a harness and a lead in the basement, and there's a trail that starts in the park. Let's take him for a little walk. Wait here and hold the door."

Steve and I watch Beckett go, both of us clearly wishing he hadn't left us here with the other.

"You have to brush your teeth before I get in that cabinet with you," I tell him. "And no licking."

"If I had a dollar for every girl who told me that, I wouldn't need your grandmother's theater," Elliott says, coming up from the alley. He looks from me to Steve. "Beckett says you're performing with him for the show."

I nod.

"He was smart. To get your emotions involved. I never should have tried to convince you rationally."

"You wouldn't have been able to convince me any other way," I say. It's not smart to antagonize Elliott, but I can't help it.

"We'll see. When the theater's mine, I'll want a full-time assistant. Pay's not great, but we can negotiate benefits."

I'm done being polite or subtle. "Elliott. I am not interested. Not in being your assistant. Not in anything else. Not ever. It's not just your hacky act or your green hair or the way you treat your brother. It's what you did to my sister. Which I won't ever forget."

He smirks. "You're cute when you're angry."

He's walking away by the time Beckett comes back outside, but as he passes, I hear him say, "I'll say one thing for you, Beckett. Your taste in summer flings is outstanding."

Something flashes across Beckett's face. Maybe anger at Elliott. Who can blame him? But suspicion might be there too, which I don't like. Before I can say anything, lightning cracks across the sky, followed, a few seconds later, by a deafening rumble of thunder.

Steve makes a sound, which, if he were anything other than a donkey, I'd call a shriek and barrels through the door I forgot to hold closed. As he takes off for the street, the skies open up. Huge, fat drops of rain pour straight down, making it almost impossible to see.

"Come on!" Beckett shouts, and we run after Steve. After taking a few steps, I have the sense to go back and grab a carrot from the bucket before turning to follow Beckett again. I run right out of my shoes as I come by the house and see Beckett up ahead on his way into the park.

Splashing through puddles, I follow, but I'm hampered by my bare feet and the wet dress clinging to my legs. I hope Beckett's got Steve in his sights. Bad breath or not, I'm going to feel terrible if this donkey becomes a runaway and takes to a life of crime because of me.

At the park, I find Steve and Beckett staring at each other from opposite sides of a merry-go-round. Beckett says to him, "You're not thinking clearly. Let me take you home." Pretty sure he's used that same tone with me.

Lightning flashes again, and Steve runs in tight little circles. I can almost hear him saying, "Help! Help! Help! Help!"

Beckett and I watch from the other side of the merry-go-round. I have no idea what to do. When the thunder stops, Steve does as well. Beckett edges toward Steve, but Steve takes a step every time Beckett does.

"I don't want to go any faster," Beckett says. "I'm afraid I'll spook him and he'll run into the street."

I don't for a minute believe that Steve is more afraid of me than I am of him, but he's more afraid of the thunderstorm than either of us is of the other, so I sit cross-legged on the merry-go-round, hold the carrot in front of me, and tell Beckett to push me over.

"You sure?"

"I got this." All part of the new me, I tell myself.

Beckett spins me slowly toward Steve, who stays where he is. When I'm right in front of him, he looks me in the eye and bends to eat the carrot. And even though he smells no better and his lips are still slimy, I keep my hand steady and reach up to scratch between his ears while Beckett slides the harness over his head and attaches the lead.

"You saved his life," Beckett says. "Now he's yours."

"God, I hope not."

Beckett winds the lead twice around his wrist so he can hold Steve close when it thunders again, and we get him back to the pen. There's a little lean-to in the corner with a pile of hay, which Steve flops gratefully into.

Beckett shuts the gate and pushes his wet hair out of his face. "Do I know how to show a girl a good time or what?"

"If you were truly gallant, you would have sent me inside while you chased that donkey."

"Are you kidding? I won chivalry tonight. My eyes haven't dropped below your chin for the last twenty minutes."

Now that he's said this, I can't not check out the way his wet T-shirt is clinging to his chest. After my bravery with Steve, I deserve a treat.

"Lia," he whispers, drawing my attention back to his face. Raindrops cling to his thick eyelashes. Sopping wet in the middle of a thunderstorm wouldn't be the worst possible place for a first kiss.

Beckett shakes his head a little, giving me a lost look. "All of a sudden, I'm having a hard time remembering why I wanted to wait."

It would be so easy to run with this. I'm pretty sure if I put my hands on his shoulders right now, he'd kiss me. But after Elliott's comment about summer flings and Beckett's fleeting look of suspicion and what's at stake with this performance, I don't want to start this until we're both sure it's real. This thing between us is like nothing I've ever felt, and I don't want to screw it up because I can't keep my hands off Beckett in his wet T-shirt.

So I step back. "You wanted to be sure you could trust me."

He looks at the ground for a minute before meeting my eyes again. "I did. I do. You still good with waiting until after the show?"

"Depends on what you mean by 'after,'" I say with a little smile.

"I'm thinking *immediately*," he says.

"That works."

Twenty-Two

WE HAVE ONE MORE WEEK IN THE PRACTICE THEATERS BEFORE WE MOVE EVERYTHING INTO THE STARLIGHT. THEO SIGNS UP FOR BACKSTAGE SUPPORT BUT SPENDS A GOOD BIT OF HIS TIME DISTRACTING EMMA FROM HER WORK ON THE LIGHTING.

By the middle of the week, the opening is clean. We combine Henry and Matilda's card tricks with our Ambitious Card routines, Guessing Objects, and my (now locked-down) Tossed-Out Deck.

During Guessing Objects, Beckett and I communicate through second-length differences in the pauses. We use odd numbers for objects and evens for colors. At the end of the week, Chase comes in to record the show and joins Emma and Theo in trying to stump us, but we're untouchable.

"Got it?" Beckett says to Chase. *One. Two. Three.* "Don't show it now." *One. Two.* "Good."

Onstage, I say, "I'm sensing money . . . or something that holds money. A wallet? A black one, I believe."

"Nice," Chase says.

Beckett meets my eyes, and I smile. Even though it's just numbers, being inside someone else's head is electric.

"What's next?" Emma asks.

"Flight," I say, strapping on the brace Chase rigged for me.

For this trick to look real, I need to appear to launch myself just as the forklift starts to go up. To keep us in sync, we're using a song, so Theo, who will be operating the machine behind the curtain, knows when to start, slow down, and stop.

As the forklift raises me into the air, I mimic flying, raising my front foot a little bit and holding out my arms as if I'm balancing. Or at least that was the plan. Beckett says he has a new idea.

He goes offstage and comes back with a giant helium balloon. It's perfect for the fun, romantic feel we're going for, and it does that essential thing of giving the audience a reason to believe in the trick.

We work out the skit—Beckett offering me a series of gifts, which I reject as clichéd (heart-shaped candy), ridiculous (a poem—I'm tempted to offer up Camden's but refrain), and too serious (a ring in a little black box). Much to my delight, he returns with the balloon. He sprinkles it with glitter, hands it to me, and I float up into the air.

After bobbing about a bit—the brace makes me steady enough that I can give a pretty good impression of movement—I let go of the balloon and float back to Beckett.

We run this again and again. The first time is a disaster. Theo brings me up way too fast, so I look like I'm getting yanked through the air instead of flying, and when I land, he pulls back before I can get free of the stand, so I'm dragged behind the curtain with him.

The last time is solid enough. We find the easiest way for me to get out of the stand is for Beckett to lift me out as part of our embrace. I wrap my arms around his neck, and he holds me against him while Theo pulls the stand back under the curtain. Beckett spins and sets me down in front of him, my back to the audience.

"That was perfect," Chase says. "Everyone's eyes will be on you. They won't see the lift withdraw."

"Make sure not to spin her too fast, though," Emma calls from the booth. "We don't want to flash the brace."

Beckett, his hands still on my waist, whispers, "Maybe we should keep practicing this part."

"Are you two done for the day?" Chase calls. "We don't all have to sit here and watch you gaze longingly, do we?"

"Chase," Beckett says, not moving away from me, "you are welcome to head home whenever you like."

"I'm out too," Theo says, and leaves with Emma.

Chase comes up to the stage to hand over the video camera. "Hey. Grandpa and Peter are working on some stuff for the school, and they're wondering about the ages of kids for the camp. What were you thinking?"

Reluctantly, breaking away from Beckett, I jump down. "Would eight to twelve work? Little kids make me nervous. They're so unpredictable, but then I worry teenagers won't listen to us."

"Eight to twelve sounds good. Especially for the first year. Probably better to start small than be too ambitious and screw it up."

I grin. "I can't believe this is actually going to happen."

"I know. I'll let you know what they say."

I wave and take the camera back to Beckett, who's now sitting on the edge of the stage. "You want to watch this on the laptop here or come home with me? I'm sure Aunt Julie will make us mini quiches. Which, now that I think about it, is an argument for staying here."

Beckett doesn't smile. Instead, he says, "Can I ask you something?"

"Of course."

"This magic camp you and Chase are doing?"

"Yeah?"

"Where are you planning to do it?"

"If we have to, at the Society. But I hope . . ."

"Here," he says.

I lift a shoulder. "If all goes well." I don't want to jinx us by being too certain.

Beckett looks at me a long time. I can't figure out why he's so serious, but anxiety makes my heart rate pick up.

Eventually, he raises his eyebrows. "But you didn't think to ask me . . . even though the theater will be half mine?"

"Oh. I didn't think you'd mind . . . You don't object to the camp, do you? The Society's running it, so they're taking care of insurance and stuff like that." I've never had a business partner before. I suppose he's right. I can't just go around making these decisions by myself.

"I don't mean about using the theater. That's fine." He waves that away like it's no big deal. "I meant about working with you at the camp."

It never occurred to me he would want this. "I asked Chase because he likes kids. And he loves magic. You . . . You're only doing this to beat Elliott."

He gives me an incredulous look. "Really? After the last two weeks . . . After I searched the entire county for a donkey, after performing that balloon trick with me . . . Is that seriously what you think?"

"I . . . I don't know." There's this undercurrent in his voice that I don't understand, and it's making me panicky. "What's going on?"

He stands, take two steps away, and comes back. Even after spending all this time in his head, I have no idea what he's thinking. "I'm just trying to figure out your plan . . . am I the endgame or a stepping-stone? Because you were really careful about getting papers signed. Whatever happens with us, you'll have a right to this space."

His words—and his lack of faith—break something in me. Since the checkpoint I have been my best self. I have memorized sequences and practiced card tricks and been all in on his ridiculous almost-dating plan. And he still thinks I might be using him?

"I'm going," I say, and move toward my bag.

"Lia," he says.

I look back. His face, both uncertain and afraid, stops me, but it doesn't dampen my anger. "I don't like who you are right now, and I don't like how it makes me feel. You need to decide who you think I am."

He shakes his head as if to clear it. "Just . . . stay . . . for a minute. Please."

I meet his brown eyes, and he looks as hurt as I am, which I don't understand. My mind maps out two versions of the next twenty minutes.

In the first one, I go home to Emma to report this betrayal and wash my hands of Beckett for good. Because I don't actually enjoy this red light/green light game of his, and if we're not going to work out, it may as well be his fault so I can enjoy the moral high ground.

In the other version, I stay here and have a conversation that is maybe difficult or awkward and might hurt my feelings or make me angry, and we get through this. Which I'm pretty sure is what I want.

"I'll stay, but you've got to talk to me," I say. "Calmly. Because whatever else we are—or are about to be—we're friends too. And at the very least, that has to mean you're not thinking terrible things about me."

Something shifts in his face, like he's coming back into himself—in this moment, with me—instead of trapped somewhere far away. My satisfaction at causing this is almost as strong as my relief.

"I'm so sorry, Lia."

I nod, because that's a good start. "What was all that about?"

"I . . . I'm having a hard time believing in this . . . in us."

"Because you're worried I'm manipulating you. Like she did?"

He nods.

This does hurt, but not in a way I can't bear.

He rubs his face. "I'm such an idiot." He gestures to the first row of seats. "Come sit?"

Our knees angle toward each other, barely touching, but I keep my hands in my lap, not quite ready to go back to where we were.

"So, clearly I have zero dating skills," he says.

"I know it would be polite to argue, but . . ."

"Fair. Obviously, I'm still . . . not quite over last summer, and it made me freak out."

I nod. "Probably I should have talked to you more about the camp. And definitely about using the theater."

He takes my hand, and I let him lace our fingers together. "It wasn't about that. I hope we win. I hope you can do it here. And . . . I hope I can help?"

"Really?" I say. Because even with all the work he's put into this, I didn't think he wanted that. I figured he no longer wanted to destroy the building, but I didn't think he wanted to spend any more time here.

"Yes. Everything with Elliott made me forget the fun parts of performing. You brought magic back to me. I couldn't believe you didn't see that. So I was hurt when you didn't ask me to help out with your camp, and it sent me down some not-great mental paths."

"I'm sorry. I wasn't trying to leave you out."

"It's not your turn to apologize. I shouldn't have been so suspicious. I should have said what I wanted." He shakes his head. "I'm not sure how many times I have to learn that lesson."

"Well . . . if we're saying what we want, I do want the camp. And I want this theater," I admit. "But if both disappeared, I'd still want to see where this goes." I give his hand a little squeeze.

"Even though I'm such a mess?"

"Even though. My own dating history isn't all that outstanding, so I get it. It's probably going to take us some time before we really trust each other." I sigh. "Seems like this is going to be more hard work than magic."

Beckett brings my hand to his mouth to kiss my knuckles, sending a little spark right up my arm and straight to my heart. "Could have fooled me."

Twenty-Three

THE DAY BEFORE THE SHOW, BECKETT LETS PETER INTO THE THEATER, WHILE EMMA AND I PACE BACKSTAGE. IN SOME WAYS, THIS IS ANOTHER CHECKPOINT, BECAUSE IF PETER SAYS WE'RE NOT READY, HE WON'T LET US PERFORM.

This is the biggest Society event in a decade. Twenty-five Inner Circle members will be here to vote on the winning act, and the other fifty people in the audience are paying twice as much for their seats as they do for Henry's and Elliott's regular shows. Thurston is going to make the announcement about the school, and Aunt Julie is doing some taping for the TV ads.

"If we put up people who don't know what they're doing," Peter said, "no one's paying to come here and learn magic."

So no pressure or anything.

When Peter and Beckett come into the theater, Emma turns to me, her eyes huge and her breathing shallow.

"Why is this so much worse than piano?" I ask.

"I don't know," she says, almost whimpering.

Theo sticks his head backstage and grins at Emma. "You're gorgeous and you're going to do great."

Emma grins back, all her anxiety vanished with his presence. "Obviously," she says.

"I'm glad we've had this talk," I say, and take my place behind the curtain.

We run the whole show, except for my one secret trick, and it's flawless.

Peter stands and claps when Beckett and I take our final bows. "That was beautiful, kids. And I'm sure it's exactly what Matilda wanted when she started this thing."

He's not surprised.

"You knew?" I ask.

He snorts. "Of course. I saw their act hundreds of times, know them both and what they're capable of. You think I didn't know who did what?"

I can't believe this. All this work. My grandmother's disappearance. And he already knew. "Why didn't you say something? Why isn't she in the Inner Circle?"

"I don't have much power in that group," he says. "I'm not a magician." Maybe, but Peter is the acting president of the Society. His voice is in a lot of ears. If he wants to make this happen, he can.

So I push him. "But tomorrow, after the show, you'll get them to admit her?"

"I'll try. Your performance will help." As he's leaving, Peter says, "Have you heard from her?"

"No, not for weeks." I'm surprised when my voice breaks a little. Beckett puts his hand on my back, and I lean into him.

"Don't worry," Peter says. "Matilda Montgomery wouldn't miss this for the world."

✦

That night, while we're getting ready for bed, I ask Emma if she thinks Mom and Dad will let me stay in Mirror Lake to do my senior year.

"Because of Beckett?" she asks, sounding wary.

"No. He doesn't live here full-time, and he's going to college next year anyway. But I want to help start this magic school. And spend time with Grandma. This is where I belong."

"You're really going to do this? Make magic your thing?" Emma's working hard to treat the idea of me being a magician as seriously as her being a pianist. She's not quite achieving it yet.

"Yeah. Eventually, maybe I'll do community theater along with magic. And I want to do a little rabble-rousing on equity stuff. I see a Girls Who Conjure club in my future for sure."

"But you're still going to college, right?"

I laugh. "Definitely. I'm not trying to get disowned. But . . . probably Madison? I don't want to be far away. Do you think they'll be OK with that?"

Emma comes to sit on my bed. "I know you don't believe this, but all Mom and Dad want is for you to commit to something."

Maybe this is true. I know Emma thinks so. But I can't forget Mom calling me a sideshow freak. "Mom doesn't really get this. Or me."

Emma shrugs, putting aside the argument. We've always had different takes on Mom. Not surprising, since she's never been anything but supportive of Emma's dreams. "You're convinced Grandma will be here tomorrow?" she asks. "That all this was part of her plan?"

"Well, maybe not all of it," I say, thinking about my failure at the checkpoint. "But, yeah, I think she'll walk through the doors of that theater right before the opening."

The doorbell rings, and I leap up, thinking, illogically, that maybe it's Grandma now, even though she wouldn't ring the bell at her own house. I fly down the stairs, Emma behind me, to find Peter at the front door.

Aunt Julie, who's been talking to him, says, "Peter has something for you, Lia."

He hands me a letter, with my name written in purple ink across the front. "Matilda asked me to deliver this to you when you figured it out."

"She was so sure I would?"

"She really was. I'm sorry, Lia. I was never entirely comfortable with the way Henry talked about the act, but he's been my client—and my friend—almost all my life." He says this as if he wants absolution, but that's not mine to grant. And I'm not sure I want to. Peter sat back and let Henry take my grandmother's ideas—even though he knew it was wrong—because he didn't want to jeopardize his own relationships. It's the same reason Henry overlooks Louis's poker games and all of them ignore what Elliott did to Helen's mom and who knows how many others.

"Thanks for this," I say, not wanting to get into the rest of it.

He opens his mouth and closes it again before saying, "Good night."

Emma and Aunt Julie both look at me curiously, but I want to read the letter on my own, so I head upstairs before opening it.

Dear Lia,

I knew it would be you. (If you don't believe me, you can ask Peter. I wrote no other letters.)

Now that you've figured it out, you're probably wondering why I didn't fight for recognition sooner. But things were so different when I was young. I didn't even have a credit card in my own name. Offstage, I was just Mrs. Henry Blackwell. So the financial security Henry offered was too much to pass up.

And the truth is, it took me a long time to feel like I deserved to be called a magician. Back then, it didn't seem strange that I was the assistant and Henry performed my tricks—or pretended to.

But the older I've gotten—and the more the world has changed—the more it bothered me. Until I knew I couldn't go through the anniversary this summer being called an assistant.

I'll always be grateful to you for making this happen. And I'll be there the night of the show. Let me know what you need. (My phone should be working again by the day of the performance.)

Love,
Grandma Matilda

PS In case you're wondering, I took my stage name from Matilda Gage.

PPS If you don't know who she is (criminal public schools!), look her up.

Twenty-Four

THE STARLIGHT HAS ONLY TWO DRESSING ROOMS—A GIANT ONE FOR A GROUP AND A SMALL ONE FOR THE STAR. PETER ASKED US TO LEAVE THE BIG ONE ALONE BECAUSE IT'S SET IT UP FOR THE INNER CIRCLE TO MEET AFTER THE SHOW, SO EMMA AND I SHARE THE SMALL ROOM WHILE BECKETT CHANGES IN THE OFFICE.

We have to get ready quickly, because we weren't allowed backstage while Chase and Elliott performed. We have a twenty-minute intermission to switch things over. Emma and I had our makeup and hair done before we came so we'd look as similar as possible. All we have to do is slide into our dresses and shoes. I haven't seen Grandma, but I'm trusting she got my text and she'll be here.

I could have given her detailed directions about what I want, but she doesn't deserve them after leaving me with only the donkey postcard, the eggs, and the order to look up Matilda Gage (fittingly, a suffragist who wrote about men stealing women's work). I sent her a picture I pulled out of Thurston's movie. She'll figure it out.

I hope.

Ten minutes before curtain, I step out of the dressing room. Chase, a duffel bag over his shoulder, squeezes my hand as he goes by. "Good luck. I did what I could."

"Are they letting you watch?"

He shakes his head. "We're not supposed to, but I'm going to try to sneak up to the booth."

Then he's gone, and a warm breeze swirling through the back of the theater draws my attention to an open side door. I peek out. Beckett's standing in his tux, back to me, hands in his pockets and head thrown back to look at the darkening sky. There is something in his pose that makes my breath catch.

Beckett turns at the sound and stills as he studies me, his gaze sliding from my face, down my body, and back up again, leaving a trail of heat behind. This is the first time he's seen me in full costume. We practiced with the dress and shoes, but Emma and I wore ponytails and regular makeup for the rehearsal.

Beckett comes to stand at the bottom of the little flight of stairs and, with a smile, holds up one finger to make a circling motion. And even though he's doing that master-of-the-universe thing again, I oblige, turning carefully in my silent heels.

"Don't take this the wrong way," he says, "but you look exactly like your grandmother."

"You're lucky my grandmother was a total babe," I say, coming down the steps.

"And a really top-notch magician."

"Yes. That too." We're inches apart now. His gaze is warm and affectionate.

"I'm ready when you are, Lia." He takes my hands. "I trust you. With the theater. And with me."

Every part of me wants to pull his mouth to mine, but instead I put my hands on the lapels of his jacket and push back a little against the smooth satin. "Not yet. When I kiss you the first time, I don't want to worry about mussing my hair or getting lipstick all over you."

"Sounds worth waiting for." He puts his hands lightly on my waist. "We've got this."

The look in his eyes steadies me. "You ground me somehow," I tell him. Not totally sure what I mean, but I know I feel more capable with him than without.

"That's funny," he says, resting his forehead on mine. "Because you make me feel light." After a few moments of silence, he moves to hold open the door. "Come on. Time to show the audience your Ambitious Card."

✦

Standing in the wings of the stage, I recite the deck, trying to bring my heart rate down. So very much is riding on this, and I've already gone down in flames once.

Beckett takes his place on the opposite side of the stage.

"Ready?" he mouths.

The house lights go down before I can answer. Beckett heads out to center stage, and the spotlight hits him.

"How's everyone doing?" he says. "Nervous? No? Just me, then."

The crowd laughs. I can't believe the way he owns this stage, or that a week ago, I thought he was only doing this to get back at Elliott. Tonight, happiness radiates off him.

"So here's the thing," he continues. "My partner in this contest happens to be the girl of my dreams."

He looks at his shoes for long enough that I worry he forgot our script, and maybe he did, because the next thing he says is something we never rehearsed. "This girl is joy in human form."

His words take up all the space inside my chest, and I grab the curtain so I don't ruin our opening by running out there and throwing myself into his arms.

Beckett returns to the script. "We're about to go back to school, so tonight's my last chance to convince her I'm worth the effort. Will you help?"

People applaud, and a few whoop.

"I think magic is even more amazing when you know a little bit about it, so I'd like to invite you into the world of Mirror Lake by having you do a trick for Lia. Sound good?"

The crowd cheers again, but in the front row, Henry and Louis look skeptical.

Beckett demonstrates the deKolta flowers, making them appear one after the other from his sleeve, pocket, and lapel. Then he asks the audience to reach down and pull out the little bags of flowers we left under their seats, and he talks them through opening one.

"Now," he says, lowering his voice as if he's sharing a secret. "Don't open the rest until I give you the signal. You'll know when."

And that's my cue.

I hurry out and give one of Matilda's wide-eyed looks of amazement at the crowd. "The audience!" I say. "They're early!"

Beckett gives me his exasperated smile. "No. You're late. Again. But now that you've joined us, can we begin?"

"But my face! My hair!" I turn to the crowd, holding up a finger. "Can you hang on for one little minute?"

They laugh.

"You're perfect as you are," Beckett says, and I swear I hear a girl sigh. Which I totally get. But I'm required to be in frantic mode.

"But my grandmother always wore flowers in her hair! I can't do the show without flowers!"

"Your wish, my command," Beckett says and gestures to the audience. The theater blossoms. Red flowers triggered by every member in the audience, hundreds already in bloom quietly blown across the stage while the spectators focus on their own efforts. The lighting turns dreamy, as if we've entered a fairy tale. And the faces out there are glowing because they've had a part in creating the magic.

"And now, Lia," Beckett says, holding a paper flower out to me. "Can we begin?" With a flourish, he turns the flower into a real rose and tucks it into my hair.

"Yes," I say.

"I don't suppose that while you're in the habit of saying yes . . ."

"No."

He sighs. "Cards then, please." I hand him the deck.

He goes out into the audience and does a couple rounds of "is this your card" tricks. We both do our Ambitious Card routines. He folds his arms and shakes his head when I kiss the back of my victim's card, but Beckett's attitude is all playful, with none of Henry's threats, and our modern audience loves it.

Next, Beckett blindfolds me onstage, and I guess the objects people hold in their laps. I'm not surprised we get every single one. I don't know if I've ever felt so in sync with someone.

When we get to the Tossed-Out Deck, I'm not even worried. The sequences are in my blood now. To build tension during the first round, I ask questions of each person before I name their card.

"When's your birthday?" Two of clubs.

"What's your favorite TV show?" Jack of diamonds.

"How many sisters do you have?" Seven of hearts.

When I get to a boy my age, I say, "What's your phone number?" Beckett shakes his head, and the audience laughs.

Then we repeat the trick. Beckett asks those with black cards to stand, followed by red. Black. Red. Black. Red. Red. Sequence seventeen. Starts with Emma on the stairs. I go down the line, pointing and saying their cards as fast as I can. The laypeople liked the first version better, but the magicians in the first three rows applaud this time. Beckett, holding the deck in his hand so it stays in view, pulls a rubber band out of his pocket, bands the deck, and tosses it right at Louis Gleason. "Fifty-two cards. Ungaffed," he says, and the deck hits Louis in the chest.

Right here onstage, I'm falling in love with this boy.

"Our grandparents used to do this next trick with a lion," I say as Beckett wheels our cabinet out onto the stage, opens the doors, and spins it to show it's empty and nothing is hidden behind it. Emma is inside, invisible behind the mirrors.

"But for some reason, Lia didn't love that idea," Beckett says.

"You wouldn't believe the red tape," I tell the audience. And I actually see Henry laugh. I suppose this was true even fifty years ago.

"We had to come up with a way to make the trick equally challenging," Beckett says.

"So we thought about what animal would make it difficult."

Beckett crosses his arms. "And I said, 'We need one as stubborn as you.'"

"And I said, 'Don't be an ass.'"

"And we had our answer." Beckett goes offstage, and drags Steve out, much to the amusement of the crowd. He struggles and swears under his breath. I never would have guessed what a ham he could be.

I climb into our cabinet and hold a carrot out to Steve with one hand while I reach into my pocket to turn off my lapel mike with the other. No need to broadcast what's going on in here to the audience. Steve just about knocks me down to get the carrot, but Beckett's playacting makes it seem like he's fighting the enclosure. The more recalcitrant the donkey seems, the better the trick appears.

When Beckett closes up the first half of the box, I put my hand over his mike and whisper, "I hate this part."

"Can't tell. You are all lit up." The longing on his face makes me forget about the smell of old donkey. I'm seventeen years old, and Beckett Blackwell's ruining me for all other boys.

He smiles. "Hold that thought."

Beckett shuts the box before turning to address the audi-ence. I shake my head to clear it of Beckett-induced daydreams and move to help Emma. She pops open one of the mirrored panels. We coax Steve in, pressing him flat against the back of the cabinet, while she and I huddle in the tiny triangle behind where the mirrors connect. Steve snorts, and I scratch his head. Performing with live animals is terrifying.

"I hate this part," Emma whispers.

"That's what I said."

We're quiet while Beckett opens the doors, revealing the empty cabinet. Another spin. This is the tricky bit. We can't leave the mirrors up because they'd reflect me and Steve when Beckett opens the doors again. So we fold them flat against the walls, their black backs matching the sides. And when the cab-inet stops, Emma slips out a secret door in the back and stands on a little ledge behind the cabinet.

When Beckett throws open the doors, Steve and I are stand-ing alone in the box. The audience applauds, and I climb out.

"Did you teach Steve the trick?"

"He's a faster learner than some," I say, twinkling up at him.

Beckett closes the doors again.

"I'm not going back in there," I say.

"Lia, we agreed. This is the trick."

"No." I call backstage, "A little help?"

Theo wheels our tower out onto the corner of the stage, and I blow him a kiss. All this gives Emma enough time to climb back inside the cabinet and hide with Steve behind the mirrors again.

Beckett spins the cabinet while I climb up onto the platform. He opens the empty cabinet, showing Steve has vanished. The faces I can see in the audience are puzzled but not yet amazed.

"Time to get back in, Lia," Beckett says.

"Absolutely not," I respond, and pull the curtains up around me. "I already smell like farm." Holding up the curtains with a rope, I curl up into a little sunken hole in the base of the tower, sliding a trapdoor over me.

Beckett spins the cabinet again, says, "Back in!" and claps his hands. Which is my cue to release the rope. The curtains drop to reveal my now-empty platform. Beckett opens the doors of the cabinet, and there is Steve, next to Emma in my dress, blond hair twisted in a complicated updo, set off with a single rose. She'll be radiating irritation, arms crossed, head turned away from Beckett and therefore the audience. As far as the crowd's concerned, I teleported from the tower to the box in seconds.

Beckett now gives a sheepish smile before saying to the crowd, "Give me a minute to grovel before the next trick?" And he wheels the cabinet off the stage in one direction while Theo wheels my tower out in the other.

Halfway down the ladder, Theo grabs my waist and swings me down the rest of the way. "You guys are killing it."

"Not done yet." I run across the stage behind the curtain in my silent shoes so I can come in from the side where Emma exited.

The flight is next. And it plays beautifully after the drama with Steve. Beckett apologizes as he offers his gifts. I am

271

unimpressed. Until he brings out the balloon. I give him a dreamy smile, and as soon as I grab the string, I float up into the air.

He pleads a bit more as I bob about, then he holds his arms out to me. "I'm sorry, Lia. No more teleportations. No more donkeys. Come back?"

I release the balloon and, thanks to Theo, who hits the musical cue just right, float down. When Beckett steps in front of me to lift me out of the stand, I lose myself in his eyes. He turns with me much more slowly than we practiced and sets me in front of him, but he doesn't let me go and I leave my arms around his neck, fingers tangled in his hair. I can't look away. I'm not even trying to remember what we're supposed to do next.

"Lia? Beckett?" Theo's voice calls over the sound system. "You remember we've got an audience out here, right?" We didn't practice this, but it's perfect. The crowd laughs.

"Soon," Beckett mouths, and twirls me out for a quick curtsy.

I slip behind the back curtain. Theo rushes out to take off the brace and help with my threads while Beckett introduces the next trick onstage.

The curtains part. Emma chose dark lighting with twinkling stars and a glowing moon for the setting. Because of a quick dusting with some kind of powder Emma found, I'm glowing, like the silver ball on the edge of the stage. The whole thing looks like a dream.

Beckett picks up the silver sphere, struggling a little to suggest weight, and blows the ball over to me. He's exaggerating his movements, appearing to make the ball float around me with his hands, and I'm minimizing mine. Dancing—oh-so-carefully with my silver hoop—I demonstrate there are no threads. I roll the hoop away.

Beckett watches for a moment. Then he puts his hands in his pockets and walks off the stage to stand beside Henry in the audience. For a second, I freeze, let the ball drop a touch, and then send it circling around me again. Most of the audience—who have no idea how the trick is done—pay no attention, but there are some surprised faces in the first couple rows, and I look right at Henry as I make the sphere obey my commands to rise, float, sink, and bob. With a gesture, I send it into the air.

Then the lighting shifts to reveal the complicated network of threads, and the audience applauds.

Beckett looks up at me from the floor, a wonderful sort of awe on his face. "This is one of those tricks that Lia and I think is more impressive when you see how it's done."

I slide the threads off my fingers and reach back to detach them from the loops in my dress before walking to the front of the stage.

"This trick," Beckett says, "also reveals our biggest illusion of the night. The fantasy that Lia was my assistant. She identified the cards, vanished Steve, disappeared herself, did all the work in the levitation and the floating orb. I just waved my hands around. Except for a few card tricks early on, my job was mostly to stand there and look good in a tux."

"Which you do remarkably well," I say.

"She's coming around," Beckett says to the audience. And he takes a seat next to his grandfather. This is my show from here on out.

Twenty-Five

I LOOK OUT AT THE AUDIENCE. "I LEARNED THAT TRICK FROM MY GRAND-MOTHER. DO YOU WANT TO SEE?"

In response to the applause, I gesture to Emma, now in the booth, and she lowers a screen, dims the stage lights, and starts Thurston's film.

Matilda calls the orb to her and dances about, managing the threads in the same way I did. Studying the faces of the men in the first three rows, I'd say only half of them are surprised. Matilda's role in Henry's act was an open secret. The film stops on the image of Matilda with the silver ball hovering above her hand. After a moment, the picture fades.

I'm about to find out if my grandmother is as good as I think she is.

With a little smile over my shoulder at the audience, I take a paintbrush, draw it across the screen, and, thanks to Emma's Photoshop skills, a new picture appears—Matilda in the same pose, but now wrinkled and white-haired.

Then there's a puff of blue smoke, which hides the screen as it's yanked up into the air. When the smoke clears, there is my grandmother, in the same pose as the painting, a silver orb floating above her hand. Goodness knows where she found the dress, because there's no way she still fits in the one from the film. And now that I look closer, I see she's got some kind of nude bodysuit on underneath. The illusion of youth this creates is nearly as impressive as her appearance from the painting.

I grin at her and mouth, "Love the hair." She's dyed it a pale lavender, because for some reason Grandma associates disappearances with pastel hair. This ruins the illusion that she stepped out of the painting, but I forgive her.

She smiles. "Yours too."

The crowd, both laypeople and magicians, are too surprised to applaud, I think, so I speak into the silence.

"Tonight, on the Society's hundredth anniversary, I'm pleased to honor my grandmother Matilda Montgomery, who performed as a magician for more than a decade, inventing and adapting magic tricks with her partner, Henry. She wasn't his assistant any more than he was hers."

Henry stands. "Pulling on a few threads doesn't make you a magician, Matilda."

Grandma comes forward to stand next to me. I unclip my lapel mike and hand it to her with the little battery pack so she can answer.

"True enough," she says, and looks at me.

But before I can speak, Thurston Carter, sitting in the center of the third row, struggles to his feet. Emma hits him with one of the spotlights. Pro that he is, he doesn't react. The theater is silent, the audience waiting. It's clear they're not sure if this is a planned part of the show or a spontaneous interruption, but they're compelled to watch.

"She brought you the lion cabinet, Henry," he says. "And the teleportation. And the orbs. And she developed the Tossed-Out Deck while she was with you. Don't bother denying it, because I remember you when. You were card tricks and mechanical props until she came along."

"Why are you involved in this?" Henry asks Thurston. "It was more than fifty years ago. You can't possibly still be angry she left your act for mine."

"At least I had an act without her," Thurston responds.

"Thank you, Thurston, darling," Grandma says.

"If you'd come to me, we could have settled this years ago," he says.

She sighs. "I know. But I really like that house. I grew quite fond of it once he moved out." Grandma glowers at Henry.

"Our agreement still holds," Henry says. "This spectacle doesn't change that."

"But it wasn't me who shared our secrets." With a little flourish, Grandma produces a paper from nowhere. "I've spent the last three months at Nirvana—a wretched retreat in the middle of the Alaskan wilderness. No technology, no talking." She shudders a little and looks at me. "No makeup."

"I'd rather sleep in that cabinet with Steve," I say. Grandma's mike picks me up, and the audience laughs.

"And no way of communicating with my brilliant grand-daughter. Or with her very helpful partner." She smiles at

Beckett. "Who might make me rethink my position on Black-well boys."

Henry looks down at Beckett. "How much of this are you responsible for?"

"Grandpa, it wasn't just your act."

"You turned on me?"

There are a lot of things Beckett could say, but he chooses the exactly right one. "You must have loved her once. Make this right."

Henry stares at him for a long moment and then nods.

I hold out my hand toward my grandmother. She comes to take it, and we bow. The first people I see leaping to their feet as they clap are Mom and Dad.

"There goes my eyeliner," I say to Grandma when the tears well up.

"No," she says, looking at me. "Everything is so much better these days. You could do an underwater escape and keep your mascara on."

The members of the Inner Circle file out a side door, off to make their decision about the contest and, hopefully, my grand-mother's membership in their ranks. Henry and Beckett join us on the side of the stage, while Peter explains what's happening to the audience.

Beckett and I exchange a look as we watch our grandparents size each other up.

"Still beautiful, Matilda," Henry says, taking her hand and kissing it.

"And still a charmer," she answers.

I don't understand this relationship. Two minutes ago, I would have sworn they hated each other, but they're both looking pretty fond. There are all kinds of ways to be in love, I guess, but I don't think I care for theirs.

After a few moments of silence, Henry speaks. "I'm sorry. I never should have made you sign those agreements. I wanted to punish you for leaving the act. And later, I was angry about William."

"You took my work. Not just after, but during. You never let people see how much I created."

"I didn't think about it that way. During, it was ours. Hiding how it was done was part of the act. And after, you didn't need it anymore. The money seemed like more than a fair trade."

She takes his hand. "I didn't realize how much it mattered to me until much later. But I had to do this. Before it was too late."

He's quiet for a bit. "If I'd given you credit, would you have stayed?"

Grandma takes a step back. "Of course not. We didn't get divorced because you took my tricks. We got divorced because you were boffing my look-alike."

Henry grins. "Fair point."

I cover my mouth with my hands, unable to believe that Grandma and Henry are standing here talking about boffing.

Grandma glances at me. "Oh, don't look so surprised. She was perfect for him. Looked just like me but never stole his spotlight."

"But much, much less fun," Henry says and extends his arm to Grandma. "Walk with me? I have an idea about how to make this up to you."

They go off toward the side of the stage, and Beckett and I turn to each other in shock (and, honestly, maybe a little bit of horror).

"If they start something up again," he says, "that won't make us cousins, will it?"

I cover my ears and scrunch my eyes closed. "Talk about something else! Right now!"

When I open my eyes, Aunt Julie's in front of me. "Do I want to know what that was about?"

I drop my hands. "No. You definitely don't."

"That was amazing," she says. "I'm so proud of you."

I wrap my arms around her. "Thank you for everything."

She whispers in my ear, "And you now have my permission to kiss that boy."

"That's a relief," I say. "Because I'd never do it otherwise."

"Smart aleck," she says as our families appear in front of the stage. As soon as I slide down, Dad wraps me in a hug.

When he lets me go, I turn to see Mom exchanging some kind of look with Beckett's dad. I glance at Beckett, who's as surprised as I am.

"Max," Mom says.

"Kristen," he says with a wry half smile. It's like seeing Beckett's expression on Chase's face. "It's been a long time."

"Not nearly long enough," Mom says archly. Archly! My mother.

"Because when it was just our grandparents, that wasn't weird enough," Beckett whispers before we get pulled into separate conversations with our families.

"Why is everyone leaving?" I ask Emma, looking out at the empty seats. "They haven't even announced who won."

"Oh, it's no contest," Emma says. "Theo says Chase yelled out 'Damn it, Elliott!' when the blades slid into the box." Chase is my hero.

"Even before that, it was pretty clear they couldn't stand each other," Mom says. "So they were no fun to watch. Unlike the two of you."

"We have a productive working relationship," I say, all innocence.

"Yeah, you do," Emma says.

Dad puts his hand on Mom's back and says, "I guess I should be grateful this Montgomery-Blackwell thing skips a generation."

"More or less," Mom says and kisses him. I feel a wave of gratitude for growing up in this family where affection is always so near the surface.

"Seriously, that was amazing, Lia," Mom says. "Not just the magic, but what you did for your grandmother. That generation of women gave up an awful lot."

"I know."

"I'm proud of you too," Dad says. "And this magic school idea is great."

"About that," I say. "I want to do my senior year here in Mirror Lake. Work on the magic school. And, if things go well back there, on the Starlight."

Mom shakes her head a little. "That's a big deal. It could affect college. The high school here . . . it's not like yours."

"I want to major in theater, so all this will probably help as much as another AP class." I know Mirror Lake High doesn't have the same classes as my school, but I can't see how that's going to make a difference in my life. And whatever my parents say, I want to go to Madison, not a fancy private school. I'd hate being any farther from Mirror Lake.

"Theater?" Mom says. "What about math?"

"You've been waiting for me to find the thing I'll stick with. This is it. I'm sorry it's not something you're happier about. Something that does Good in the World." I put the capital letters into my voice.

Mom touches my face. "I only have to look around to see you're doing good in the world. If this is what you want, you should do it. When you stand onstage with your granddaughter, I don't want it to be because of something you regret." Dad puts his arms around us both, and Emma does too.

At that moment, I can't imagine being any happier. But I'm proven wrong when Thurston Carter comes out ten minutes later to announce that Beckett and I are the new owners of the Starlight Theater.

I go back up onstage with Beckett and look around the theater, taking in its faded curtains and cracked seats. It's the most beautiful thing I've ever seen. And it's mine. Or ours. Which, maybe, is even better. Beckett points out at the remaining members of the audience, and I turn to face them. Although the theater's half-full, the crowd makes a ton of noise.

Then Henry steps between me and Beckett, putting a hand on both our shoulders. "Come with me. There's something I think you'd like to see."

I look at Beckett, who shrugs, and we follow Henry to the door of the large dressing room. "Technically, this is only for members, but I don't think you two are going to have any trouble getting through that final vote." He smiles. "And besides, Matilda wants you there, and while it may have taken me seventy years, I'm learning that my life is easier if I give Matilda what she wants."

He opens the door.

Four rows of chairs fill the dressing room. Almost every one is taken by an old white man. A few people stand on the sides, including Louis, who sees me and winks. I'm not quite ready to be back on winking terms with him, though, so I give a low-key wave and turn toward the front.

Grandma's up there with Thurston. She blows me a kiss. Then she nods to Thurston.

He looks out at the crowd, and even though he leans on his cane, I can see the charisma that made him one of the greats.

"We're here to induct a new member." He pauses for applause and then turns to Grandma. "Matilda Montgomery, inventor of Donkey and Clowns, adapter of Abbott's magic spheres, and national performer, welcome to the Inner Circle. An honor long overdue."

The crowd applauds again, more enthusiastically this time. I look at Henry beside me. He doesn't seem angry, only a little rueful.

Then Thurston steps closer to Grandma and says something quietly. Looking him in the eyes, she says something back. This must be the second oath. While I'm curious, I'm glad I can't hear. I don't want to know the words until I get to say them for myself. When Beckett takes my hand and squeezes, I know he's thinking the same thing.

Thurston makes a gold medallion on a burgundy ribbon appear in his hand. If I'm totally honest, I saw the move, but if I'm still that good at ninety, I won't complain. He hangs the medal around Grandma's neck, and she kisses his cheek and whispers something in his ear. His expression is almost unbearably tender.

The audience gets to their feet and applauds, but Peter steps in front and quiets them. "We have one further announcement. As many of you know, largely thanks to Matilda's granddaughter, the Society of American Conjurers will be starting a magic school soon." He glances at Grandma and smiles. "And tonight, I'm thrilled to ask my friend and former client Matilda Montgomery if she'd be willing to become our school's first director."

Grandma steps back and puts both hands over her heart. She obviously wasn't expecting this any more than I was. I just barely hear her say, "I'd be honored."

"Montgomery girls for the win," Beckett says as the crowd of people swarms forward, but in just a few moments, Grandma fights her way back to us.

She grins. "This is why you're my favorite."

"I knew it," I say. "I'm so proud of you."

She touches my face. "Back at you, granddaughter. But promise me something?"

"Anything."

"Don't wait a half century to go after what you want."

"I don't plan to."

"OK. We'll talk tomorrow about this school of yours. Tonight is for celebrating." She looks over at Beckett. "So far, you seem to be the best of them. I'd like to see that continue where my granddaughter is concerned."

"Yes, ma'am."

"You'll do," she says, and goes to talk to Henry.

That is one conversation I don't want to hear, so I take Beckett's hand to pull him toward the door. I've been waiting a long time for the next item on the agenda.

But instead of the empty theater I expect, the stage is full of families waiting for us, and we get pulled in different directions again. Adults ask about the show and the school.

Mae, who's there with her grandmother, hands me a bouquet of flowers. "You were so good," she says.

"Thanks. For coming and for the flowers. You too, Mrs. Kowalski."

I'm about to move on to the next group waiting when Mae takes my wrist and pulls me back to her. She goes up on her toes to whisper in my ear. "You have to teach me how to add in that kissing-the-card part next."

I laugh. "OK, but you have to teach me how to have a long-distance relationship."

She smiles, a little bashfully. "Will do."

A few minutes later, I see Abby and her brothers. Their mother says, "She cannot wait for that camp next summer. You made a fan, for sure."

I'm not a suffragist, or the first woman president, or even the first woman admitted to London's Magic Circle (Debbie McGee, 1991), but I do feel like a little bit of a pioneer. And I love that I get to do it in a sparkly dress and heels.

After Abby's family says goodbye, I search for Beckett and spot him on the opposite end of the stage. When I meet his eyes, he mouths, "Can we get out of here?" I respond, "Back door?" while holding up my hand to show five minutes. He salutes.

I'm moving toward my dressing room when someone grabs my wrist.

Elliott.

When I yelp, a few people look over, and I wave to show I'm OK.

"Don't be like that," he says. "I'm not a predator."

I cross my arms and look at him incredulously.

"I was barely out of high school when that thing happened with Emma." That thing! "I'm not the first teenage boy to do something stupid. And I think we're even on that now."

"Not nearly," I say. "And what about Helen's family and all the other private readings?"

"Most of that wasn't a big deal. I predicted long lives, true love. People left happy. A couple of times, it got out of hand." I'm not sure if I believe him. And I can't stop thinking about Elliott sending Chase into traffic. And eight thousand dollars is a lot of money. "I want in on the school. Grandpa will listen if you tell him you changed your mind."

"No," I say quickly. Even if it's just adults, Elliott doesn't need to be anywhere near people learning to do this.

"You'll need a mentalist."

"Not the way you do it." But I think about Thurston and Henry, who are much older but seem like they can change. Cutting Elliott off from everything he knows probably isn't going to make him a kinder person.

"Here's the deal. We have a year before we open doors. That's plenty of time for you to make a good-faith effort. But that means no more talking to dead people and no being creepy around girls."

"I'm not creepy."

"You are the mayor of Creepville. But maybe you can learn not to be. And you need to return the rest of the money to Helen's mom."

"The rest?" he says.

"Beckett and I gave you a head start. Which is more than you deserve."

"What do you mean?"

I purse my lips, trying to decide if I should tell him. Probably there's not going to be a better time than when we're surrounded by dozens of people.

"Maura—who took your pictures—doesn't work for a studio. She was employed by a . . . um . . . I guess you could say a nonprofit that Beckett and I started to get Helen's family their money back."

Emotions flash so fast on Elliott's face I barely recognize them. Confusion, understanding, embarrassment, anger, resignation. And maybe . . . respect?

"So . . . no TV show, then?" Figures this is what he'd care about.

"Yeah, I made that up."

"You're good. Maybe as good as I am."

"Faint praise," I say. "Beckett sent her family the first check he got from my grandmother too, so you're halfway there. But the other four thousand needs to come from you."

"What if I say no?" he says.

"We don't need you. We have more out-of-work magicians than we need to teach."

Elliott stares at me.

"And remember, Beckett and I don't have to let you perform here. Ever again. And you know how he feels, so tell me when you decide. I have to go." I'm already past the five minutes I promised.

"Fine," Elliott says to my back. "You win."

"Oh, and you have to apologize to Chase," I add before going into my dressing room.

"For what? He completely screwed me over tonight."

"For letting him get hit by a car."

"That was ten years ago! Dude needs to let it go."

"Apologize!" I say, and shut the door.

I speed-change, throwing my dress and heels on the floor and pulling on a sweatshirt, leggings, and flip-flops. I'll come back tomorrow and clean up. I grab a makeup wipe and clean my face, not bothering to put anything back on.

Except lip balm.

Because I have plans.

Finally, I grab my purse and phone and sprint for the back door. When I push it open, I find Beckett, now in a sweatshirt and jeans, leaning against the railing at the bottom of the stairs.

"Lia Sawyer," he says as the door shuts behind me, "you are always worth the wait."

Twenty-Six

I SCRAMBLE DOWN THE STAIRS TO TAKE HIS HAND, MY FACE ONE BIG QUESTION. HE TUCKS A STRAND OF HAIR BACK INTO MOUNDS OF CURLS STILL COILED ON MY HEAD. *KISS ME, KISS ME, KISS ME.* I'M BOUNCING ON MY TOES.

He grins. "We're so close now. We may as well do this right."

"What does that mean?" I say, unable to believe he's putting this off again. If he thinks we're going to ask my parents' permission, he's out of his mind.

"Back to the beach?"

Of course. Could he be any sweeter? (No. He actually, empirically, could not.)

"OK."

I lean my head on his shoulder as we walk, appreciating the little bit of coolness in the night breeze and not wanting to do anything other than be in this moment. There are so many things to talk about. The show tonight. The theater. The school. College. My plans to stay in Mirror Lake. And us.

But I don't want to do any of that right now. I only want to anticipate.

I've never waited so long for a first kiss. Usually it was days, but sometimes hours, and every once in a while (like with Chase) minutes between when I first thought about kissing a boy and when I did it. Which was fun.

But this is real. And it's Beckett. So I like it better.

The steps that lead down to the beach take us right to our chairs. Around them, candles flicker in glass jars.

I look up at Beckett. "How?" There's no way this could have been set up before the show.

"Magic," he says.

I give him a look.

"Chase," Beckett admits. "I explained about 'no dibs,' but he still wanted to apologize."

When we get closer, we find a folded-up blanket and a little cooler. Beckett spreads the blanket out in front of the chairs, amid the candles. I curl my legs underneath me when I sit, so I can get as close to him as possible.

"Are you hungry?" he asks. "Do you want something to eat?"

I shake my head and smile in a way that should make perfectly clear what I want. His eyes wander over my face.

"Can I take down your hair?"

I nod. He takes the rose out first and hands it to me. I watch his face while he pulls out the bobby pins, throwing them one by one onto the blanket. He looks entranced. Which is how I feel.

My curls slide down my neck, each one a caress. When my hair is finally down around my shoulders, he smiles. "You look like the day we met."

"Two months, two days," I say. It feels both longer and shorter.

"Exactly how long I've wanted to kiss you."

"Please tell me that's what's happening next."

He nods and leans toward me. I come closer too but let him close the last distance between us. After all his delays, I need to know he wants this.

Beckett's kiss is reverent. He is gentle and slow and adoring. His hands trace my jaw, my neck, and my hair so carefully—as if he can't believe he gets to touch me. I wind my arms around his neck, drawing him closer, because even this last inch of space between us is too much, and he's being much too cautious.

In response, he slides one hand into my hair and presses the other against the small of my back, and I am entirely undone. Too lost in him to remember to be bright or charming or fun. Or to think about doing this right.

I am just Lia. Kissing Beckett. Like I was made to fall for a Blackwell boy.

Later, he leans against the chairs, and I sit between his legs, resting my back against his chest. We say very little, spending our time looking at the water and tracing each other's hands with our fingers. Every once in a while, I tilt my face up toward his, testing this new power of mine to make him kiss me whenever I want.

It's wonderful. Every time. And I'm relieved. In my heart of hearts, I was a little worried that Beckett was putting off this part because he wasn't good at it. I'm happy to find no remedial work is necessary.

"What?" Beckett says, looking down at me, suspicious.

"Nothing," I say, but I can't help grinning. I love the way he reads me, even when I don't want him to.

"Lia," he says.

"Fine. I thought it was possible you wanted to put off kissing me because you didn't want to reveal your inadequacy until after I was committed."

"Flattering," he says.

"I assumed you'd respond to instruction."

"All pointers are welcome."

"But none are needed," I say, and kiss him again.

Eventually he says, "Would it be super unromantic if I ate something? I'm starving."

"As long as I don't have to move, feel free." I want to spend as many moments as I can sheltered in his arms.

"I don't want you to go anywhere." He kisses my neck.

"More," I command.

I feel him smile against my skin. Obediently, he trails kisses up to my ear. Then he whispers, "If you don't let me have some food, I will waste away, and we won't be able to do this anymore."

"Fine," I say, nestling back against him. "I'll control myself."

Beckett digs around in the cooler, finding a sandwich for himself and a container of cut-up strawberries and a little tub of cheese and whole wheat crackers for me.

"Is there chocolate?" I ask.

"Yes, but you know you want this first."

He's right. I do. It's hard not to be all thrilled he knows this. Camden never really got how I ate. He seemed surprised every time I reminded him I was a vegetarian, and he somehow thought that meant I didn't eat sweets. It's weird: My whole relationship with Camden—from meet-cute to ugly breakup—lasted less time than I've already spent with Beckett. Even though this was our first kiss, it's hard to think of tonight as the beginning. Maybe because it feels so close to the end.

"How much time do you think we have?" I ask, even though I'd rather not know the answer.

"Tonight? That's up to you. My parents are in a hotel because they can't stand staying with Grandpa, and he doesn't care."

"Not tonight. Us. Together."

"I don't know? Sixty, seventy years, if we're lucky. We can't all be Thurston Carter."

I scoot back a little bit to look at him, although I stay pressed against his leg. I can't bear not to be touching. "You don't mean that."

He strokes my cheek. "Can we just see how it goes?"

I'm about to ask when he leaves for college when I realize that I don't even know where home is for Beckett. "I can't believe I never asked this, but where do you live when you're not here?"

"Two months and you still haven't typed my name into a search engine?"

"Some of us aren't naturally suspicious."

He shakes his head. "But . . . you weren't curious?"

I pat his leg. "Don't worry. We can work on that ego."

"Shorewood," he says. "I live in Shorewood."

"Get out!"

He grins.

"We live in Whitefish Bay." I grew up two miles from Beckett. I've cheered at his high school.

"I know. Convenient, right?"

"Not really," I say. "You'll be in Madison. And I'll be here."

"You're not going home?"

"I want to see this through. I don't want to hear about it long-distance and come back when it's all done."

"You'll have to leave all your friends. You won't know anyone."

"I'd leave them next year anyway. Emma's already gone. And, I haven't asked yet, but I hope I'll know one person here."

Beckett's confusion clears after a moment. "Chase."

"He wasn't totally excited about going back to your parents' without you, and I want to start an after-school program this fall to practice for the summer camp. And I need Chase for that. He's really good at close-up work."

Beckett gives me a look. "So I've heard."

"Don't do that jealous thing. It's boring."

"I'm not jealous. Chase said he kissed you to get me to do something."

"Hmm." If saying that is what it took for them to get over it, I can live with it, but as someone who was there, I think Chase kissed me for the exact same reason I kissed him—he wanted to play a little, which was nice enough, but now that sort of thing just seems . . . a little pale and uninteresting. For all the light between us, there's this seriousness to my connection to Beckett that's grounded in who we are together. It's the thing that made him agree to share the theater with me, and honor my grandma in the show, and throw that deck of cards at Louis. The thing that made me want to get that money back for Helen's family and stay even when he flipped out. Now that I know what this is like, I don't think I'm interested in a relationship without it.

"When do you have to be in Madison?"

He brings my hand to his mouth and kisses my palm. "Two weeks. But that doesn't have to be all tragic. If you stay in Mirror Lake, I'll be forty-five minutes away. We'll figure out how to see each other."

"But do you want to be that boy? Locked into a boring long-distance relationship with his hometown girlfriend?"

"One. It's not really long-distance. On a Friday afternoon in the summer, it takes more than forty-five minutes to get from one end of Mirror Lake to the other. And two. Boring? My magician—con artist—business partner girlfriend? I don't think so. You felt that onstage tonight, right? It wasn't just me?"

I nod. Performing live magic is like dancing on a tightrope in a windstorm. Living in that space with someone else was wildly intimate. Even in front of a crowd.

"We'll do more shows. Because I can't live in a world where we don't get to do that again. You'll help your grandma start the magic school. And I'll figure out what I want to do with my life. And sometime in there we'll do a few normal, date-y things. For the experience."

"Like prom?"

"If we must. I'll work at your camp next summer and keep an eye on the old guys. And when you're ready, I'll sell you my half of the theater, and no matter what happens, we'll get out of this before we hate each other."

I'd like to say that could never happen, but I know too much about Henry and Matilda's story to argue. Although I hope living in a time that allows me to be a whole person will make it easier for us both to find happiness.

"So that's our plan?"

"Yep. Do magic. Fight crime. Fall in love." He grins. "Not necessarily in that order."

"Do you think that can really happen?" I ask, afraid to believe.

"For us? Absolutely."

"Because we're friends?"

"Because we're magicians." He cups my cheeks with both hands and turns my face up to his, but instead of kissing me, he whispers, "Do you know what 'abracadabra' really means?"

Without moving away from him, I shake my head a little.

"It's from Arabic. 'If I say it, it is so.'"

I can't believe I met a boy who turns the language of magic into love poems. I want to tell him a hundred things. That I've never felt so wholly myself as when I was on that stage with him. That he makes me feel both brilliant and beautiful. That when I'm with him, I don't have to hide any part of who I am. But instead of saying any of that, I lean in so my lips barely touch his, and I whisper, "Abracadabra."

Acknowledgments

As always, all the thanks to my agent, Elizabeth Bennett. On this one, you taught me that I only need half as many characters as I think I do. I am also so grateful to my editors Emily Daluga and Maggie Lehrman. I'm so lucky to have found people who also like that space between love stories and geeky little obsessions, like math and magic. I really appreciate the way both of you helped me find the emotional center of a story that could have stopped at the sparkly bits.

Thank you, also, to everyone else at Abrams who made this book a reality—designers Heather Kelly and Deena Fleming, managing editor Marie Oishi, copy editor Sara Brady, proofreaders Regina Castillo and Esther Reisberg, production manager Rachael Marks, marketer Megan Evans, and publicist Mary Marolla. It means so much to have a physical book that looks as happy as the story I wrote. Also, I'm so lucky to have illustrator Andi Poretta on board again. Your ability to get cute on the page continually amazes me.

This is the first book I had beta readers for, and I'm thankful to everyone who helped fill early plot holes, fix pacing, and get the level of detail in the tricks right. Annette Dodd, Julie Ferguson, Maggie Maxwell, Kat Seeling, and Ginger Switzer all gave me thoughtful comments that made the story better.

I started dreaming up this book while listening to the absolutely bonkers lyrics of One Direction's "Girl Almighty." I love this song, but it makes zero sense. The only way I could think of to get a girl to float through the room on a big balloon was stage magic, and so I decided to write that story. I wouldn't have been able to do it without Penn and Teller's Master Class, *The Expert at the Cardtable* by S. W. Erdnase, *Fooling Houdini: Magicians, Mentalists, Math Geeks, and the Hidden Power of the Mind* by Alex Stone, and *Hiding the Elephant: How Magicians Invented the Impossible and Learned to Disappear* by Jim Steinmeyer. I'm grateful to the handful of magicians who were willing to share some of their secrets.

Finally, thanks so much to my family. Mom and Dad, I am always grateful for your support, and Dad, I'm especially grateful for your toast at our wedding, without which this book wouldn't have had an ending. Sophie and Chloe, I hope you both find the thing you love most in the world and go after it, however weird and wild. And Perry, thank you for always letting me show up as whoever I currently am. I love you all.